PRAISE FOR *WATCH FOR ME*

"Deliciously creepy with a twist you won't see coming!"
—Helen Hardt, #1 *New York Times* bestselling author

"I read spellbound as Tom Harper's life is demolished brick by brick. Assured, remorseless writing, that grabs the reader and doesn't let go. Highly recommended."
—Michael Ridpath, author of *The Diplomat's Wife*

"I absolutely loved this book. One of the best I've read in ages—gripping, thrilling and pretty scary!"
—Alex Pine, author of *The Christmas Killer*

"This is an outstanding novel that got its hooks in me from the first page. I love the laser-focused storytelling—the terror of Ali Page is evident in every line. It's like a clinic on how to write a thriller, every beat of the plot is perfectly placed."
—Chris Rhatigan, publisher of All Due Respect Books

"Compelling reading...Psychologically gripping...Haunting storytelling. Young, attractive—and mentally unhinged—Ali Page is some men's dream girl, but one man's worst nightmare. *Watch for Me* will have you flipping the pages until the cathartic surprise ending."
—Bryan Quinn, author of *The Package* and *No Good Deed Goes Unpunished*

"Riveting, from the beginning to the end. Once again, Bodenham catches you by surprise with his twists. Capturing the essence of the Pacific Northwest, *Watch for Me* is a must read."
—Tracie Ingersoll Loy, author of
the *Hartz Island Mysteries*

"When Tom helps young Ali Page to find a new home, he knows that something isn't right. When she begins to obsessively text him, his world falls apart. As we enter the dark mind of a fantasist living amidst the claustrophobic confines of an island, we plunge into a disturbing world with no way out. This is an unsettling tale of one woman's illusions that leave devastating consequences in their wake."
—Jackie Bateman, author of *Straight Circles*

"Martin Bodenham's *Watch for Me* gives us a stalker villain for the ages with Ali in this fast-paced, tightly-written thriller that calls to mind *Fatal Attraction*, except Ali will do more than boil your bunny; she's out for blood and ultimate destruction!"
—Lee Matthew Goldberg, bestselling author of
The Mentor, *The Ancestor* and
the upcoming *Stalker Stalked*

WATCH FOR ME

BOOKS BY MARTIN BODENHAM

Shakedown
The Geneva Connection
Once a Killer
Crime and Justice
Watch for Me

WATCH FOR ME

MARTIN BODENHAM

Down & Out Books
3959 Van Dyke Road, Suite 265
Lutz, FL 33558
DownAndOutBooks.com

Cover design by BookCoverPro

ISBN: 1-64396-215-9
ISBN-13: 978-1-64396-215-3

To Jules, for your patience, love, and friendship

Chapter 1

How many standout memories are there in an average lifetime? For most of us, a handful of events delineate our lives: the moment we fall in love, the day we marry, the birth of a child, the end of a serious relationship, the death of a loved one. Maybe a couple more if people stop and think about it. For me, it's different. One brief period is forever seared into my mind: the time Ali Page returned to Vancouver Island. It overshadows everything else. And while the passage of time hasn't lessened the trauma, five years on I've gained some sort of perspective, a way of compartmentalizing the terror she visited upon my family that summer.

The irony is, if she hadn't been the daughter of friends, I would never have taken her on as a client in the first place. I tried to explain I wasn't the right person. My tiny real estate brokerage focused on single-family homes around Owen Bay where I lived. What did I know about the Victoria condo market? Ali needed a downtown specialist; someone who knew the patch. But her parents wouldn't give up. "You're the only broker we trust," they kept saying. "With you, we know she won't make a mistake." And when flattery didn't work, they piled on the guilt. "We've already promised Ali you'll help her…She's desperate to find a place before she starts her new job."

According to Marie, I've always been a people-pleaser. A soft touch, she calls me. My wife says I find it impossible to say no.

1

She's always been thicker-skinned than me. Marie's a cynic; she thinks people will take advantage if you let them. Call me a sucker, but I don't like disappointing anyone, least of all friends and family. Long story short, I caved and agreed to act as Ali's buying agent. One small favor that would change our lives forever. What is it they say? No good deed goes unpunished? I soon discovered what that meant.

Over the space of two months that summer, I reckon we visited every condo building in the downtown area, some several times over. By my last count, we'd looked at over seventy properties and still we weren't close to finding one she liked. There was always something not right, something holding Ali back. It was as if she kept inventing reasons not to buy—the price was too high, the layout was wrong, the place was too small, the street was noisy. You name it, she came up with every excuse.

Sure, I understood it was a big step; it would be for any twenty-eight-year-old buying her first property. As British Columbia's capital, Victoria has always been an expensive part of the province, so a mistake could prove costly. I got that. Even so, Ali's persistent reluctance to commit was hard to fathom. Wasn't she supposed to be under pressure to find somewhere fast?

It didn't add up.

At first, I put Ali's caution down to her profession. Lawyers can be indecisive. After all, they're paid to look for problems, right? Before she returned to the island, Ali had been working for a major law firm in Vancouver, advising clients on M&A deals. I wasn't entirely sure what those were, but from the way her father described them to me, they sounded important. She'd always been bright. I remember that from her late teens before she went off to study at UBC on the mainland. Even then it was obvious she'd end up pursuing some high-powered career. Her family lived a couple of blocks from us, and she used to babysit our daughter, Freya. After Ali went off to college, we didn't get to see her that often; her visits back home were fleeting and usually on the weekends when I was busy with open houses and showings. Besides her intelligence, my other lasting memory of Ali as a teenager was her incredible shyness. Withdrawn, some might say.

As we shot around town looking at properties, I soon realized nothing much had changed. Our conversations were one-sided. Nine times out of ten, I'd be the one asking questions, offering an opinion on something in the news, or commenting on a TV show, hoping to stimulate a discussion. Hardly anything came back, and on the few occasions when Ali did string a sentence together, her responses seemed forced, unnatural, stilted in a funny sort of way. The truth is, for an intelligent woman, she sure came across as shallow.

The hardest times were when we were alone in my car, driving from one property to another. That's when I felt the most pressure to fill the long, uncomfortable silences. Clients and their realtors don't have to like each other, but it certainly helps if they can get along. In the end, I accepted her as she was, and CBC Music on the car radio became my refuge when I ran out of things to say.

So, you can imagine my surprise and relief when I arrived at my office one afternoon, and my assistant told me Ali had just been on the phone asking me to make an offer on a property we'd visited a few days earlier. I wrote it up immediately and sent it over for her signature. Given it was a full-ask bid with only a couple of standard conditions, I was optimistic it would be well received. An hour after we submitted it, I heard from the seller's broker. Accepted.

I was delighted for Ali and I knew her mom and dad would be relieved, too. I'd learned from conversations with her father, as much as they loved having their daughter back on the island, they were concerned she was getting too comfortable living at home again. As many parents have discovered, once adult children return to the nest, it can be hard motivating them to move on.

Ali was at work when I called her. "Congratulations. Your offer's been accepted."

"Okay," she said, not even a hint of excitement in her voice. When Marie and I bought our first place, you'd think we'd won the lottery we were so pumped. With Ali, nothing.

"We got there in the end. You must be pleased."

"Huh?"

"I was beginning to worry we wouldn't find anywhere. At least now you'll have your own place again."

"Listen, I can't talk right now. I have to go." She terminated the call.

When you've been in the real estate business for as long as I have, very few things are surprising, but Ali's strange reaction was one of them. The condo we'd found her was only a ten-minute walk from her new law firm. It was in a great, safe location, and the price was fair. I knew Bank of Mom and Dad was helping with the deposit and that she'd easily be able to afford the mortgage since we'd looked at many more expensive units during the search. What was not to like?

As I said, something wasn't right.

That evening was "Dine-out Wednesday." Marie and I started the tradition soon after Freya was born. Spending quality time together once a week was important to us. It was an opportunity to take a moment out from our busy work schedules—Marie taught English at Owen Bay High School—to catch up as a family. There had been a time when Freya would join us, but now she was sixteen, she was way too cool to be spending evenings with her parents, so the two of us headed off to one of our favorite places for dinner.

The Dockside restaurant sat on the waterfront, and our window table looked directly across the fifteen-mile-wide Strait of Juan de Fuca toward the majestic Olympic National Park in Washington State. Even though it was early June, thick snow still covered the highest mountain peaks in the distance. The floor-to-ceiling windows were open, so we could hear the wind whipping around the rigging of the yachts in the marina. If you closed your eyes, it sounded like a chorus of alpine cow bells.

Marie ordered pan-fried salmon fillet while I went for my usual—halibut fish and chips. For my money, The Dockside served the best fish and chips on the island. Believe me, I'd tried a good few restaurants to put that assertion to the test. Shortly after our food arrived, a cruise ship approached. All summer, they made regular stops at Victoria's Ogden Point on their way north from San Francisco or Seattle before heading along the rugged BC coast toward Alaska. Marie and I had long been saving to take the same trip for our twentieth anniversary, less than two years away.

My phone pinged. When I picked it up off the table, I saw it was a text from Ali. *Thanks for all your help finding my new condo.*

So, she was pleased, after all. Maybe I'd caught her at a bad time when I called her earlier. Quickly, I tapped out a reply. *You're welcome. I know you'll be very happy there.*

Immediately, my phone pinged again. *Part of me wishes they hadn't accepted my offer.*

Ali was suffering from buyer's remorse. I'd seen this emotional reaction so many times before, particularly from first-time buyers. Once the contract is signed, suddenly the purchase becomes real, and the magnitude of the mortgage debt can seem daunting. That explained why her reaction had been so muted; she was nervous. She had no reason to be. The Victoria market, while pricey, had always been a good long-term investment. Plus, she was a senior associate at the biggest law firm on the island with a great career ahead of her. All she needed was reassurance.

You have nothing to worry about, I replied. *I'm certain you've done the right thing.*

Her response came back instantly. *I'm sad we won't get to spend more time together.*

I wasn't sure what to make of Ali's words. Our long days together must have been tedious for her, too. Surely, she was relieved she no longer had to put up with me prattling on. I assumed she was just being polite. We Canadians are like that.

I fired off another reply. *Now the real fun begins. You get to enjoy your new home.*

Ping. *No, seriously, I wish I hadn't bought it. I will miss you. XOXO*

I didn't respond this time. I kept reading her text, searching for an innocent explanation. What was she trying to say?

"Trouble?" Marie asked.

I looked up from the phone. "Sorry?"

"You haven't touched your food, Tom. From the worried look on your face I thought maybe someone was shafting you on a deal again."

"It's nothing. Just a client raising a few points."

Marie threw me one of her looks, as if to say: *I know what you're like. Don't let anyone walk all over you.*

My phone rang, so I quickly muted it and put it in my pocket. I can't explain why I didn't share the texts with Marie right away. They were confusing. I guess I didn't know what to do. What did Ali mean when she said she'd miss me? For weeks, she'd hardly said a word to me and now this. Her messages seemed completely out of character.

When we arrived home around eight thirty, Freya was in the den watching one of the property-buying shows on HGTV. Part of me hoped one day she'd take over my brokerage. I'd never mentioned it to her; I didn't want to put her under any pressure career-wise. She was still way too young to be thinking about things like that, anyway. But she seemed to have a genuine interest in the real estate business and had a good way with people, which always helps.

While Marie put the kettle on to make us some tea, I went upstairs to the study. Sitting at my desk, I took out my phone. Twenty-three missed calls. Worried that one of our transactions was falling apart, I navigated to the recent calls screen. All of them had come from an "unknown" number. Strange thing

6

was, when I called my voicemail, there were no messages. Then I noticed the red circle on the messages icon. Thirty-seven unread texts. Thirty-seven. I'd be lucky if I received that many in a week, let alone in the space of two hours.

A chill ran through me the moment I opened the app. All of them were from Ali, and they were still coming in. My stomach muscles tensed when I scrolled down to the first unread text.

I mean it. I'll miss you. XOXO

The next five repeated the exact same words and were all timed within a few minutes of each other. Many of Ali's messages had been sent multiple times, and the content appeared increasingly unhinged the more I read.

I really enjoyed our talks when we were on our own.

You're the only one who really gets me.

We have a connection. You see it too, right?

I just called you. Pick up the phone.

I want to pull out of the condo purchase. You'll think of a reason, won't you, Tom?

How cool would it be to spend more time with each other?

I know you want the same as I do. I see it in the way you look at me.

WHY DON'T YOU ANSWER MY CALLS?

Please pick up the phone.

Tom, are you there?

Is she with you?

Is that why you're ignoring me? She's with you, isn't she? I get it.

Don't worry, Tom. I'm here when you're ready.

I'll always be here for you.

My heart lodged in my throat when the study door opened. The phone fell out of my hand and bounced on the carpet.

"Tom," Marie said, "your tea's getting cold."

"I'm sorry," I said, scrambling for the phone on my hands and knees, so Marie didn't pick it up. "I completely forgot." Quickly, I powered it down, pangs of guilt running through me.

Marie cocked her head to one side. "Are you okay? You look flushed."

What could I say? My brain was still trying to process what I'd just read. I knew one thing: Marie must not see Ali's messages. What on earth would she think? "I'm not sure my fish was right." I patted my stomach. "I'm not feeling one hundred percent, to be honest." As I spoke, I could feel my cheeks getting warmer.

"Come downstairs and sit for a while. Work can wait for once. It'll still be there tomorrow."

Chapter 2

Best Buy had a sale on and, according to one of Ali's new co-workers at the law firm, the deals on computers were awesome. In need of a more powerful laptop to replace the brick she'd been using since she graduated from UBC, Ali went to check them out. Right after her last client meeting, she left the office, walked to the Broughton Street parking lot, picked up her VW Golf—the one her father had bought a couple of years earlier as a present for winning a big promotion—and headed over to Uptown Mall on the northern edge of Victoria.

The shopping center's rooftop parking area was packed when she arrived just after six thirty. Eventually, at the end furthest away from the escalators, she found a few empty spots and pulled into one. She grabbed her purse from behind the front passenger seat, applied fresh lipstick in the vizor mirror, then took out her phone. Near the top of her list of messages was the last text she'd received from Tom when he'd been trying to set up an appointment to view another property a few days earlier.

Ali tapped out a quick thank-you note for his help on finding her condo. Staring at the phone, she waited for him to reply. Moments later, her face lit up when his message came in. She fired off another text and then, after a couple of exchanges, he stopped responding.

She sent another. *I mean it. I'll miss you. XOXO.*

Ali waited in the car, her eyes glued to the phone. No reply.

Twice she speed-dialed Tom's number then killed the call when his voicemail answered. She sent the text five more times, one immediately after the other. Still no response.

While her mind was preoccupied, a vehicle pulled into one of the spaces next to her. Seconds later, a tapping sound broke her concentration. She turned her head and saw the rear door of a black SUV rubbing against the side of the Golf as a mother struggled to get her young son out of his child seat. Ali threw the woman a dirty look, but she appeared completely unfazed. For the best part of a minute, the door kept banging against Ali's car.

When Ali inspected the damage after the woman left, she found a slight, barely visible indentation in a rear panel. Dark flecks stuck to the cloth she used to wipe her vehicle's silver paintwork. Other than the one tiny dent, there was no other obvious damage.

She locked the car, checked her phone again, then ran across the parking lot. Slowed down by her toddler, the owner of the SUV was only a few feet ahead when Ali reached the escalators. At the ground level, they turned left and made their way into the supermarket.

Ali followed them.

The little boy made a beeline for one of the plastic shopping carts made up to look like a red fire truck. His mother lifted him into the driver's seat, but he was having none of it. Soon, his crying drowned out the cheap instrumental version of a Michael Bublé song coming out of the tinny ceiling speakers. Eventually, unable to placate her son, she allowed him to walk alongside her, and, magically, the wailing stopped. Ali picked up a shopping basket and tailed them, pausing to examine items on the shelves each time she caught up. Whenever the woman was distracted, the young boy would wander off, and she'd have to go chasing after him. As he ran up and down the aisles, a broad smile on his little face, the other shoppers beamed back at him in encouragement. All except Ali. Stone-faced, she looked right through him, her eyes trained on his mother.

Right in front of the canned vegetables section, the toddler fell over, grazing his head on one of the shelves. When the woman ran toward her screaming child, Ali spotted her opportunity. She sidled up to their cart and inspected the shopping inside. It didn't take long to spot what she needed—a triple-pack of Gillette razor refills. With her back to the security camera in the roof-corner of the building, she checked to make sure no one was watching, reached for the razors, and slipped them into the woman's open purse hanging from the handlebar. Seconds later, Ali wheeled the fire truck over to the mother.

"I didn't want to leave your purse unattended," Ali said.

"That's really kind," the woman said. "Thank you so much."

"Is there anything I can do to help?"

"He'll be okay." She was stroking her son's bright red forehead. "He's a big boy."

Ali smiled then made her way toward the checkout area. For a quarter of an hour, phone in hand, she waited next to the bakery section, the aroma of freshly baked bread wafting through the air. With one eye on the aisles, she called Tom, but his voicemail kicked in. She tried texting. Nothing came back.

By the time the fire truck appeared, the little boy was sitting quietly in the seat. Ali watched him grabbing at the display of chocolate bars alongside the line for one of the checkouts. She abandoned her basket on the floor and rushed to the customer service counter near the exit.

"I don't wish to make a fuss," she said to the member of staff. His name badge read: *My name is Anton—Assistant Manager—How can I WOW! you today?* "But I just witnessed someone stealing."

Anton looked confused for the few seconds it took for his brain to engage. "Have they left the store, madam?" he asked.

"No. She's over there." Ali pointed. "The woman in line five, the one with the young boy. It's her."

"What exactly did you see?"

"She put something into her purse. I saw her take it out of her cart."

"Are you absolutely certain?" Anton's tone was skeptical. Either that or he couldn't be bothered to deal with the hassle. "Could you be mistaken?"

"I'm sure. Look, would you prefer if I spoke to the manager?" Anton's chubby cheeks reddened. "I'm sorry, madam. I'll deal with it. Thank you for letting us know."

Ali walked away and stood outside the store until the woman came out, wheeling her shopping. Seconds later, Anton and what looked like a uniformed security guard approached her. It was too far to hear their conversation, but soon things appeared to get heated. The mother waved her arms about and kept pointing to her son. He started crying again.

Then she shouted, "Take a look if you don't believe me," thrusting her open purse toward the guard. He reached into the bag, shook his head, and retrieved the razors.

"I didn't put them there," she continued.

When she stepped back, the guard placed a hand on her shoulder while Anton held onto the cart. A small crowd stopped and stared as they led the thief back into the store. Ali turned and walked away.

Great news. Laptops were, indeed, discounted by fifteen percent at Best Buy. Ali even managed to pick up the one she wanted—the latest Dell XPS 13-inch. When she carried her shopping back to her car, the SUV was still parked next to it, but there was no sign of its owner. She sat in the Golf with her door wide open, using it as a shield to prevent anyone from seeing. With the ignition key gripped in her right hand, she slowly carved the four-letter C-word into the body of the SUV.

Before she left the mall, Ali checked her phone for any reply from Tom. Nothing. The moment she pulled into her parents' drive, she tried calling him, but again it went to voicemail. For another fifteen minutes, she remained in the car, bombarding him with texts.

Chapter 3

I left my cell phone off all night. Early the next morning, I went for my usual run along the beach. As mine was a largely sedentary job, I liked to squeeze in a jog most weekdays before heading into the office. My father had put on weight in his later years and died from complications arising from diabetes. I was determined not to let that happen to me.

The cool air drifting north from the Puget Sound filled my lungs, the increased oxygen in my blood helping me think. During the night, sleep had been impossible with a million thoughts churning over in my mind in a fruitless search for answers. I must have replayed every moment Ali and I had been together over the last couple of months, and there was nothing I could remember doing or saying that could possibly have given her the wrong impression. Hell, at forty-eight, I was twenty years older than her—old enough to be her father. What made her think I was interested in her? It was utter madness. For the life of me, I couldn't comprehend why she thought there was something going on between us. I was dreading what I'd see on my phone when I powered it back up.

Turning away from the beach, I ran up Sea Street then along Tanner Avenue, which would eventually take me toward home. Marie's face kept flashing in front of me. I knew I ought to show her what was on my phone. Marie would know what to do; she always did. But, even though I'd done nothing wrong, the idea of sharing Ali's nonsense with my wife worried me. Taken at face value, Ali's words looked damning. *We have a connection... She's with you, isn't she?...I'm here when you're ready...I'll always be here for you.* What would Marie think? What would any wife think? I couldn't blame her if she thought I'd been up to something. No sane woman would write those texts without a lot of encouragement, right? But if I didn't tell Marie, and she later found the messages, that would be far worse. Then she'd assume I was hiding them from her. How would I ever explain that away? I was damned if I did and damned if I didn't.

Tires screeched, followed by a car horn blaring. Suddenly, I was torn away from my thoughts. A car skidded to a halt a few inches from me. I'd been crossing the street near the golf club, and the vehicle seemed to appear out of nowhere. It was entirely my fault; my mind had been elsewhere. Burning rubber clung to the air as I waved sorry to the woman behind the wheel. She shook her head and drove away before I could check to see she was okay.

Leaving the busy road behind me, I jogged up the quiet street toward Bob and Sonya Page's house. Ali's silver Volkswagen— license plate: THX DAD—was parked outside, as it was most mornings when I ran past. Setting out from home that day, part of me had thought about taking another route to avoid their place. But I'd done nothing wrong. Why should I change my routine for that woman? Wouldn't that be the act of a guilty man? For a moment, as I approached her parents' home, I slowed down, wondering whether I should knock on their door. Confront Ali there and then. Show Bob and Sonya their daughter's crazy messages. Make Ali answer for her outrageous behavior.

I didn't stop. I bottled it and continued running. If Marie was likely to misinterpret the texts, what would our friends think of them? Naturally, they would side with their daughter. In all probability, they'd assume the worst and think I'd been leading her on. It could end up being embarrassing for everyone.

Two minutes later, I was home. I jumped in the shower while

Marie prepped coffee on the Nespresso Pixie machine we'd treated ourselves to last Christmas when Hudson's Bay had one of their sales on. With warm water washing over me, I reached a decision: I wouldn't show Marie Ali's texts, least not before I'd first found out what was going on for myself. Our relationship was strong, and we trusted each other completely, but it hadn't always been like that.

Twelve years earlier, I'd had a brief affair with another woman, a mortgage broker with whom I did a lot of business. It lasted no more than a month, and I swear it was the one and only time I looked outside our marriage for intimacy. It was stupid, and to this day, I still don't understand what led me to act so selfishly. It was nothing more than sex. I knew that then, and I know that now. There was never any love there. That much was obvious to us both. Marie is the only woman I've ever truly loved. It's crazy, really—the massively important things we risk for a foolish moment of distraction from our daily routine.

While there was no excuse for my self-centered behavior, I can tell you I was the one who ended the hollow affair. For months after, the guilt kept eating away at me until I could take it no longer. So, one evening over dinner, I confessed it all to Marie. Told her everything. At first, freeing myself from that suffocating burden felt liberating, but I soon realized I should have kept quiet. Understandably, Marie was shocked and devastated. I knew I'd never be unfaithful again, so what purpose did it serve to tell her? It's not as if telling her diminished my infidelity in some way. All it did was destroy her trust in me forever. You want to know the real motivation for my confession? Simple: it eased my conscience. That's why. It was all about me, to make me feel better. Yet another selfish act, one I came to regret almost as much as the affair itself.

And because Marie has always been a much bigger person than me, to save our marriage, she worked through the hurt, the anger, the loss of trust, even the betrayal. She found the strength to forgive me and move on. Not once did she hold that shabby, meaningless episode against me.

I didn't deserve her. I still don't.

One thing was clear as I jumped out of the shower: I wasn't about to let Ali jeopardize my precious relationship with Marie. I would never let that happen.

By the time I was dressed, I'd formulated a plan. I would call Ali that morning and demand an explanation. I'd tell her to back off and leave me and my family alone. Then I'd sit down with Marie that evening and show her what was on my phone. Hiding it from my wife, when there was absolutely nothing going on, wouldn't be the honest thing to do. It didn't feel right. This time, it wasn't about my conscience; it was about transparency. Our marriage was strong enough to cope with the truth. Certainly, we had nothing to fear from the ramblings of a young woman's deluded mind.

My plan lasted only the few minutes it took me to drive to the office and power up my phone. Forty-three new texts appeared on the screen when it came back to life, causing me to spill half a Tim Hortons take-out coffee down the front of my shirt. Brenda, my assistant, looked up from her PC and came running over when she heard me swear.

"Are you okay?" she asked.

"I'm sorry." I was holding the shirt fabric away from my skin to ease the burning.

Brenda handed me a box of Kleenex from her desk. "Here. Use these."

"Thanks." I placed my phone face down in case she was looking. "It's my own fault. I didn't have the lid on properly."

After Brenda returned to her desk, I closed my office door, cleaned myself up with more Kleenex, then called to check my voicemail. Nothing.

My heart was racing when I opened the messages app and scrolled down. Ali's texts went on and on about our "special connection" and how she was "dreaming" about spending whole days with me again once I'd found a way to pull out of the contract for her condo. This is going to sound strange, but the more I read, the more I began to feel sorry for her. Clearly, she had serious psychological problems and needed professional help. This was far from normal behavior for a sane adult woman.

But when I reached her final text, my sympathy vanished, replaced by anger and frustration.

Saw you running by the house this morning. When you slowed down and looked up at my window, I felt warm inside. ☺ I get it. You can't talk right now, but this was your way of letting me know you're there for me. I saw you smile when I dropped my towel for you. Watch for me tomorrow! XOXO

What planet was she living on? It certainly wasn't the same one as the rest of us. I hadn't looked at her window. I didn't even know which room she used. And to imply I had been watching her get changed was perverted. This had to stop right now before things got out of hand. Contacting Ali from my office would have been awkward; the walls were thin, and there was a risk Brenda would overhear my conversation. What I wanted to say to Ali wouldn't be nice, far from it. Something like that needed privacy, so I grabbed my jacket and car keys and left the office.

On the way out, Brenda waved me to stop. "Are you leaving?"

"Something important has just come up," I said, continuing to move toward the front door. "I have to go out for an hour or so."

"What about our ten o'clock listing appointment?"

"I'm sorry, Brenda. Can you handle that one on your own? This really can't wait." I hated dumping on Brenda like that, but I didn't wait around for her to debate my request. Moments later, I was in my vehicle and heading in the direction of town.

I found an empty spot on Dallas Road and pulled over. The cold wet fabric of my shirt stuck to the seatbelt when I released it, pulling the sticky coffee-stained patch away from the hairs on my chest. I reached into the glove compartment for some of the tissues Marie kept in there. While I used them to dab my skin, I stared toward the ocean, wondering what I was going to say to Ali.

A few hundred yards away, the car ferry to Port Angeles was leaving Victoria's inner harbor. On board the top deck a group of passengers waved as it sailed past Breakwater lighthouse. Marie, Freya and I had taken that crossing to the US countless times on short trips to Seattle and, when time permitted, further down into Oregon.

Whatever I said to Ali, she had to hear exactly how I felt about her and her unwanted attention. With my tendency to avoid conflict, I could already hear Marie's voice in my ear: "Don't let her walk all over you, Tom." Even if I had to be rude, it was critical she was left with no misconceptions or ambiguity. Despite what she thought, we didn't have a relationship and there was never going to be one. *Make sure she gets it.*

I watched the ferry sail out of view before closing the car window and picking up my phone.

"I've been waiting for your call," Ali said after only one ring. I detected no shame in her voice. Instead, she sounded almost excited to hear from me.

"What's going on?" I made a poor job hiding the anger boiling inside me. "Why on earth have you been sending me all those messages?"

"Come on, Tom. We both know you feel the same as I do. Don't insult my intelligence by pretending—"

"I don't know what you think is happening here, but I don't have any feelings for you. The whole idea is crazy."

"I'm not stupid, you know. I've seen the way you look at me. You just don't like to admit it."

"What are you talking about?"

"Remember when I used to babysit Freya and you would drive me home?"

"That was years ago. What's it got to do with—"

"Even then, we had a certain chemistry. I've never forgotten. Don't make out you don't know what I mean."

"I have no idea what you're talking about. Really, I don't."

"No one else is listening. You don't have to pretend with me."

"Listen, I'm sorry if I've given you the wrong impression. If I did, it was completely innocent. You need to understand there is nothing between us. There never has been."

"You know that's not true."

Why wasn't she listening to me? It was like we were talking different languages. "I don't know how else to put this, but you're just a client. There's nothing special about—"

"That's funny. Then how come you agreed to help me find a place? You could have said no, but you didn't. You told me yourself you don't cover the downtown market and yet you jumped at the chance to work with me."

"I only agreed to help as a favor to your mom and dad. It had nothing to do with how I feel about you. Ask them. They'll tell you I didn't want to do it."

"Dad told me you were super excited."

"That's just not true."

"I'll admit when we first started looking at properties, I wasn't sure if you still felt the same way about me. You seemed a little distant, but it soon became apparent what we had before was still there."

"This is insane."

"I picked up your signal."

"What are you talking about?"

"When you started confiding in me, I knew it was for a reason."

"What? I've never confided in you."

"Not everything is spoken, you know. The problems in your marriage were written all over your face. I got it; you were testing me, seeing how I'd react, seeing if I still cared for you."

She was inventing things. No wonder her texts made no sense. "Marie and I have a great relationship. I wasn't sending you hidden messages. This is all in your head."

"Why are you acting as though I'm making this up? Just last

week, didn't you tell me you wanted to go on a vacation to Europe, but Marie wouldn't go? Did I imagine that? I could see how upset you were with her."

She was twisting my words. I remembered mentioning I'd really like to take a European trip one day, but Marie was concerned about the cost. We certainly hadn't argued about it. There was no secret meaning in what I'd said. "I wasn't upset at all. I was just making conversation."

"Yeah, right. Maybe I'd believe you if that was the only time, but you were always moaning about her, checking to see how I'd react."

I wasn't getting through to her. It was time to be direct. "The truth is, Ali, I really didn't like spending time with you at all. In fact, I was relieved when you found a place. I was glad it was over."

"Then what about this morning? Explain that to me. I saw the smile on your face when I dropped my towel for you. You look up at my window every time you run past the house. Try telling me that doesn't mean anything."

Why was she doing this? None of it was based in reality. "I didn't look at you. I didn't even know you were there. I've been taking the same route for years. Most of that time, you weren't even living at your parents' house."

"Why won't you admit how you feel? There's no shame, you know. I've already told you I feel the same."

What more could I say to persuade Ali I had no feelings for her? This call was quickly heading in the wrong direction. As hard as it was, if I was going to get through to her, I had to risk being cruel. "Let me be absolutely clear. There is nothing between us. There never was and there never will be. And now you've found your condo, I don't want to hear from you or see you again. Is that understood?"

"I know you don't mean that."

"Don't send me any more messages. Don't call me. Don't come anywhere near—"

"It's Marie, isn't it? I get it. Even though you're desperate to get out, you feel guilty. That's because you're a decent man, Tom. It's one of the things I love about you."

"Listen, I want you to stay the hell away from me."

There was a brief pause before she spoke. "Don't worry," she said, "take all the time you need. I know you can't just walk away from your marriage, even if it is toxic, not after all those years. I get that. Just know that I'm here for you when the time is right."

"You are fucking crazy. Do you know that? You keep away from me. Do you hear?"

When I ended the call, I was shaking. I caught my reflection in the rear-view mirror. My eyes were shiny, my face pale. The fact that she still believed there was something between us after I'd been so clear, proved Ali was suffering from some sort of psychosis. She was seeing things that weren't there. In her mind, our relationship was all too real. Realizing that was terrifying. For the first time in my adult life, I didn't know what to do.

Together with his two brothers, Nick Bladen ran a small financial advisory firm in Sidney, a quaint seaside town about fifteen miles north of Victoria. Nick and I had been friends since our college days at UVic. He was Freya's godfather. My mom was one of his clients, like many of Sidney's retired community. I trusted him. Naturally, he was the first person I thought of for advice on what I should do about Ali. So, before I left Dallas Road, I called Nick and arranged to meet him for lunch that day at the restaurant in the Sidney Pier hotel, one of Marie's favorite spots for Dine-out Wednesdays.

When I arrived at the table, Nick was already there, staring out of the large window, a half-empty glass of white wine in front of him. "Looks beautiful today," he said, nodding his head toward the ocean.

To the east, some seventy miles away on the US mainland,

21

Mount Baker dominated the horizon with half its mass under snow, gleaming in the sun. Often when I visited Sidney, the mountain was obscured by cloud, but not today. For once, it looked like it did on the postcards sold in the gift shops up and down the town's Beacon Avenue.

"I hope you haven't been waiting long," I said, shaking his hand before taking a seat.

"I got here early." Nick threw me a quizzical look. "Man, you look exhausted. What happened to your shirt?"

"It's a long story." I grabbed the menu. "In fact, that's one of the reasons I'm here. I need to pick your brains."

Nick grinned. "I can recommend a great laundry service."

"No, seriously, I want your advice on something."

"Then lunch is on you."

One of the waiting staff came over and took our order. After the minimum amount of small talk, I shared with my friend everything Ali had done. The only thing I held back was her name. I read out some of her texts to give him a flavor of what I was up against and told him about my telephone conversation that morning. If I wanted Nick's take on what I ought to do, he needed to hear the whole story. He listened without interruption.

"She's a good twenty years younger than me," I said as I finished. "What she sees in me, goodness knows."

Nick pushed his empty plate to one side. "What does Marie think?"

"I haven't told her yet?"

He raised his eyebrows. "You have to. You can't sit on something like this."

"I don't want to upset her. Those texts could easily be misinterpreted. What if she thinks I've been seeing this woman?"

"Better she hears it from you than the person sending them. How would you feel if she found them on your phone and you'd said nothing?"

"You're right. That's been worrying me."

"Not easy, I know." Nick emptied his wineglass. "How well

22

do you know the parents?"

"I've known her father for over ten years. He's a senior officer with the Mounties. He and I are volunteers at the air cadets near the airport. That's how we met. Like me, he's ex-air force. They live near us in Owen Bay, and we meet up for dinner every now and then. I'd say they are good friends. Why do you ask?"

"I was thinking you could start there. Maybe have a quiet word with them. You said she's still living at their place. Do you think she would listen to them?"

"I'm not sure that's such a good idea. It wouldn't be an easy conversation." I finished the last of my penne. "What would I say? 'Your daughter's a bunny boiler. Please tell her to leave me alone.'"

Nick wrinkled his nose. "Yeah, I see your point. No parent wants to hear that about their kid. Man, you sure pick them."

"I didn't choose any of this, remember? I wish I'd never laid eyes on her."

We ordered a couple of decaf coffees and stared out of the window toward the pier. A group of people stepped off a small whale-watching boat. They all wore broad smiles, so I assumed they'd seen some orcas or a humpback out in the strait.

"Do you mind if I ask her name?" Nick asked, breaking the silence.

I hesitated. I wasn't sure what it would add. If I held back now, though, would he think I was hiding something? "If I tell you, it has to remain strictly between us."

"Sure. I'm not going to share it with anyone."

Leaning across the table, I whispered, "Ali Page."

Nick's face took on a glaze of confusion. "Not Bob and Sonya's daughter?"

I flinched. "Yes. Do you know them?"

"When you said he works for the Royal Canadian Mounted Police, I made the connection. They're clients of ours. Have been for years."

Sometimes, I despise living on an island. It's almost impossible

23

to keep anything private. "Listen, you can't say a word to them about this. This conversation has to remain between the two of us."

Nick held up his palms. "Don't worry, Tom. I won't say anything. I promise."

I glanced at the clock on the wall. "I must be getting back." Had I known the Pages were clients of Nick's firm, I'm not sure I would have confided in him. "I've been out of the office all day. Brenda will be wondering what's happened to me."

"I met their daughter last year," Nick said. "They brought her with them to their annual client review."

"She comes across as perfectly normal when you first meet her."

"I remember she asked some penetrating questions about her parents' investment portfolio. Isn't she a lawyer in Vancouver?"

"Not any longer. She just joined a firm in Victoria. That's why I was helping her find a condo."

I paid for lunch, then we left the restaurant together and strolled up Beacon Avenue toward Nick's office. Just before we got there, he tapped me on the shoulder and threw me a knowing smile. "As well as being smart, I remember Ali Page is quite a looker."

I stopped. "What's that got to do with anything?"

"Nothing, I guess. It's just that most men would be flattered to receive attention from a young, good-looking woman like her." He frowned. "You sure you're not overreacting?"

Driving south down the Pat Bay Highway, I couldn't stop thinking about Nick's parting comments. Over lunch, I thought he'd truly understood how worried I was by Ali's unwanted attention. But it was as if he was making a joke of it once he knew what she looked like. It wasn't funny. Far from it. And her fixation with me was anything but flattering. How could he think that? What if it had been the other way around? If I had sent Ali those texts, do you think for one moment Nick's reaction would have been the same? Hell, no.

I was a grown man, but I don't mind admitting, as I headed back to the office, I felt scared and alone. I knew Ali wasn't going to go away and I had no idea how to make her stop.

Chapter 4

Nick was right about one thing: even though I knew it would upset her, I had to tell Marie. If she found out from someone else, or discovered Ali's texts on my phone, I'd never forgive myself. How would I explain hiding them from the woman I loved?

After dinner that night, we sat in the den while Freya went upstairs to her room. Our daughter would spend hours chatting with friends on Instagram or WhatsApp or one of the multitude of other social media platforms we crinklies know little about, so that was my opportunity to have a quiet chat with Marie.

Marie turned on the TV to catch the end of Anderson Cooper's evening slot on CNN.

"Would you mind if I turned that down a moment?" I asked, reaching for the remote control. "I'd like to discuss something with you."

Marie threw me a look as if to say: *You must be crazy; it's Anderson Cooper*, but said, "Okay."

"I'll record it for you."

I hit the red button on the remote then turned off the TV. Immediately, my mouth felt dry. There was no easy way to say what I was about to share. A vivid memory flashed into mind: Marie's horrified reaction that time I confessed to having an affair all those years ago. This was bound to stir up those old emotions. I detested Ali for putting us in this awful position.

"You remember last night," I said, "when I told you I had an upset stomach?"

"You thought your fish might be off."

My tongue felt like it was coated in sand. I cleared my throat. "Well, that wasn't actually what was troubling me. It was something else." From Marie's mystified expression, I could tell she was already concerned where this conversation was going. But I'd started, so I had to continue. "I should have told you about it then, but I wasn't sure how to handle it."

"Spit it out. You're starting to worry me."

"Believe me, that's the last thing I want. It's the only reason I've sat on this since yesterday."

Marie sighed. "What is it, Tom?"

I took a deep intake of breath and picked up my phone from the coffee table. "I need to show you something on here—some messages. Before you read them, you need to understand I've done nothing to encourage them. Please understand there's not a shred of truth in what she says."

"Who are you talking about? You're not making much sense. What messages?"

"Bob and Sonya's daughter."

Marie made a face. "Ali?"

"Yes." I held my phone in the air. "There are messages on here from her. They started coming in when we were at the restaurant and they kept coming all night. They make no sense. You have to believe I did nothing to—"

Marie grabbed the phone out of my hand. "For goodness sake, let me see." She fumbled with the screen. "What's the password for this thing?"

My heart pounded the inside of my ribcage, and I could taste the bile rising in my throat. *Please, Marie, don't think I'm having another affair.*

I told her the passcode then watched as she hit the messages icon. I'd planned on showing the texts in chronological order, but I couldn't stop her. Even though the phone was upside

27

down, I could see she was reading the last one first: *Saw you running by the house. When you slowed down and looked up at my window, I felt warm inside.* 😊 *I get it. You can't talk right now, but this is your way of letting me know you're there for me. I saw you smile when I dropped my towel for you. Watch for me tomorrow! XOXO*

The muscles in Marie's jaw twitched as she read on. Scrolling through the earlier messages, she hardly blinked. At one point, I thought she was going to say something, but she covered her mouth with her hand. When I could watch her no more, I looked down at the carpet, imagining what horrors she must be thinking right now. After what seemed like an age, she placed the phone on the table and stared at me. She said nothing; she didn't need to. Her expression alone commanded an explanation.

I could feel blood rushing to my cheeks. Just tell her the truth. She will understand. "I swear I've done absolutely nothing to encourage this. I promise, Marie. Nothing. When they started coming in last night, I was as shocked as you—still am. They make no sense. All day, I thought of nothing else. I kept asking myself why she would do this. She must have a mental illness, because this fantasy she's created is all in her mind."

"What does she mean when she says she'll be there for you?" Marie asked. "And what's this 'connection' she's talking about?" Her eyes began to water. "Why would she say those things?"

"I have no idea. You know how hard it was for me working with her. I kept telling you how difficult she was, how she hardly said a word to me all those weeks." I pointed to my phone. "And then all of a sudden those appeared. It's like someone else sent the texts."

Marie picked up the phone again. "I want to see what's on here before yesterday."

"Absolutely. I've nothing to hide. All you'll see are messages arranging to meet for showings, that kind of thing."

When Marie finished scrolling, she looked at me. "I want you to promise me something."

28

"Anything."

"I want you to swear on Freya's life you haven't done anything to encourage her."

"Look, I know what you must be thinking."

"I need you to say the words, Tom."

"I swear on Freya's life I've done nothing to cause this. I realize how it looks, but I promise this is all in her head. It's not real. Please believe me, Marie. I wouldn't do anything to jeopardize our marriage. Ever."

Marie tossed the phone on the table and looked away. "You don't know how much I want to believe that. For heaven's sake, the girl's not much older than Freya."

I went over to Marie and tried to cuddle her. "Don't," she said, recoiling. "I need to process this." I tried again. "Don't touch me."

"I'm sorry." I returned to my armchair. "This has been playing on my mind all day. I wanted to tell you last night and then again this morning, but I've been struggling to process it myself."

Freya walked into the den. "Dad," she said, "my laptop's playing up again. Can you take a look at it for me?" She looked at Marie. "Are you okay, Mom?"

Marie wiped her eyes and forced a smile. "I'm fine, honey."

I stood and put an arm around Freya's shoulders. "Come on. Let's see what's up with your machine."

When I returned from Freya's room some fifteen minutes later, Marie had made us both peppermint tea and she was watching Anderson Cooper with the sound muted. I noticed my phone wasn't in the same position as I'd left it.

"Have you talked to her?" Marie asked, her gaze glued to the TV screen.

"Ali?"

"Who else do you think I mean?"

"I called her this morning."

"And you were going to tell me that when, exactly?"

I went over to the sofa and sat next to her. "I'm not holding back anything. I was going to tell you everything this evening, I promise. I called her this morning, looking for an explanation."

Marie turned toward me. "And what did she say?"

"Things went from bad to worse. You don't want to hear it."

"Tell me what she said."

"It's crazy stuff. I really don't want—"

"Just tell me."

"She talked about the chemistry between us." Marie flinched. "She pretty much made out I'd led her on."

Marie cocked her head. "How exactly?"

"It was all nonsense. She seemed to think when I talked about our family, perfectly normal things like our vacations or where we'd been to eat and so on, there was some hidden meaning. Like I was trying to send her signals about how I felt about her. As I said, it's crazy."

"And this morning? Did she expose herself at the window?"

"I have no idea. I ran by their house, as I do every morning, but I certainly didn't look at her window. I've no idea what room she sleeps in. Why would I? The woman's a fantasist."

Marie turned toward the TV again. After a minute or so of silence, she asked, "Have you told me everything? I don't want to find out there's more, Tom."

I didn't have the heart to tell Marie what Ali had said about waiting for me to end our marriage. My wife was distressed enough as it is. What good would it do to tell her that? "There's nothing more to tell."

Chapter 5

Although I didn't like being so aggressive the day I called Ali from my car, spelling out exactly how I felt about her seemed to have worked. Weeks went by without a word from her. That said, every time my phone went off, my whole body tensed, not knowing if it was her trying to reach me again. Concentrating on anything for more than a few seconds was impossible without a persistent background feeling of dread weaving its way into my consciousness.

When the closing day for Ali's condo purchase arrived, I expected her to try to contact me, but she didn't. It probably helped that I got Brenda to handle the closure formalities for our firm. After that, with each day that passed without hearing from her, I grew a little more confident Ali had moved on.

Most mornings, I was still running, but I was taking a different way home to avoid the Pages' house. Even after her father told me Ali had moved out of their place and into her new property, I stuck to my alternative route just in case she was back visiting her parents. I took no chances.

Things were frosty at home. With Marie going out of her way to avoid being on her own with me, Dine-out Wednesdays were the first casualty. Then she began staying at work longer than usual, leaving much earlier in the mornings, and going shopping with Freya on those few days I was around. No matter how many times I tried to explain I hadn't sought Ali's attention,

Marie seemed unconvinced. She never came out and accused me of anything. She didn't have to. After eighteen years of marriage, I could tell how she felt from the tone in her voice and the way she projected some of her anger onto Freya. I'd betrayed her once. What was to stop me doing it again, only this time with a much younger woman? I hated Ali for resurrecting that ghost from the past.

Then the calls began.

This time on our home phone, not my cell. Always from a withheld number and around the same time of night—just after Marie and I had gone to bed. At first, I answered them, but there was never anyone on the line. They would continue for an hour or so—sometimes three or four calls, and at other times more than twenty—and then nothing until the following night, when they would start over. It had to be Ali.

You can imagine the impact they had on our relationship. Death by a thousand cuts. Each call feeding Marie's suspicion and widening the gulf between us. But that wasn't all. Most nights Marie and I went to bed between ten and eleven, but the exact time would vary. The creepy thing was the calls would start the precise moment we turned our bedroom lamps off. Ali must have been watching our home. How else could she know?

Immediately after the first call each night, I'd go back downstairs to check outside our property. I looked up and down the road for Ali's Golf. I knew she had to be hiding close by, but not once did see her or the car. When I returned to bed, invariably, Marie would tell me I had to do something to "fix this" and that "we can't go on living this way." Exactly what I was supposed to do about it wasn't clear. If Ali was trying to drive a wedge between me and Marie, she was succeeding.

When it was clear the calls weren't going to stop, I started putting our phones on silent mode before we went to bed. While that gave us a chance to get some sleep, I was uncomfortable being out of contact all night. My mother lived alone in Sidney and the previous summer she'd fallen badly when getting out of bed in the middle of the night. She called me, and Marie and I rushed over there to help. Fortunately, we got there in good time. Just as well, because we soon discovered her hip was broken. While that had long since mended, she'd lost some of her former confidence and now seemed permanently unsteady on her feet. Turning off the ringer volume on our phones created a dilemma. While it eliminated one source of stress, it caused another. I'd never forgive myself if it meant missing another emergency call from Mom.

Marie was right about one thing: Ali's intrusion into our lives had to stop. So, when I was alone at work on one of Brenda's days off, I called Ali's cell phone. It went to voicemail. "Call me back," was my terse message.

Twenty minutes later, she returned my call. "I've been waiting to hear from you," she said.

"I thought I was perfectly clear when I told you to leave me alone."

"I have left you alone. I've been giving you the space you need, exactly as I said I would."

I'd promised myself I would control my temper this time, but it was far from easy. "Bullshit. You've been calling our home every night. I know it's you."

"You seem upset."

"You think?"

"Did you ever consider how hard it must be for me waiting?"

"You're not listening. If you continue—"

"Okay, okay, so I called you a few times. I just wanted to hear your voice. Don't get mad. I wasn't trying to hurt you. You can hurt me if you like."

Ali was living in a parallel universe. She'd lost all grip on reality. The last thing I wanted was to indulge her lunacy by dragging out the conversation any longer than necessary. I'd made my point. She now knew that I knew it was her making the calls to our home, not that she seemed concerned. Hell, she'd even admitted it.

"If you continue to harass me, I'm going to report you to the police. I don't want to do that, but you're leaving me no choice."

"There's no need to be aggressive. I've hurt you. I get it. When we're together, I promise I'll make it up to you a million times over. You'll see."

I killed the call. It was a mistake contacting her. Big mistake. I knew it the moment she started speaking. How do you rationalize with someone like that? My fear was by reaching out to her, I'd just given her more encouragement, made things much worse. She now knew her calls were getting to me. If she was so brazen about watching our home and phoning late at night, what else might she do? Someone that divorced from reality was dangerous.

My phone pinged, sending my gut into spasm. It was a text from her. I should have deleted it immediately, but I couldn't stop myself from reading it.

I'm sorry, Tom. Forgive me. I need to learn to be more patient. Know that I'm still here for you.

Placing the phone on my desk, face down, I could see my fingers were trembling. Then it pinged again.

Let me make it up to you. Come and see what I've done with the condo you found for me. I know you'll love it. I bought a new king-size bed. 😊

When was this going to end? If I was going to prevent permanent damage to our marriage, I knew I had to do something quickly. I would have to go to the police and report her.

Chapter 6

The Owen Bay Police Department was our local, municipally controlled police force. I mention that because it was separate from the Royal Canadian Mounted Police, the country's federal policing operation. Given Bob Page was a serving senior officer at the RCMP detachment on the island, that distinction was a crucial consideration for me as I entered OBPD's building next to the fire hall. The last thing I wanted was Bob to hear that I'd reported his unstable daughter.

Explaining to the woman on the other side of the protective glass panel why I was there was embarrassing. While I was spelling it out for her, there were two young men standing in line behind me, and they could hear everything I was saying. They chuckled when I told the receptionist I needed to report being harassed by a woman. When I took a seat in the waiting area, they smirked at me and nudged one another. *Juveniles.*

I still hadn't worked out what I was going to say. Reporting a theft or property damage was one thing. In those situations, there would normally be tangible evidence, something I could show the police. They could take fingerprints and photograph the scene. This was completely different. I didn't have such proof, so how was I going to get them to understand the full impact Ali's disturbing behavior was having on my family? Despite the frustration and anger rising inside me, I knew containing my emotions would be crucial; facts mattered to the police much more than feelings. Whatever happened, I had to come across as measured in my meeting with the officer. Besides, as far as I knew, Ali hadn't yet done anything illegal.

Even though I'd lived in Owen Bay for most of my adult life, I had never been inside our local police station. Let's just say the décor was austere, and that's being kind. The cheap wooden seats in the waiting area looked like they'd been bought second-hand from *Used Victoria* or some other classified-ads website, and I swear the pot plant standing in the corner was plastic. No living plant could survive under a layer of dust that thick. On the cream-painted wall opposite me was a bunch of posters covering all manner of society's ills: opioid addiction, missing persons, domestic abuse, the crime-stoppers hotline, you name it. I couldn't believe all this was going on in our sleepy, conservative neighborhood. This was a world I knew nothing about, but for the men and women in this building, handling these serious issues was an everyday experience. I toyed with the idea of leaving. Would the officer I was about to meet think I was wasting his or her time? Like Nick, might they think I was overreacting?

Outside, I could hear men shouting to each other. I leaned toward the window and saw some of the fire crew cleaning one of the fire trucks in front of the fire hall. It was a blisteringly hot day, and it looked like the one with the hose was having a bit of fun spraying his colleagues with cold water.

"Mr. Harper," said the uniformed officer in a booming voice when he appeared from a side door.

I stood and shook his hand. "That's me."

Sergeant Manning was a big man—huge shoulders, thick neck, and hands that were twice the size of mine. From the back, he looked like a football lineman as he led me down a windowless corridor. He was much younger than me, too; around thirty-five or so. If I was a criminal, he'd be the last person I'd want to run into in a dark alley late at night. Anyway, he seemed friendly enough as we took our seats at the tiny table in one of the cramped interview rooms.

36

"I hear you want to report some harassing behavior," Manning said after taking down a few of my personal details.

"Yes," I said, feeling more nervous than I had anticipated. "It's a sensitive matter involving the daughter of some friends of ours."

"The daughter's the one being harassed?"

"No. She's the one doing it."

Manning leaned his head slightly to one side and pursed his lips. "I see. And who exactly is she harassing?"

"Me."

Manning threw me another quizzical look before scribbling something on his pad. "Okay. You said her parents are friends of yours, so I take it you have a name for her."

"Ali Page."

"Ali Page." Manning wrote down the name.

Maybe I was imagining things, but the sergeant's expression revealed a slight flicker of recognition. Did he know her? That was unlikely; she hadn't been back on the island that long. Also, Manning was a few years older than Ali, so they couldn't have gone to Owen Bay High School together. Was it possible her behavior had already caused her to show up on the police's radar? Maybe I wasn't the only one she was tormenting. Then another explanation came to mind: did Sergeant Manning know Bob Page? I wondered whether to continue.

"Her father works for the RCMP," I said, scrutinizing Manning's face for clues. "This won't get back to him, will it?"

"No reason for it to. We're not part of the RCMP."

"I know that, but I'd hate him to..." I stopped myself. I needed Manning's help, so the last thing I could afford to do was alienate him by implying he wouldn't treat everything with professional discretion. "I'm sorry. I didn't mean to suggest anything."

Manning remained stone-faced. "How old is Ali Page?"

"Twenty-eight."

"Okay, so we're not talking about a kid up to no good.

37

What's she been doing to upset you?"

I told him the whole sordid story: how I was a local realtor helping Ali find her condo as a favor to her parents and how we'd spent weeks together looking at properties, during which time the conversations had been limited at best. Fact is, I hardly knew much about her. When it came to the disturbing texts, I summarized the content. I told him how they'd started only after we'd found her a property to buy. I explained how they'd stopped for a while, but then the late-night phone calls began. As I shared my story, I could feel my muscles tensing. The stress of the past few weeks came flooding back.

Manning heard me out, making one or two notes while I spoke. When I finished, he leaned back in his chair and crossed his arms. "Has she threatened you in any way?" he asked.

I paused before answering. There had been no overt threats, but that didn't mean I didn't feel threatened by Ali's actions. "Her behavior is unsettling. Anyone can see that. And my wife is worried by it, too."

"But has she threatened to harm you or your family?"

"No. Not in so many words." Maybe I hadn't described Ali's harassment properly because I didn't seem to be getting my point across to the officer. What Ali was doing felt intimidating even if she hadn't actually threatened us.

"Hmm."

"I hope that won't prevent you from talking to her. She needs to understand the effect she's having on my family and that there will be consequences if she continues."

Manning scribbled another note on his pad. "Has she had any physical contact with you since you found the condo for her?"

"No. I haven't seen her since then. Thank God. All communication has been by phone or text."

"All one way?"

"I don't follow."

"Have you sent her any messages or tried to phone her?"

Where was Manning going with all these questions? He should be focusing on Ali's actions, not mine. Did it matter that I had called her to get her to stop harassing us? "I've called her twice in the last few weeks, but only to tell her to leave us alone."

Manning used his fat fingers to stroke the short bristles of his goatee. "Do you have the text messages with you?"

"Yes, of course." I reached into my pocket and pulled out my phone. "Would you like to see them?"

"Please."

I unlocked the phone, found Ali's texts, and handed the handset to him. He took a while to read through them, the expression on his face remaining impassive throughout. When he finished, he handed it back to me.

"You can see why I'm so concerned," I said.

"They don't look threatening to me," Manning said.

"I'm sorry. Did you read them all? Anyone can see—"

"Looks to me like there's a little more going on here than you're telling me."

Was he serious? Anyone reading those messages would know the sender was unstable. "I don't understand. There's nothing else going on. I've told you everything."

"Clearly, Ms. Page is under the impression she is, or has been, in a relationship with you. Can I see the messages you sent her?"

"There are none."

"Where are they?"

"There weren't any. That's what I'm trying to tell you. This is all in her head. There is no relationship. There never has been. The woman's young enough to be my daughter, but for some reason she won't leave me alone."

"A few moments ago, you said you called her."

"Yes, but only to tell her to back off."

"You sure there are no texts from you?"

"If they existed, they'd be on my phone."

Manning's arms were crossed again. "How do I know you haven't deleted them?"

39

"It doesn't work that way. If I'd sent her anything, they would show up in the conversation string. You can see all the communication is one way."

"Right now," Manning said, pointing to my phone, "her messages don't look like harassment to me."

"Does that mean you're not going to do anything?"

"There's nothing we can do. It seems to me you've got yourself into a little domestic difficulty, but that's not something for us."

Why wasn't he taking this seriously? Sure, I could see Ali's texts looked bad when taken out of context. That was why I'd been concerned about showing them to Marie weeks earlier. But Manning seemed to be completely ignoring what I'd just told him. I had done nothing to encourage her. And yet he was all but accusing me of leading her on.

"There must be something you can do," I said, my voice laden with incredulity. "Can't you go see her and warn her off? I'm sure that would make her think twice about doing it again."

"I'm sorry, Mr. Harper, but unless she makes physical contact with you, there's little we can do to help. We're not here to intervene in domestic disputes."

"What am I supposed to do? Wait until this crazy woman attacks one of us? Is that what you want?"

Manning closed his pad and stood. "I suggest you keep a diary. If she makes physical contact with you, make a note of it. If it gets to the point where there's a threatening pattern, we'll take a look at it again."

"That's it? You're not even going to speak to her?"

"Right now, there's nothing we can do."

Chapter 7

For weeks, I heard nothing more from Ali. Even her late-night calls to the house stopped. Despite what he said, I wondered if Sergeant Manning, or someone else from OBPD, had decided to pay her an informal visit. Maybe they'd warned her she was now on their radar. Certainly, Ali's silence seemed more than a coincidence. Thankfully, the respite from my stalker caused the ice to melt at home. Marie stopped hiding out at school and began talking to me again in a civil tone, although she was careful to avoid mentioning my tormentor by name.

Partly because we weren't talking at the time, I didn't tell Marie about my meeting with Manning. But that wasn't the only reason. If she knew the police had trouble buying my story, it would only give her more reason to suspect there was something going on between me and Ali. Given the fragility of our relationship, it wouldn't have taken much to unnerve Marie, so I kept quiet about my visit to our local police station. I was confident, in the fullness of time, the truth would come out, and Ali's instability would catch up with her. Then everyone—the police and Marie, included—would see her for what she was. Until then, I decided to keep my head down, hoping her silence meant she'd become fixated on another target.

Throwing myself into work became a welcome distraction. Fortunately, there was plenty to do. Spiraling house prices in the Vancouver area seemed to be creating more demand for properties on the island, where they were less expensive. Since the spring, there had been a marked pickup in buyer inquiries for the greater Victoria region. As a result of what was fast becoming a sellers' market, local realtors witnessed a late summer surge in new listings, and my firm picked up more than its fair share. At the pace we were working, we looked set for a record year in sales. Even Brenda's son started helping us out with our weekend open houses because we were struggling to handle the workload. If Freya had been old enough, I would have roped her in, too.

The bubble soon burst. And I don't mean the property one. I was sitting in my office, grabbing a late lunch, when I received another text from Ali.

Come outside. I'm across the street. I don't want to hurt you.

A cocktail of anger, fear, and resentment welled up inside me. How much longer was this going to go on? I placed my half-eaten turkey wrap on my desk and walked to the window. Standing to one side so I couldn't be seen, I lifted one of the slats in the blind and peered through. Even though it was almost three o'clock, and its lunch trade had long since subsided, Tim Hortons directly across the street was still busy. As far as I could tell, Ali wasn't in there. I looked down the road then quickly dropped the slat when I spotted a silver VW Golf. I couldn't make out the license plate, but it had to be her car.

What the hell did she want from me?

The phone pinged again. *I know you're in there, Tom. I saw you earlier. All I want is to talk.*

I toyed with the idea of calling Sergeant Manning. OBPD was only a five-minute drive away. If he came right away, he'd see for himself that I wasn't making things up and catch her in the act. But I already knew what he'd say: "There's no law against parking on the street. She's not threatening anyone."

Ping. *Please, Tom. I need five minutes of your time.*

My office phone rang, startling me. I returned to my desk,

picked it up, and listened.

"Tom?" Ali was on my direct line.

I hesitated. "What do you want?"

Brenda must have detected from my voice there was a problem because she made a face at me through my open door. With the phone pinned to my ear, I reached over, closed the door, and returned to my seat.

"I just want to talk," Ali said.

"I'm not interested."

"Didn't you get my text? I'm parked right across the street from your office. Come outside so we can talk."

"I have nothing more to say to you. Please, just leave me alone."

"I can't do that. In your heart, I know you don't want that either. What we have is special. We can't just throw it away as if it means nothing."

She paused, no doubt waiting for me to say something, but I remained silent. I didn't know what else to say.

"I've tried to give you some space." Ali continued. "I haven't called you, I haven't texted you, I've left you alone so you could deal with Marie in your own good time."

"Am I supposed to be grateful?"

"There's real beauty in what we have, Tom. It's perfect. Be honest. You see it, too, right?"

I put the phone down and held my head in my hands. My breathing was shallow, and I was convinced I could hear the blood racing in my head. What was it going to take to stop her? Part of me wanted to run across the street and wring her neck for putting me through this. But I knew that's exactly what she wanted. She was looking to get a reaction out of me. That way she could paint herself as the victim. I wasn't going to fall for it.

My desk phone rang again. I left it to ring until I realized Brenda might answer it for me. I opened my door and saw she was about to pick up the call. "Please, Brenda, don't pick it up. Leave it."

"It's no trouble," she said. "I can take a message if you're busy."

"No. I don't want to speak to them. Don't answer it." My tone was more hostile than I'd intended.

Brenda looked confused but did what I asked. I shut the door again and returned to my desk.

Another message came in on my cell phone. *Please don't ignore me.*

I walked to the window, making sure I wasn't visible from the outside. She was still parked across the street, sitting in her car, looking directly at our building. My cell pinged again.

You can't pretend I don't exist.

Then, about a minute later, *I look at you and see the rest of my life in front of my eyes.*

I heard a car engine start, and her silver Golf pulled out into the road. As it passed my window, she was looking straight ahead, but even from the side I could tell she was crying.

There was no guilt seeing her upset like that. The over-whelming emotion coursing through me was cold, penetrating terror.

Chapter 8

Monday evenings were for marksmanship training at the air cadet squadron where I volunteered my time, helping kids between twelve and eighteen years old develop skills in teamwork and leadership. In an age when many think teenagers spend their days glued to their smartphones or gaming consoles, it was rewarding to see the young members of our squadron show that misconception for what it was. Wrong. Seeing them mature over those formative years was a rewarding experience for us volunteers, and it gave me faith in the future of our country. Freya had been a member of the squadron since she was twelve and, in that time, she'd grown into a confident, outgoing young woman—quite some contrast to the shy, introverted girl she was before. I was proud of who she had become, in no small part thanks to the life skills she'd learned as an air cadet.

A skilled marksman himself, Bob Page was one of our volunteer shooting instructors. You could see from the permanent smile on his face he was in his element teaching the cadets how to adjust their sights for improved accuracy, demonstrating breathing techniques to reduce the chances of pulling on the trigger when aiming, and showing them general gun safety procedures. There was nothing Bob didn't know about guns and how to use them properly.

My role was mostly in support, scoring the cadets on their target shooting and consoling those who weren't as good as some of the others by finding something else they were proficient at and building on that. That's what I liked about the programme. The range of activities was wide enough for us to find something to suit all individuals and so bring out the best in each of them. If I had my way, all young people would sign up for the cadets or something similar. I'm convinced it helps them develop into rounded and fully contributing adult members of society.

As usual, we had the evening's activities wrapped up by nine. Bob caught up with me in the parking lot just as I was approaching my car. Without making it obvious, I'd done my best to avoid him all night. Although he had no reason to know I'd reported his daughter to the police, nonetheless I felt a twinge of panic when he tapped me on the shoulder.

"I've been meaning to have a word with you," he said.

I turned and braced myself. If he challenged me on it, how was I meant to explain why I'd gone to the police without spelling out the ugly details of his daughter's behavior? Bob was a friend; the last thing I wanted was to offend him. Even if I told him, he'd struggle to believe it, anyway. I know I would if someone told me that Freya had done half the things Ali had.

"It's about Ali," Bob continued.

He knows. If I wasn't careful, this conversation could turn nasty quickly.

"I haven't got much time right now," I said, pressing the remote to unlock my vehicle. "Do you mind if we pick it up next week?"

"No problem. It's not urgent. We had dinner with Ali yesterday. We've hardly seen her since she bought the condo. I can't tell you how pleased she is with her new place. She's delighted. Wouldn't stop talking about it all night."

"That's great she likes it so much." Even I could hear the relief in my voice. Bob knew nothing about my visit to OBPD, after all. "Took a little longer than we might have wanted, but we got there in the end."

"That's my daughter," Bob said, his face beaming with pride.

"She takes her time over most things, but once she finds what she wants, she goes all out to get it. There's no stopping her."

Ain't that the truth. I turned away and opened my car door. "As long as she's happy."

Bob tapped me on the shoulder again. "You certainly made a big impression on her."

I looked at him, wondering what was coming next.

"She's always quoting you," he continued. "Tom thinks this, or Tom thinks that. That's not how Tom would describe it." The smile disappeared from Bob's face as he relayed his daughter's comments about me. I swear he seemed jealous. "I don't know what your secret is, but she's got some sort of crush on you. Good thing you're married, buddy."

The sides of my face felt warm. What was I supposed to say in response to that? "Anyway, good to see you, Bob. I have to get going I'm afraid." I climbed into my car.

Bob held my door open and leaned in. "Hey, we can have a proper catch-up on Saturday."

"Why? What's happening Saturday?"

"You guys are coming over for dinner. Didn't Marie tell you? Sonya spoke with her over the weekend. It's our turn."

"I'm sorry. She may well have said something. Things have been so hectic at work recently. I may have missed it."

The truth was Marie had said nothing to me. I'd remember something like that. What I didn't understand was if we were talking to each other again, why hadn't she told me about it?

"Ali said she's coming over." The smile was back on Bob's face. "As soon as Sonya told her you're coming, she said she'd like to be there. I tell you, she's your biggest fan."

"Okay." I pulled on the door, and Bob released it from his grip. "I guess we'll see you Saturday."

Driving down the Pat Bay Highway, all I could think about was why Marie had kept quiet about the Pages' invitation. She knew full well what I'd think about it; there was no way we could go. Why on earth hadn't she come up with a good excuse when Sonya called her? It was obvious sitting across the dinner table from Ali would be a nightmare for all of us.

It wasn't going to happen.

Chapter 9

The narrow stretch between the islands of Galiano and Mayne was my favorite part of the crossing to the mainland. On both sides of the car ferry, I loved how you could almost touch the trees as they carpeted the land all the way to the water's edge and how the houses nestled among them clung to the sides of the steep rock. Regular as clockwork, the ferry coming in the opposite direction approached, and the passengers on the open decks waved when we sailed past each other. Once out of the pass, we were only half an hour or so from the terminal at Tsawwassen. Countless times in the past, I'd spotted a pod of orcas or humpback whales in that expanse of deep water known as the Strait of Georgia.

I drove off the car ferry and headed north on Route 99 toward Vancouver. The crowded highways on the mainland and their maniacal drivers cutting in and out of lanes to gain a microscopic advantage always reminded me how lucky we were living on Vancouver Island, where the pace of life was less frenetic, and the people seemed to have more time for each other. It continually baffled me why so many folks chose to live in large cities, my sister Bekah included.

It was Bekah's forty-fourth birthday, and for as long as I could remember I'd made the trip to West Vancouver where she lived to buy her a birthday lunch. It was our annual tradition. As the only siblings, she and I had always been close growing up. Since she'd moved to the mainland in her early twenties, however, we'd not seen each other as often as we would have liked. Life and work seemed to get in the way. But we made up for it by regular phone conversations, more so after Dad died almost five years earlier. Bekah liked to hear from me how our mother was coping on her own, particularly after Mom broke her hip last year. Trouble was Mom was fiercely independent and detested being fussed over. Even if she had a problem, she wouldn't say much when my sister called her. Most weeks I'd go see Mom at her place in Sidney, primarily so I could see for myself she was okay. I'd always call Bekah on my way home to give her an honest update. That way everyone was happy.

In my view, the best part of the drive, once I'd run the gauntlet of Vancouver's downtown traffic, was leaving the city behind and heading over Lions Gate Bridge, seeing Grouse Mountain rise in front of me. This area had some of the highest-priced real estate in the country. It sounds weird a country the size of Canada struggling for space, but the steepness of those mountains to the north meant pretty much every spare inch of building land had already been taken. Whenever an old property came onto the market, it would be razed to the ground and a much larger mansion erected in its place, normally taking up the whole lot. Yard space was considered an expensive luxury.

We met at Bridget and Freddy's, an unpretentious seafood restaurant on Palmerston Avenue. Bekah had raved about this place for years, but it was my first time and now I could see why she rated it so highly. The food was delicious, and the views from the deck toward Lions Gate Bridge and behind it the steel and concrete high-rises of downtown were stunning.

Mainly, we talked about family stuff. Like us, Bekah and her dentist husband, Mike, had one daughter. She was the same age as Freya, sixteen, going on thirty. We lamented how fast they were growing up and how soon we'd be agonizing over college choices and all that. We talked about Mom. As she always did, Bekah apologized for not being able to visit her as much as she'd like. I kept telling her not to worry and assured her she was doing well. Two hours of non-stop talking whizzed by.

After our server brought us coffee, Bekah asked, "And how about you, Tom? How are you doing?"

I could tell from the concerned look on my sister's face this was no casual question. After weeks of little or no sleep, I looked a wreck. "I'm fine," I said. "Just a little tired from all the work we have on right now. The market's gone crazy."

She reached across the table and placed a hand on top of mine. "Are you sure it's just work? You seem quite down. Not like you at all."

Hiding things from Bekah was impossible. I always said she would have made a great psychotherapist; she was good at picking up unspoken communication and a great listener. While I was desperate to share with her what was troubling me, I didn't want to put a dampener on her birthday. That wouldn't be fair.

Typical, Bekah. She wouldn't give up; she kept poking and prodding until I gave in. Eventually, I told her the whole story, even letting her read all Ali's text messages.

Her jaw hanging open, Bekah's face was ashen when she handed my phone back. "I don't know what to say, Tom," she said. "The woman seems...what's the right word?...delusional?"

"That's putting it politely. I've never come across anyone like her. For weeks, I've had this constant fear, dreading what she's going to do next. No wonder I look so worn out."

"Explains a lot. When you arrived today, I thought you looked gaunt with all the weight you've lost. I was worried you might be ill or something. I'm glad you told me."

"When I was working with her, there was no hint of what was to come. It's like someone has taken over her body. I don't recognize the woman doing all this. I can't think of anything I've done to set her off. I treated her exactly the same as my other clients. You know me, Beks. While I like to have a good chat, I always treat my clients with respect. I know where the boundaries are."

"There's really no need to explain. I know you're not like that. It's just not the man you are. You're a professional."

A wave of relief washed over me. Finally, someone was listening. "I can't tell you what it means to hear you say that."

Bekah squeezed my hand again. "It's incredible the police won't help. For all we know, she could be dangerous. You must be worried sick."

"That's an understatement. I'm not sleeping well. It's difficult concentrating on my work. I don't mind admitting to you this whole thing is terrifying. I just want it to go away."

"What does Marie think? She must be worried out of her mind."

While we were close, Bekah knew nothing about the affair I'd had many years earlier. Without that knowledge, she couldn't properly understand Marie's reaction. As much as I trusted my sister, some things needed to remain between me and Marie. They were private.

"She's really anxious," I said, before drinking the rest of my coffee.

We sat in silence for a while. I was hoping I wouldn't be pressed for more on Marie's thoughts, and Bekah, no doubt, was racking her brains for something helpful to say or do. She was always the pragmatic one in our family—the fixer. But I could tell the situation with Ali was testing her, too. There was little anyone could do until Ali stepped over the line and threatened me. And so far, she seemed too clever to do that. I had reread her texts many times, and Sergeant Manning was right; they contained nothing an independent observer would consider an outright threat. Yes, I found them intimidating—no, frightening—but that didn't seem to count for much under the law. I had no choice. I had to wait until she actually harmed me or threatened to do so. Until then, I'd have to cope with not knowing what she was going to do next. The stress of waiting, powerless and in the dark, had become a living hell.

Bekah drummed the table with both hands. "You need to

speak to a lawyer," she said. "You can't just wait to see what this woman does next. We have no idea what she's capable of. You said she just moved from Vancouver. Do we know what prompted her move back to the island?"

I nodded. "It does seem a strange move. Most professional people her age leave the island to go work in the big city, not the other way around."

"I suspect there's a story there. Anyway, there must be something a lawyer can do to put a stop to her, right?"

"If the police can't help, do you really think a lawyer's going to be able to?"

"It has to be worth a try. If nothing else, you'd have someone independent making a record of her harassment. That could come in useful as evidence one day."

"You're right," I said. I couldn't sit around waiting for Ali's next move. It was too passive. Although it was a long shot, contacting a lawyer was something I could do to regain an element of control over my life. "Who knows what legal remedies there might be."

"Do you have anyone you can go to?"

"Not really. I used a small firm in Victoria when I set up the brokerage, but they're probably not the right ones to use for something like this. I'll need to ask around."

Bekah frowned. "I think you should stay out of Victoria. The place is too small. She's a lawyer there, and if her father works for the RCMP on the island…"

"I'm going to need someone from outside the area."

"Let me make some inquiries, Tom. I'm sure Mike and I can find you someone good in Vancouver. Give me a day or two and I'll call you when we've found one."

I paid for lunch, and we walked outside to the parking lot, where Bekah gave me the biggest hug. She seemed not to want to let go of me. "Take care, Tom. And try not to worry too much about all this. We'll deal with it, I promise."

"I feel a whole lot better already," I said, holding both of her hands tightly. "I'm sorry I was so downbeat on your birthday. I'll make it up to you, Beks."

"Don't be silly."

I watched my sister drive away before I headed back to Tsawwassen to catch the five o'clock ferry to the island.

At last, I had a potential way forward, a way to wrestle back some control.

Chapter 10

Next morning, I was sitting in my office when my sister called. "That was quick," I said. "You found a lawyer already?"

"Not yet," Bekah said. "That's not why I'm calling." This time she was the one who sounded down. "I was going to call you last night, but I changed my mind. The last thing I want to do is pile on more pressure."

"What do you mean?"

"You're under enough stress right now without me adding to it, but this morning Mike persuaded me it's best you hear what happened. He said I shouldn't sit on something like this."

"You have me worried, Beks. It's not Mom, is it?"

"No, nothing like that. Besides, you'd be the one to hear first if it was her."

"What is it, then?"

Bekah remained silent for a few seconds, then she said, "Yesterday afternoon..." She sighed. "I hope I'm doing the right thing telling you."

My sister was the most grounded person I've ever known, but she sure sounded scared on the phone. "Please, just tell me. I'd rather know."

Another loud sigh from the other end of the line. "When we left the restaurant, I didn't go straight home. I headed over to Park Royal to do some shopping. I parked the car and was in and out of the mall within an hour. Maybe a bit longer."

"That's quick for you," I said, trying to lighten the mood a little.

"Yeah, I know. Anyway, everything seemed fine. I got into the car and drove home. Mike came back around six. When he walked into the house, he looked at me and said, 'Have you seen your car?'"

"What was wrong with it?"

"That's exactly what I said. He told me I had to see it for myself, so I followed him into the garage. He led me around to the front passenger side and pointed. And there it was, scratched into the paintwork, right across the door." Bekah's voice rose in pitch as she spoke. "The word BITCH. And I'm not talking a light scratch. Oh no. The letters had been carved into the body. You can actually feel the gouges in the metal where a key has been used. And the car's only three months old."

My guts twisted inside. I knew instantly who was responsible and I was sure Bekah had to be thinking the same thing. I walked around my desk and pushed the door closed. "Do you think this could be—"

"It's her," Bekah shouted. "It has to be her. There's no way this is a coincidence, Tom."

"Where did it happen?"

"I know it wasn't there when we left the restaurant."

"It definitely wasn't there. I would have noticed it as you drove away. Must have been at the mall."

"I think so. But why didn't I notice it when I returned to the car?"

"You probably just got in the driver's side. Sounds like you wouldn't have seen it unless you walked all the way around."

"I honestly can't remember what I did. But there's nowhere else it could have occurred." The strain in Bekah's voice was palpable.

"I'm so sorry, Beks. This is all my fault. I'll pay for it to be put right. I know that won't begin to—"

"No, Tom. That's not why I told you. In the grand scheme

of things, the car doesn't really matter. It can be fixed. What matters right now is what this signifies: she must have followed you all the way to the restaurant. How else would she know you were going to be there? Think about it. Who does something like that?"

I didn't want to believe it—the implications were terrifying—but my sister had to be right. There was no way Ali was there by chance. She had to have tailed me from home that morning, then onto the ferry and all the way to West Vancouver.

"She probably sat there watching us have lunch," Bekah continued.

My throat tightened. "You don't think she thought you and I were...seeing each other?"

"I don't know. If she was watching us, she might well have thought something was going on between us. How would she know we're brother and sister? Someone with a twisted mind like hers could easily jump to the wrong conclusion. Why else would she write bitch on my car? She's a fucking sicko."

"She must have seen you leave the restaurant and followed you to the mall. I left the parking lot right after you. I didn't see anyone else leaving, but I wasn't looking either."

"I hope to God she didn't follow me home."

I could feel the rage welling up in my chest. Not only was Ali trying to ruin my life, but now she'd also brought my sister into her warped little world. "I very much doubt she would have done that," I said, trying to sound calm and reassuring. "After she damaged your car at the mall, I'm certain she would have disappeared quickly. If she waited around for you to return, she would have risked being caught if someone spotted what she'd done. She's too smart for that."

"I hope you're right, Tom. I dread to think what it means if she knows where I live."

"Did you call the police?"

"After what you told me, I wasn't sure what to do. But Mike was adamant, so we called them. Not that they could do much about it. They told us it was difficult to do anything as there were no witnesses and I didn't even know for sure where it happened."

"Did you tell them about our conversation? How it's obvious who did it?"

Bekah didn't respond immediately. "I thought about telling them," she said, "In my heart, I know it's her, but the problem is there's no evidence. Do you think I made a mistake not saying anything about her?"

I couldn't blame Bekah for not telling the police about Ali. Given the experience I'd had with my local police department, it was unlikely they would have believed her anyway. In my case, I had text messages to back up my allegations, and still they said they could do nothing to help. While Bekah didn't say as much, I sensed the real reason she kept quiet about Ali was because she was scared. Since there was a chance Ali now knew where she lived, her caution was perfectly understandable.

"If I were in your shoes, I would have done the same thing," I said. "You're right; we don't have any proof it's her."

"If you think I was wrong, I could always go back to them. I'm sorry if I've let you down."

"No, Beks. This is my problem, not yours. I need to sort this out. I should be the one apologizing. But for me, none of this would have happened to you."

"Promise me you'll be careful, Tom. We now know she's dangerous. This could turn nasty if you don't watch out."

"I'll be careful, I promise. Last night I thought some more about your idea of seeing a lawyer. I definitely think it is the right way forward. If the police won't act, I have to find out if there's anything else I can do to stop her. A good lawyer will know what the options are."

"Mike said he has someone in mind. He knows them from the gym he goes to. He's going to have a word tomorrow. If they pan out, we'll give you the details right away."

"Tell Mike I really appreciate his help. Is it okay with you if

I tell the lawyer about the damage to your car?"

"Of course. If they are going to advise you properly, they need to know everything."

"Thanks. I'm so sorry you've been dragged into this. I promise I'll do everything I can to make her stop."

"Take care, Tom."

Chapter 11

I waited until Thursday evening, when Freya was sleeping over at a friend's house, before broaching the subject with Marie. I had been hoping she was going to tell me about it before now. After all, she'd known since the previous weekend we'd been invited to the Pages' on Saturday. What was the big secret?

"Bob told me we've been invited round to theirs for dinner," I said, right after Anderson Cooper's show finished.

"Yes, that's right," Marie said. She couldn't have been more casual about it if she'd tried. "It's this Saturday. Didn't I tell you?"

"No, you didn't tell me. That's something I think I'd remember." I made a poor job masking the sarcasm in my voice. "Were you planning on keeping it to yourself?"

Marie shrugged. "I must have forgotten. Sonya and I arranged it a few days ago." She kept watching CNN.

I waited for her to elaborate, but she didn't. "You know we can't go, right?"

Marie looked right through me. "Is there a problem? You don't have any meetings or late open houses. I checked your calendar. Besides, we don't have to be there until seven."

"It has nothing to do with my schedule. You know full well why we can't go. I'm amazed you agreed. It would have been much easier to come up with an excuse when Sonya was on the phone. Now we run the risk of offending them."

"We've been many times before. I don't see the problem."

"C'mon, Marie, let's not play games. You know exactly why we can't go this time."

"No, I don't, actually. Care to enlighten me?"

Why was Marie being difficult? She had to know it would be uncomfortable for both of us. "She will be there," I said. "Their daughter will be there."

"Yes, Sonya told me."

I threw my palms open. "That's why we can't go. Not after all the trouble she's caused us. The last thing I want is to go there and pretend what she's done doesn't matter. It does. It's unforgiveable. We're not going."

"Bob and Sonya are our friends. They've done nothing wrong."

"Why are you making this so difficult? We can't go if Ali's there."

"You told me it's all in her head."

"It is, but can you imagine the atmosphere with her sitting there?"

"If you've done nothing wrong, I can't see why you have an issue. On the other hand, if you have something to hide, then I would understand your not wanting to see her. Which is it, Tom?"

"Really? So, this is a test for you? Thanks for your faith in me."

Marie shook her head. "It's not a test. We've simply been invited over by good friends. Where's the harm in that?"

"When are you going to believe me? Listen, for the hundredth time, I have not done anything. If going to this stupid dinner will prove that to you, then I'll go, but I think it's a big mistake. Just remember I warned you."

Marie knew I'd been to see Bekah for lunch earlier in the week. So far, I hadn't told her what happened to my sister's car. I wondered whether to do so now. If she heard how scheming and dangerous Ali was, then maybe Marie would be as keen as I was to avoid her. But I decided to keep quiet about it. Explaining the late-night phone calls had been hard enough. I didn't want to give Marie any more reasons to suspect me. If she knew Ali was following me as far as Vancouver, what would my wife think? That I was doing something to lead her on? I couldn't risk it, not until I'd been to see the lawyer I was hoping Mike had found me. With luck, the lawyer would have a solution, one that I could share with Marie. If she saw that I was taking legal action then, maybe, it would put her mind at rest once and for all.

We were still arguing as we walked from our house to Bob and Sonya's. Well, to be more accurate, I was doing my best to persuade Marie we were about to make a big mistake, but she wasn't listening. She hadn't heard one word of my protests over the last few days. I'm sorry to admit part of me thought she was looking forward to watching her husband sitting across the table from his tormentor.

How was I supposed to act over dinner? Smile and pretend Ali had done nothing wrong? That didn't seem right. The mood I was in as we turned into their street was anything but conciliatory. I knew it wouldn't take much for the rage inside me to boil over. I don't think Marie truly understood how the next few hours had the potential to blow up in our faces, ruining our relationship with the Pages forever. If she had, she would not have been so adamant about going.

Bob and Sonya lived in an Arts & Crafts-style, gray-painted house that was typical for the area. My heart red-lined when Marie rang their doorbell. Seconds later, I heard footsteps on the other side of the front door, and my body flooded with adrenaline.

Sonya appeared in the doorway. "Come on in, guys," she said, smiling. Bob was standing right behind her. We handed over a bottle of Bob's favorite Okanagan red and a bunch of hand-tied flowers Marie had bought from the expensive florist in Owen Bay. Kisses were exchanged, then we all filed into the kitchen, drawn by the smell of cooking.

Fortunately, Ali wasn't there. Relief. Maybe she wasn't coming, after all. Bob poured us all large glasses of Prosecco while Sonya stirred something on the cooktop.

"Couldn't Ali make it?" Marie asked, her face a picture of disappointment.

"She's on her way," Sonya said. "She called earlier to say she'll be a little late. Something to do with work. She's working all hours right now, no doubt trying to make a good impression at her new firm."

My stomach convulsed as Sonya spoke. I was trapped. The devil was on her way, and there was no escape. While everyone else sipped their wine, I emptied my glass.

"What about Simon?" Marie asked.

Simon was Ali's younger brother. The same age as Freya, he was in many of the same classes as her at Owen Bay High School. I knew what Marie was up to. She was only asking about their son out of courtesy. She already had all the information she needed. Ali was still coming.

"He's out with friends," Sonya said. "We hardly see him these days."

"He and Freya seem to be getting quite close," Marie said. "They're always together when I see them at school."

"I didn't know that," I said. Knowing how weird Ali was, I wasn't sure how I felt about her brother hanging around with our daughter. He'd always seemed a nice enough kid to me, but then I would have said the same about his sister until recently. "You never mentioned it to me."

Marie threw me a foul look. "That's because you've been preoccupied lately."

I climbed back into my box and the conversation moved on.

After a few minutes, we sat in the living room. Every now and then, Sonya would pop into the kitchen to make sure everything was as it should be. Marie joined her, offering help, leaving Bob and me putting the world to right. Small talk, but it kept my mind from dwelling too much on what was to come. After I downed my third glass of Prosecco, my nerves eased a little. I was never much of a drinker, but that night alcohol was my only way to cope.

Just as we were about to take our seats at the large rosewood dining table, I heard a familiar voice in the hallway. "Only me." Ali must have let herself in with her own key. Despite all the drink I was consuming, suddenly my mouth felt dry.

"Sorry I'm late," she said, kissing her father on the lips when she walked into the dining room. She was dressed in a skin-tight short skirt and a white blouse, under which I was convinced she wore no bra. Was she sending me a message? "I've been working in Vancouver most of the week. I only got back in this evening. The ferries were heaving."

Vancouver. Proof she was there earlier in the week. Subtle as a brick in the head. The night was going to be much worse than I'd anticipated. If she was like this now, what other stunts was she about to pull?

"Don't worry, princess," Bob said. "You're not late at all." He took a step back and admired his daughter. "You look beautiful." Her eyes lit up. "Isn't she beautiful, Tom?"

I nodded slightly. Enough to acknowledge Bob, but not enough to upset Marie too much. Maybe I was seeing things that weren't there, searching for explanations for Ali's weird behavior, but the relationship between her and Bob seemed a little strange to me. Lecherous would be the way I'd best describe the look on Bob's face. Too close for comfort for my taste.

Ali gave her mother a quick peck on the cheek. Marie arched her body away when Ali walked over to kiss her. Then Ali turned to me, threw her arms around my waist, and gripped me tightly. In the corner of my eye, I could see Marie watching us. After an uncomfortable couple of seconds, I tried to slip free from Ali's embrace.

"How's my favorite realtor?" Ali asked when I succeeded in extracting myself. "I haven't seen you for ages."

The woman had some balls to stand there and act as if there was nothing wrong. It took all my strength not to rise to the bait. I responded with a thin half-smile.

"I've seated you there," Sonya said, pointing Ali to a chair, "right next to Tom, just as you asked."

I didn't dare look at Marie. I didn't need to; I could feel her laser-like stare penetrating me from across the room.

We sat at the oblong table, Bob and Sonya at each end, Marie opposite me, Ali on my right. Without making it obvious, I focused my attention on Bob to my left. Now and then, Sonya asked me a question, forcing me to turn in her direction. Ali would wait for her mother to finish then lean forward and engage me in some inane conversation. Her positioning must have been deliberate because her blouse kept falling open, and from that angle, I couldn't help seeing the exposed side of her breast. I tried not to look at Marie, but just once I caught her eye. From her expression, it looked as if she was drinking bleach from her wineglass. I couldn't blame her for being furious. It was exactly what I feared would happen.

After the starter, Bob and Sonya took our plates away. While they were busy in the kitchen, Ali smiled at Marie and said, "Your husband is a genius."

In return, Marie made a strange face, a mix of confusion and contempt.

"The condo he found for me," Ali continued, "is awesome. I couldn't have done it without him. I'm really sorry I stole him away from you for so long." As she spoke, under the table, Ali rubbed the top of my right thigh with her left hand. I had no idea if Marie could see what was happening. I wanted to throw up. "At times, I felt like his second wife, we spent so much time together. You're a lucky woman."

Marie glanced at me then glared at Ali. "That's interesting," she said, but the look on her face said something completely different: *I know you're fucking my husband, so don't play games with me. Pathetic little slut.*

When I could take no more, I stood. "I'm going to see if Sonya needs a hand," I said, leaving the room without looking back. I went to the bathroom, splashed cold water over my face, then stared in the mirror. Dark bags hung under my eyes, standing out against my pale skin. I couldn't allow the night to go on like this. It was turning into a slow car wreck, and I was powerless to stop it. Marie was going to crucify me when we got out of there. Ali had just confirmed my wife's worst fears, and there was nothing I could do or say to counter it. Ali had to have planned it this way all along.

When I returned to the dining room, everyone was seated, and the main course was laid out on the table.

"I cooked your favorite, Tom," Sonya said. "Halibut."

"Talking of fish," Bob said to me before I sat. "Ali just asked whether any of us know of a restaurant called Bridget & Freddy's in West Vancouver. Apparently, it has the best seafood in BC."

"Your sister lives out that way, doesn't she, Tom?" Sonya asked.

"Er...yes...she does," I said, feeling light-headed. I had to get out of there.

Ali turned and looked at me. "You really should tell her to try it. A group of us went there for lunch this week. I'd say it's the best fish restaurant I've ever eaten at."

I didn't sit down. My head was spinning. I gripped the back of my chair for balance, looked at Marie, and said, "You know that upset stomach I had a while ago? I think it's come back again." I grimaced. "I'm really sorry Sonya, but I don't feel too well. I think I need to go home and lie down for a while."

"You do look faint, Tom," Ali said. "I hope it's nothing serious."

Minutes later, we were walking home, Marie always a few steps ahead of me. Not a single word was spoken.

Chapter 12

Wearing a thin black tracksuit and Nike running shoes, Ali sat in her VW Golf playing with the iPad she bought at the Best Buy sale the same day she picked up her new laptop. Every now and then, she glanced through the windshield toward Tom's house some fifty yards away.

At six fifteen, some movement caught her attention. Tom and Freya left their property and got into his car. Ali pulled down her baseball cap, slid lower in the seat, and watched them drive away. Shortly after, Tom returned on his own and went back into the house.

Half an hour later, he and Marie emerged, locked their front door, and walked in the opposite direction from Ali's VW, on their way to her parents' home for dinner.

From their raised voices through the open car window, it sounded like they were having an argument, but she couldn't make out what they were saying. She waited for them to disappear around the corner before grabbing the brown envelope sitting on her front passenger seat and climbing out of the vehicle. She slipped the envelope into the large front pocket of her tracksuit top and crossed the street.

An elderly couple said hello as Ali approached Tom's house. She stopped and made a fuss over their puppy.

"Lovely dog," she said, kneeling. "I love dogs. What breed is it?"

"A border collie," the old man said, while the puppy jumped up and licked Ali's face. "We just got her. She needs a lot of walking."

"She's beautiful. So much energy at that age." Ali sprung to her feet and smiled. "You folks have a wonderful evening."

As if she lived there, Ali strolled up the driveway, past Tom's car, to the front of the Harper residence. She stopped and waved goodbye to the couple. Only when they were out of sight did she walk around the side of the property. Back there, because of the mature shrubs and bushes, no one could see her from the road. By pulling down a sleeve of her tracksuit, she was able to cover one hand. She used it to try the handle of the back door, but it was locked.

A few yards away, on the side of the detached garage, was a door that looked like it hadn't been painted since new; flakes of old paint were peeling off, exposing bare timber underneath. Either the door was warped, or the frame was out of line, because it didn't fit flush to the garage wall. Ali gripped the handle with her covered hand, and the door opened. She glanced over her shoulder then walked inside.

The place reeked of freshly cut grass from a Honda lawnmower next to the entrance. Along one wall, a large aluminum ladder was supported on brackets. On the opposite side were three bicycles hanging from special fixtures. In the middle of the double garage stood Marie's red Mini Cooper S and behind it, running the length of the back wall, was a wooden bench. On top sat a leaf blower, a weed whacker, and several smaller power tools. Underneath was a gas power washer. Right next to it were two gray metal storage cabinets.

One of them was unlocked. Inside, on shelves, were smaller containers filled with screws and nails of varying sizes and a few hand tools. Stacked neatly beneath the shelves was a bunch of "Sold" signs with the Harper Realty logo printed on them. Ali cupped both hands in her sleeves, took the signs out of the cabinet, and placed them on the concrete floor.

Nearby, a lawnmower kicked into life. Ali went to the front of the garage and peered through one of the high windows. Across the street, a man was about to start work on his lawn. She returned to the back wall and retrieved the brown envelope from her pocket. Inside the cabinet, she found a clean dry spot and placed the envelope there. She picked up the sold signs from the floor and carefully stacked them, so they hid the envelope completely.

Lawnmower-man took another twenty minutes or so to finish the work on the front of his house. Ali waited in the garage, killing time by inspecting Marie's car. It was locked. Inside, on the front passenger seat, were a few schoolbooks, an open box of chocolate Turtles, and a cell phone charger. When the neighbor disappeared around the back of his house with the mower, Ali slipped out of the side door, lowered her cap, and jogged back to her car.

Moments later, when she pulled up in front of her parents' home, she watched the front of the house. The lights were on in the dining room, and her parents were there, chatting with Tom and Marie. They looked as though they were about to sit down at the table. Quickly, Ali removed the tracksuit. Underneath, she had on a short skirt and white blouse. High heels replaced her running shoes before she walked up to the front door, retrieved a key from her purse, and let herself in.

"Only me," she shouted.

Chapter 13

Golf is a game I'd long found incomprehensible. What's the point in paying to take a slow walk while trying to whack a tiny ball into a small hole with a bent stick? I know some folks call it exercise, but no one I ever saw on a golf course looked like they broke a sweat, not even in the summer. And in the winter months, with all the rain we get in this part of the world, the players always looked decidedly cold. I just didn't get it.

However, the Sunday after our non-dinner at the Pages', the penny finally dropped. Call me a slow learner, but I only realized that morning a lot of people go out with their golf clubs to avoid spending time with their spouses. When they don't have work as an excuse, it's a great reason to get out of the house for a while. When I went to the driving range off Blenkinsop Road, near Mount Douglas, more than half the customers there were middle-aged men on their own. Like me, they spent an hour or so beating the hell out of golf balls. While it helped reduce some of my pent-up aggression, more important, it gave me a welcome break from the cold shoulder treatment I was getting at home.

Marie hadn't spoken a word to me since we left Ali's parents' place, not even when we went to collect Freya from her overnight stay at her friend's house first thing that morning. If we hadn't promised our daughter breakfast at her favorite diner, almost certainly Marie wouldn't have come.

Our daughter picked up on the tense atmosphere immediately

when she jumped in the car. "Are you two not talking again?" she asked.

I changed the subject. "What's this about you and Simon, then?" I asked.

Freya blushed. "It's nothing."

She quickly focused her attention on her iPhone. I wanted to ask a few more questions to find out how our daughter felt about Ali's brother, but it was clear the conversation was closed. Part of me was uncomfortable Freya was seeing Simon. However, I wasn't in a position to say anything without having to explain to our daughter what Ali had been doing. That would have been tricky, so I bit my tongue.

Marie stared out of the window while I drove to the diner. I wasn't angry with her; I had no reason to be. She was only reacting to the evidence in front of her and, from her perspective, it looked damning. The messages on my phone were bad enough, but the charade we'd both witnessed at the dining table the night before was something else. To say I was furious with Ali would be a massive understatement. I wanted to tear her head off for what she was putting me and my family through.

When I woke up in the spare room that morning, I thought long and hard about going to see Bob. I wanted to tell him what his daughter had been up to and get him to make her stop. But it wasn't just how he might react that prevented me from going over there. Something else held me back. An image kept flashing in front of my eyes: the way he'd interacted with his daughter at dinner. To my mind, there was a level of intimacy beyond a normal father-daughter relationship. I know I was biased against Ali, so there was a risk I was seeing things that weren't there. But if I was correct, and there was something unhealthy going on between them, it could help explain why Ali was so screwed up, particularly if it had been going on since her childhood. If there was even a slight chance I was right, I certainly couldn't risk confronting Bob. There was no telling what that might unleash.

71

Besides, it didn't make sense to do anything before I'd spoken with the lawyer Mike and Bekah were finding for me. Without first learning what my legal remedies were, I could unknowingly do something that might prejudice my position.

By coincidence, when I returned from the driving range, Mike called to give me the lawyer's contact details. Turned out that his friend from the gym wasn't the right person to help, but his buddy had recommended an attorney by the name of Karen Collins. Mike had gone to a lot of trouble on my behalf, and I didn't want to appear ungrateful. But I had to tell him I wasn't sure how I felt about a woman legal adviser. Not that I had anything against a woman professional. That wasn't it, at all. It was the nature of my problem—being stalked by a female—that made me nervous. So far, apart from family, I'd only spoken to men— my friend, Nick, and Sergeant Manning—about the harassment, and they'd both struggled to believe me. Would a woman be more understanding of the threat I felt from Ali? At first, I was doubtful, but I was soon persuaded otherwise.

Mike told me I was worrying over nothing. Collins was the best, he kept saying. According to Mike's friend, Collins dealt with this kind of thing all the time and she was a real "ball-buster." That was good enough for me. I needed a bruiser on my side, not someone who would think I was overreacting. By the end of our phone call, I was even starting to think it might be an advantage that my lawyer was a woman.

Tuesday morning, a little before eleven, I walked into the thirty-second-floor reception of Saunders, Whyte and Collins on West Georgia Street in downtown Vancouver. The place reeked of money—white-painted walls with original artwork, expensive fresh flowers in giant vases on the front desk, and hordes of serious-looking people in glass offices, none of whom would have been out of place on the TV series *Suits*.

Karen Collins came to collect me from reception. She was a

lot smaller and younger than I had imagined. On first impression, she didn't live up to the image of the battle-scarred, street-fighting warrior I had in mind after my discussion with Mike but looks can be deceptive. We shook hands and I followed her into one of the meeting rooms. It had a great view of Vancouver Harbor and the mountains beyond. Sure beat my modest offices in Owen Bay, overlooking a Tim Hortons and a branch of TD Bank.

"You're a realtor, right?" Collins asked as she poured us both coffee out of a carafe on the table.

"Yes," I said. "I have a small brokerage on Vancouver Island."

"I hear the market's going crazy over there, too."

"I can't complain since it's how I make my living."

"Then I'm assuming you don't have kids."

"Actually, we do. Freya's sixteen."

Collins waved her hand down through the air. "They don't cost much at that age," she said, a look of nostalgia on her face. "My two boys are from the 'boomerang generation.'" She made finger quotes in the air. "Both in their late-twenties and I can't get rid of them. Believe me, I've tried. Only way I can think of is if I fork out a huge deposit, so they can buy their own place. Like that's gonna happen. It'd cost me a shit-load in this market."

"They could always move to Victoria. It's still a lot cheaper over there compared to Vancouver."

Collins made a face, as if I was crazy making such a suggestion. "Yeah, but all they have for kids over there are provincial government jobs, right? I didn't shell out all that money on their education so they'd end up working for them." She drained her cup. "Anyway, how can I help you?"

I was glad to move on. I couldn't afford to waste much more time, given my lawyer's fixation with money. Mike had already warned me Collins wouldn't be cheap, and I was beginning to see why.

"I'm being stalked," I said, "and I need your help to make it stop."

"Do you know who's doing it?"

"Of course."

"Not always the case. I've had plenty of situations where the perpetrator is a stranger."

"Not this time. It's our friends' daughter."

Collins narrowed her eyes. "It's a woman?"

Here we go. Someone else with a problem accepting a woman could stalk a man. When was anyone going to take this seriously? I didn't know what was worse—putting up with the torment from Ali or no one believing me.

"They can be the worst," Collins continued. "I've seen things that would...well, let's just say, they can be a lot of trouble."

Did I just hear correctly? Did someone finally understand things from my perspective? *Hallelujah.* "Don't I know it."

"Former relationship?" Collins asked.

I bolted upright. "No. I've never had a relationship with her. Why do you think—"

Collins raised both palms. "Hey, I'm not here to moralize."

"Then why do you ask?"

"Because former girlfriends...partners...whatever we're sup-posed to call them nowadays can be some of the most difficult to stop, believe me." Collins held up the carafe, offering more coffee. I declined, then she poured another for herself. "Tell me about this woman."

For the next quarter of an hour, I downloaded everything. Collins listened, nodded occasionally, and made a few notes as I spoke. Nothing I said seemed to shock her, not even the damage done to my sister's car. I got the impression she'd heard it—and probably much worse—all before, and I found that strangely comforting. I wasn't alone.

"Doesn't surprise me the police didn't do anything," she said when I'd finished. "There's not enough evidence to act."

"Maybe not when I went to see them, but what about Bekah's car? That hadn't happened when I went to OBPD."

"Even if Ali admitted she was in West Van at the same time

as you, it's not enough to pin her down. For them to act, the police would need witnesses. Someone who saw her damage your sister's car."

"What about all the phone calls and non-stop messages? Don't they add up to stalking?" I asked.

"Criminal harassment. The crime is called criminal harassment. Stalking is just a part of it. I'd say from what you've told me, there's certainly a pattern of behavior. That's important. But we need something else, too."

"What more do the police want before they'll act? She's already damaged property. Surely, we don't have to wait until she attacks one of us?"

"Did you tell the police you fear for your personal safety?"

Before I responded to Collins, I tried to recollect the conversation I'd had with Sergeant Manning. "I don't think so. Not in so many words, anyway. But it was obvious to him I was worried, not knowing what she might do."

"That's the problem. You can't assume anything. A lot of people out there don't take this kind of behavior seriously enough. Unless they've seen it before, they don't think a woman's harassing behavior can cause a man to live in fear for his personal safety. They are completely wrong."

Collins really did understand what I was feeling. Thank God Mike found her. "I thought I was pretty clear."

"Trust me. You must be explicit. You have to say the words. What Ali is doing is making you fear for your own safety or that of a family member."

"I wish I'd spoken to you before I went to the police. I would have handled it completely differently. Do I need to go back and see them?"

Collins shook her head. "No. Leave that to me," she said. "Just as the police told you, I want you to keep a diary. In it, I need you to record everything that happens: messages, phone calls, when she comes near you, and so on. Then write down how those things make you feel. Even if the phone rings at night and no one is there when you pick it up, I want you to record it and note how you feel. Understood?"

"I can do that. I started a record after I went to see the police. Now I'll start adding how it makes me feel."

"Good. In the meantime, I'll contact the police on your behalf and set in motion an application for a peace bond."

"What's one of those?"

"A court order. Don't hold your breath. It'll take weeks to get it if we are successful. But once we have it, she'll be forbidden from making any contact with you."

"Given her behavior so far," I said, "she's likely to ignore it. She doesn't care."

"That would be a big mistake since it's a crime to break any of the conditions. For her, as a lawyer, getting a criminal record would be a major problem."

At last, I had an action plan. A way forward. With my lawyer's help, I could see a route to preventing Ali from ruining our lives any further. "I can't tell you how relieved I am to know there's a way through this mess."

"One more thing," Collins said, waving her right index finger at me, "and I can't stress this enough. Do not, under any circumstances, contact her. Don't rise to the bait if she contacts you. Make a note of it in your diary and let me handle it."

"Don't worry. I'm going nowhere near her."

Chapter 14

Exactly one week after the disastrous dinner with the Pages, our doorbell rang. Marie and Freya were in the den watching a movie starring Tom Hanks on Netflix, while I was in the kitchen working on my laptop. Well, the truth is I was pretending to work so as to keep out of Marie's way.

"I'll get it," I shouted. As I left the room, I glanced at the clock on the kitchen wall: ten past nine. Late to be bothering people at home on a Saturday night.

There was nobody there when I opened the front door. Panic rose in my throat. Was this her again? Since my meeting with Collins, I'd had nothing to record in my diary. It was as if somehow Ali knew I'd been to see a lawyer and was keeping out of my way. I looked up and down the street. One of our elderly neighbors was walking her new puppy on the other side of the road. She waved. I waved back, wondering if she'd seen anyone at our door. I returned to the kitchen, half-expecting the bell to ring again.

"Who was it, Dad?" Freya asked, when she came to fetch a drink minutes later.

"There was no one there," I said. "Probably just kids playing games."

"It's a great movie. You should come and watch it with us. You love Tom Hanks."

For the past week, I'd done my best to keep a low profile.

Sure, Marie and I made a special effort to be civil whenever Freya was around, but otherwise the temperature in our home was Siberian. I'd always measured how angry Marie was by the length of her silence. She wasn't one to scream and shout. Never had been. If she didn't like something, she'd have a quiet moan. But, if something really got under her skin, she'd say nothing at all, internalizing her anger. Over the years, I'd learned to keep out of her way when she was giving me the silent treatment. It's not that I was being pig-headed. Far from it. I'd much rather have talked about our issues than let them fester. But Marie wasn't like that. She needed time and space on her own. Soon enough, I'd get a signal when she was ready to communicate. Then I would try again to explain how there was absolutely nothing happening between Ali and me. Never had been. Never would be. In her heart, I felt certain Marie knew that already.

I pointed to my laptop. "Sorry, Freya, I've got too much work to do. Maybe tomorrow night we can watch another movie?"

"I get it," she said, closing the fridge. "You and Mom still aren't talking. There's no need to pretend."

Half an hour later, the doorbell rang again, three times in quick succession. I grabbed a flashlight from one of the kitchen drawers and ran to the front door. It was dark outside; our road only had streetlights at each end, making it difficult to see much. I walked along the sidewalk, scanning and listening. No footsteps. Nothing. She couldn't have disappeared that quickly. I turned around and switched on the flashlight, using it to illuminate the bushes outside our house. Again, nothing. I walked past the garage at the back of our property and searched the yard. No sign of her.

I went back inside the house and picked up the dog-leash. "I'm going to take Lucy out," I said, clipping it onto our golden retriever's collar. Lucy, who'd been half-asleep on the den floor next to Freya's feet, gave me a funny stare, as if to say, "What is this? I've already been out tonight. Get with the programme."

"Who was it at the door, Dad?" Freya asked. "Kids again?"

"I'm not sure, honey, but I'm going to take a look around outside. See if I can spot them."

Marie threw me an accusatory glance and shook her head slowly. I could tell she was thinking it was the same person as I had in mind. She probably thought I was up to something. Like this was a charade to spend time with Ali. So, for Marie's benefit, I said to Freya, "You can come with me if you like."

"I'd rather watch the movie," she said.

"Okay, I won't be long."

I made sure to pull the front door completely shut behind me and, this time, I walked in the opposite direction. Whoever had rung the bell would be long gone by now, but I had something else in mind. At the end of our street, I turned left and walked two blocks. Lucy kept pulling on the leash, trying to turn us around. This wasn't our usual circuit, and she knew it.

At the next four-way stop, I turned right and killed the flashlight. A third of the way down the street I reached the Pages' home, and there it was, just as I'd suspected: Ali's Golf parked on their driveway. She wasn't at her condo; she was here in Owen Bay. Probably watching me right now. That was enough evidence for me. All this would go in my diary, whether the police considered it proof or not.

Nothing more happened that night. If Ali had seen me outside her parents' house, maybe she was worried I might knock on their door and cause a scene if she persisted. Even the next few nights, there was no ringing of our doorbell, no calls to the house, and no texts on my phone. Other than that disturbance on Saturday night, I'd still not heard from Ali since my meeting with Collins. Could it have been kids all along? I wouldn't have bet my life on it.

It didn't take long for my suspicions to prove well-founded. The following weekend, her car appeared in our street after dark. And it was there every night after that. Not right outside our property; usually twenty or thirty yards further up the road and visible from our house, much like the time she'd parked across the street from my office. The weird thing was not once did I see her park the vehicle.

Last thing every night, when I took Lucy out, I'd walk by and check out the Golf. Quite often, the engine would still be warm, but Ali was never in the car. She was nowhere to be seen. When I'd get out of bed in the early hours to go to the bathroom, I'd always look out of the window, and the car would be gone. Not once was it there in the morning. What was she doing out there in the middle of the night? The anxiety was eating away at me. In a strange sort of way, the uncertainty was harder to cope with than her calls and texts. At least with those, I knew what she was up to.

While everything went into the diary, keeping a written record didn't feel enough. It was too passive. At one point, I wondered whether I should be reporting Ali's nocturnal activities to the police, but Collins advised me against it when I called her for advice.

"Just keep the log I told you," she said, "and make sure you record how it makes you feel."

I was sick and tired of writing down the same emotions: fear, anger, threatened, powerless. How did she think I was feeling? There had to be more we could do. She kept saying we had to do things the right way and there were no shortcuts. I asked about the peace bond application and why it seemed to be taking ages, but Collins told me it would be several more weeks yet, and that frustrated the hell out of me. It was alright for her; she wasn't living through my ordeal.

"These things take time," Collins said.

Although it was maddening, Collins still sounded super confident and kept assuring me this would end well, provided I remained patient, followed her advice, and didn't do anything stupid.

* * *

Then Ali became more brazen, and things turned a lot more sinister.

Marie took Freya away for a couple of nights, visiting Marie's sister in Abbotsford on the mainland. On her previous visits, Marie had never stayed overnight, preferring to sleep in her own bed. Abbotsford was only an hour's drive from Tsawwassen terminal, so the trip could easily be done in a day if she caught the last ferry. Plus, I knew she didn't have much time for her know-it-all brother-in-law, so choosing to stay at their place was out of character. It was obvious the real reason was to get away from me for a while. I said nothing, of course. The space was welcome; the tension between us was difficult for all of us. Certainly, it wasn't a healthy environment for our daughter.

On Marie and Freya's second night away, Ali's Golf failed to turn up. I kept waiting for it to appear outside the house. With the girls away, I could look out of the windows as often as I wanted without having to explain what I was doing. Anyone watching me keeping guard that night would have been right to question my sanity. Peering out at the street became an obsession.

Just before midnight, when I was convinced the car wasn't going to show up, a text pinged on my phone. I picked it up from the bedside table, knowing it had to be her.

Come outside. I know Marie is away. I want to speak to you.

For once, I didn't feel anxious. More a feeling of mild exhilaration. This message was going to go straight into my log. The wording of it was damning for Ali. It proved she had to have been watching our house. How else would she have known Marie was away? Also, the time of night worked against her. Who sends a text to someone asking them to come outside their home at midnight? Finally, Ali had overplayed her hand. I was confident it would make great evidence, even Collins would be excited.

The phone pinged again. *I know you're there. Come outside*

so we can talk.

Keep them coming, you mad witch.

I slipped out of bed and glimpsed through the blinds. Without the bedroom lights on, my eyes could see perfectly well into the dark. Across the street, I saw a figure dressed in black. It was her, and she was looking directly at our house. Bold as brass.

Part of me wanted to go out there and shake some sense into her, but I could hear Collins's words in my ear: "Just record it in your diary."

Not this time. That wasn't enough. The woman who'd been making our lives hell for weeks was standing outside our home taunting me. Why should I sit back and let that happen? While I was putting on my track pants, the doorbell rang. She wasn't going to go away. For a moment, I thought about getting my pistol out of the safe. I used it for target practice at the range, and this was the first time I'd ever considered using it for self-defense. If that maniac broke into our home, she'd have it coming.

My phone pinged again.

We need to talk, Tom. I'm not going away.

That was it. Either I go outside and tear her to shreds or I call the police. Sanity prevailed. I had more than enough evidence, so I decided to call the police. Now would be their chance to catch her in the act and bring an end to this madness. I picked up the receiver for the landline and punched in 911. It took several wasted minutes explaining to the operator why my situation was an emergency. At first, he made me feel like I was wasting their time. He suggested I file a report at OBPD the following day. It was only when I mentioned I'd already reported the woman to Sergeant Manning that he began to take my concern seriously. Even then, I sensed he was reluctant to do much about it.

"Okay, sir. We'll try to get a patrol car out there as soon as we can, but I have to tell you we are busy."

Even though I had no confidence he was going to do anything, I thanked him, vowing to myself, once this was all over,

I'd file a formal complaint. No one should be made to go through all this with such little support from the authorities. What were we paying them for? Once again, there was an underlying assumption that as a man I ought to be able to deal with the small matter of a woman showering me with attention on my own. No wonder some people take the law into their own hands. I'd always been against vigilantism and citizens seeking their own remedies. In a civilized society, I'd always believed there was no need for such things. That way was a road to chaos. But my complete lack of faith in the police was making me think otherwise.

Throughout the call, our doorbell kept ringing. When I got off the phone, I can't tell you how much I wanted to open the door and take out my frustration on Ali. She had it coming to her. Far from certain the police would turn up, I wasn't sure how much longer I'd be able to sit and endure the insanity going on outside our home.

Finally, half an hour later, the harassment stopped. The ringing ceased and there were no more texts. I'd left the lights off in the house, so I could continue to look out of the window without being seen. I scanned up and down the street. She wasn't there. I crept downstairs and stood behind the front door, listening for any movement outside. Silence.

I had just returned to the bedroom when I heard a vehicle in the road. When I looked, to my amazement, it was an OBPD patrol car slowing down outside our house. The officer turned his head in my direction, then he drove off. I couldn't believe it. Was that all they were prepared to do? Was that neighborhood policing? All I could think was how different it would be if a woman on her own had reported a man outside her house in the middle of the night. The police would be all over him like a rash and rightly so.

The injustice made me want to throw up.

Some twenty minutes later, I was lying on top of my bed, fully clothed, eyes wide open, constantly alert for any sound or movement. I knew she would return. It was only a matter of time.

What was I supposed to do then?

I don't know how, but I guess I must have fallen asleep because the doorbell shocked me when it rang. I jumped off the bed and ran to the window. The patrol car was back and it was parked outside our house. My heart was racing when I ran downstairs to get the door. Had they apprehended her?

"Mr. Harper?" the male patrolman asked when I opened the door. He looked in his mid-twenties, athletic build, square jaw. He was alone, and over his shoulder I couldn't see anyone in his car.

"Yes," I said. "Please come in." I stepped aside and allowed him into the hallway.

"Is there some place we can talk?" His accent sounded French-Canadian to me, similar to Brenda's.

"Of course." I pointed him in the direction of the kitchen.

We sat at the kitchen table. "You reported a stranger outside your house," the officer said.

"Not a stranger," I said. "I know exactly who she is. In fact, I gave her name to the dispatcher when I called."

He looked at his notebook. "Ali Page?"

"That's right. She's been harassing me for weeks. I reported it all to Sergeant Manning when I came to the station a few weeks back."

The officer threw me a blank stare and made a note in his book.

"Didn't they tell you that?" The tone of my voice revealed more of my frustration than I would have liked. "I explained it all to the dispatcher. The woman has been making my life a nightmare. Then tonight she turned up around midnight, ringing my doorbell and hammering on the door. She kept sending me texts as well." I held my phone toward him. "You can see for yourself."

The officer had a quizzical look on his face as I spoke. "That won't be necessary," he said. "I've spoken to her."

"You did? Where is she?"

"I caught up with Ms. Page a couple of blocks away."

"That's great. Thank goodness you managed to catch her."

He angled his head. "She says she was out running."

"Running? Is that what she told you?"

"Said she often runs late at night when the air is cool. I do that myself sometimes when I come off shift."

"I bet she didn't tell you she was right outside our house."

"I asked her if she had been running down your street, and she said yes. She was quite open about it. Told me you're a family friend and that you often look out for her running past."

"That's a lie."

He recoiled. "She said when she noticed you waving at the window tonight, she stopped for a chat."

"That's just not true." My hands were clenched under the table. "I wasn't at the window. I was in bed, like most people at midnight. She texted me and then rang my doorbell."

The officer's eyebrows knitted together, as if he was finding it hard to believe what I was telling him. "She tells a different story."

"I bet she does. Mine isn't a story. That woman wouldn't recognize the truth if it hit her in the face."

"She says when you opened the door to invite her in, the first thing you mentioned was your wife is away. Is that right?"

"No. I never even talked to her."

"So, your wife is here?"

"She's in Abbotsford visiting her sister."

"I see. Then how did Ms. Page know that?"

"She only knows my wife is away because she's been watching our house for weeks."

"Hmm." The officer made some more notes. "Anyway, she said it didn't feel right coming in with your wife away—said it spooked her, so she decided it was best to carry on with her run."

"I can't believe what I'm hearing." I shook my head no. "What's she doing in Owen Bay, anyway? She lives downtown. She has no business being here in the middle of the night."

"As a matter of fact, she was quite open about that," the patrolman said, folding his notebook closed. "Apparently, her parents live nearby. She gave me their address and invited me to contact them if I needed to. Said I could go back to their house with her tonight if I wanted."

"I hope you weren't taken in by any of that. She's devious. You cannot believe a word she says. I think she's suffering from some sort of psychosis."

"That's interesting. Are you a doctor?"

"No. I'm a realtor."

"I see. She told me she's a lawyer in Victoria. Even gave me the name of her firm. She also said her father is a superintendent with the RCMP here on the island and that he'd be pleased to vouch for her, if I need to corroborate anything. She seemed perfectly balanced to me."

"Balanced? The woman is crazy."

The officer stood. "My advice, Mr. Harper, is don't go opening your door to young women when your wife's away."

"Are you serious? Is that it? Because her father is a police officer, you believe everything she says. This is outrageous. I didn't open my door to anyone. Why would I call for your help if I was the one inviting her in?"

He raised a palm at me. "No need to get angry."

"I'm not getting angry. I'm trying to explain what happened. It makes no sense for me to call you if I wasn't worried about her. She's dangerous, I tell you."

"Look, we get calls for all sorts of reasons." He started moving toward the front door. "They're not always for the reasons people say."

"What's that supposed to mean?"

He stopped and turned in the doorway. "Maybe you realized you'd spooked the young woman when you invited her in with your wife not here. This time of night let's just say that could be misinterpreted. Were you trying to cover your tracks? It's not really for me to—"

"Here, take a look." I thrust my phone in his direction. "Read the texts for yourself. I didn't invite her in. She's the one who contacted me. I'm not covering up anything."

"Good night, Mr. Harper." The patrolman turned and returned to his car.

Chapter 15

I lay in bed, flirting with sleep. Thank God Marie hadn't been here to witness tonight's humiliating spectacle with the police. I couldn't wait to tell Collins what just happened. It would take a lot to surprise my lawyer—she'd seen just about everything as far as criminal harassment was concerned—but even she'd be shocked by my treatment at the hands of OBPD.

The way I was feeling—alone, powerless, vulnerable—I wasn't sure I could take much more. I'd never been a violent man, but everyone has a breaking point, and I could sense mine was close.

My heart jumped into my throat when our home phone rang on the bedside cabinet. In case Marie had to reach me while she and Freya were away, I'd left the volume turned up. Instinctively, I reached for the receiver but stopped short of picking it up. Marie always used my cell number; it couldn't be her. It had to be Ali. Even if I answered it, I knew there'd be nobody on the line, so I let it ring. This time I wasn't going to play her game. She wasn't going to get her cheap thrill.

The phone rang out four more times over the next few minutes, and each time I left it alone. I couldn't put up with this all night, so I got out of bed, unplugged the unit from the wall socket, and put my cell on silent. Turning on my side, away from the phones, I worried she might come to our house again and what would happen if she turned up at our front door. I wasn't fearful for my own safety, only hers.

Luckily for both of us, I didn't have to find out, because sometime between two and six thirty, when my alarm went off, I must have dozed off. I dragged my exhausted body out of bed and hit the shower. No run that day. Although it was the last thing I needed, ahead of me was a busy schedule of potential client meetings. Plus, at some stage, I had to get hold of Collins to fill her in.

As usual since Marie and I had stopped communicating, breakfast was going to be a cup of Tim Hortons coffee at my desk. I wasn't in the slightest bit hungry. Fact is, I hadn't eaten much in weeks. I could tell by the amount I had to pull in my belt how much weight I'd lost. I grabbed the car keys off the console table in the hallway then noticed the flashing light on our main phone.

The digital display indicated there were four new messages, all of which must have come in overnight as I'd checked it before going to bed. They had to be from Ali. I thought about deleting them right away, but if she'd left something incriminating on the voicemail system, I'd need it as evidence. I punched in the security code and hit play, bracing for a tirade of vitriol.

"Tom...Tom...are you there?"

Panic choked off my breathing at the sound of Mom's voice. She sounded weak, frightened.

"Tom...it's Mom...please pick up the phone."

"I think my head's bleeding...please help me."

"An ambulance...I'm not sure..." The last message was faint and incoherent. At the end, it sounded as if she'd passed out.

My head was spinning, my heart pounding. *Please, not Mom.* She must have fallen again and somehow managed to get to the phone. As it had been hours earlier, I prayed she'd been able to contact the emergency services and that they'd reached her in time. I'd never forgive myself if something happened to her and I'd not been able to help because I'd turned off the damned phones. *Please, Lord, tell me she's still alive.*

When I reached for my cell to make sure it was off silent, there were three messages on there as well. Still unable to breathe, and fearing the worst, I hit the voicemail icon and waited for them to play, dreading what I was about to hear.

"Tom, it's Bekah. Has something happened to Mom? I just got a call from her number, but she didn't leave a message. It's...er...a little after two in the morning right now. I've tried calling her number, but there's no answer. Call me, will you? Don't wait until tomorrow. Just call me to let me know everything's okay."

Bekah sounded frantic. I knew how helpless she must be feeling. The ferries to the island didn't run overnight, so it wasn't like she could jump in her car and come over from the mainland to check on our mother. I waited for the next two messages to play.

"It's Bekah again. Just after three thirty. Please call me back, Tom, even if you don't know what's going on. I just need to...I just...call me, please."

Then came the message that chilled my veins. "Mr. Harper, this is the emergency department at SanPen." SanPen was short for the Saanich Peninsula Hospital just outside Sidney, the nearest hospital to where Mom lived. They had a small emergency department there. I tried to convince myself it was potentially good news they were calling. It meant Mom must have been able to summon their help. Plus, if it was something more serious, they would have taken her to Victoria General. "Your mother was brought in tonight. She has been transferred to Vic General. Can you please contact us?"

The relief was short-lived. From Mom's messages, it sounded like she'd suffered a head injury, and now I knew it was serious enough for her to be taken all the way downtown. Immediately, I called the ED at SanPen.

I was right; Mom had fallen at home and had suffered a serious blow to her head. They had transferred her to the General for specialist assessment and a possible procedure to relieve the pressure on her brain. *Her brain.* They gave me a contact at the hospital, and I called them right away. I soon learned Mom was in surgery, had been for some time. They couldn't tell me anything more until she came out.

Right after the call, I jumped in my car and headed to the hospital. On the way, I called Bekah to put her in the picture. She sounded hysterical when she picked up the phone. I apologized for not telephoning her earlier and explained that I'd not received her messages until the morning. I was honest about it; I'd turned the phones off because of the harassment, which is why I'd missed Mom's calls, too. I didn't go into details about what had happened last night. It was neither the time nor place. The priority right then was Mom. Besides, there was no point worrying my sister any more than she was already.

Bekah's initial shock upon hearing the news about our mother was short-lived. She soon turned into action mode. She would come over to the island later that day, just as soon as she could get onto a ferry. On the way, she'd stop at Mom's condo in Sidney to collect some clothing and any other essentials she would need when she was out of surgery. She kept saying Mom would be okay. Bekah's optimism was infectious, and it lifted my spirits. With so much self-blame weighing me down, I can't tell you how badly I wanted to believe that Mom would get through this.

I was still on the phone with my sister when I arrived at the hospital parking lot. Before we finished our call, Bekah asked if I needed anything.

"Just you, Beks," I said. "That's all I need."

I can't imagine many more horrific images than an elderly parent in an unconscious state lying in a hospital bed, a bandage wrapped around her badly swollen head. Mom had come out of surgery minutes before I arrived. She was drained of all color, frail, and suddenly looking very old for her seventy-nine years. Sitting next to her intensive care bed, I was riddled with guilt. Since Dad died, I must have told Mom hundreds of times to call me if she ever needed help. Day or night. It didn't matter. And yet, the one time she really needed me, I wasn't there for her. Logically, I knew the outcome would have been the same, but I couldn't stop blaming myself for turning the phones off. I kept imagining her alone, lying on the floor, desperate for me to answer her calls. I should have been there, offering love and support while the ambulance crew was on its way. She must have been so scared on her own. The thought of what might have happened had she not been strong enough to call 911 terrified me.

An hour later, the consultant stopped by and assured me the operation to remove the pressure in Mom's head had gone as well as we could have hoped. All we could do now was wait. Only when she was brought out of the induced coma, he said, would we know if she had suffered irreversible brain damage.

Brain damage.

I'm not an overly religious person, but I don't mind admitting I sat there and prayed to some higher power that Mom would pull through this. I promised I would do whatever was necessary to help her recover. Even though it would be awkward, given my current relationship with Marie, I vowed I would try and persuade Mom to move in with us once she was discharged from hospital. Normally a strong, fiercely independent woman, I knew she'd resist. But I hoped, with Bekah's help, we'd be able to convince her, even if it was just for the few weeks, she needed to regain her strength.

When my phone pinged, I assumed it was Bekah letting me know what ferry she was on. Instead, it was the devil responsible for making me miss Mom's cry for help.

I clicked on the message. *I forgive you, Tom.*

I choked back the bile rising from my stomach.

Chapter 16

On the MLS system for almost nine months, my listing on Ocean Drive was one of the most expensive properties I'd ever represented. The five-thousand-square-foot, single-family home sat well back from the road, hidden behind a giant set of 'don't mess with me' wrought-iron gates. And the views from its waterfront location were to die for. A truly great spot. Sure, it needed more than a little updating, like many of the original houses in Owen Bay. That's what gave them character. The place was built in the 1930s and hadn't been modernized much since, but the bones were good. In the sellers' market we were witnessing, the property should have sold a long time ago. The problem was obvious: the asking price. It was way over the top, probably by some twenty-five percent. I'd tried to advise the overseas owner his price aspirations were too high before I took on the listing, but he wouldn't listen. If it hadn't been such a trophy sale, I would have walked away back then. I should have done. Given the amount of time and money I'd wasted on it, I'd long since regretted not listening to my gut.

We had a flurry of interest in the first couple of months, but the offers were immediately rejected by the owner, even though I thought they were quite respectable. He wouldn't even counter. Later, a few developers tabled bids on the basis the house would be torn down and a new home built on the site, but their offers were even lower. Still the owner wouldn't budge. Over the last three months, we had shown only two prospective buyers around the home. Neither one made an offer. The market had spoken. This was now a zombie listing.

So, you can imagine my excitement when I walked into the office about a week after Mom's accident and Brenda told me we'd had some interest in the property.

"It's a couple," she said. "They're from Calgary and, apparently, they were over here last week and took a drive by. They looked through the gates and 'fell in love with the place'. They're cash buyers and want a large house on Ocean Drive before the start of the school term."

"Did they ask why it had been on the market so long?" I asked.

"Didn't even mention it. I got the impression they're serious. Serious enough to fly back in this weekend just to view the property. The appointment is set for two o'clock on Saturday."

"It's about time we had some good news on that one. At its current price—"

"Funny thing is, she didn't seem at all fazed by the price. And you'll like this. Her husband is a property lawyer, so she said they're not working with a realtor."

I grinned at Brenda. When a buyer isn't working with another realtor and he or she is able to draft their own offer, the selling broker gets to keep all the commission rather than losing half of it to the buyer's agent.

"If they make a half-decent offer," I said, holding up my crossed fingers, "I hope our owner doesn't walk away again."

"How's your mom doing today? Any more news?"

"Not yet, but the doctor is talking about bringing her out of the coma in the next couple of days. We should know a lot more then."

"If you need me to handle the appointment this weekend, just let me know."

That was kind of Brenda as it was my turn to be on duty that weekend. But with my mother's situation, I'd been away from the office more than I would have liked, and Brenda had stood in for me on too many appointments already.

"Thanks, but I should be okay to handle it. Anyway, my sister will be around if one of us needs to be at the hospital."

"I get it. You want all the glory if we sell Ocean Drive."

"Am I really that transparent?"

Bekah and I were both at Mom's bedside when they brought her out of the induced coma. She looked confused when she first opened her eyes, but the moment she saw my sister and me, she smiled and asked what happened. Over the next few minutes, we knew we had our mother back. It didn't matter she was weak and unable to care for herself. Time would take care of those. The most important thing was she seemed okay in herself. Later, even the consultant told us he was surprised by her recovery, although he kept stressing to his patient how she needed to take tiny steps; the road ahead was going to be a long one.

"Don't worry," I said. "She'll be staying with me, so I can keep an eye on her."

Mom frowned. I thought I knew what was coming, but she surprised me. "I think that would be for the best, Tom." That more than anything told us this was, indeed, going to be a long recovery.

I kissed Mom on her cheek. "Freya's going to love having you at home with us." She squeezed my hand, and a wave of relief washed over me.

Saturday afternoon, I left Bekah at the hospital with Mom and headed over to our listing on Ocean Drive to meet the couple flying in from Calgary. From the way Brenda had described her conversation with them, I had a good feeling about these people. Brenda wasn't easily excited and was normally a good judge of character. Countless times her instincts about people had proven to be right. She was my secret weapon, helping us separate real buyers from tire-kickers, saving my firm a lot of wasted time and effort. If Brenda thought these folks were the real deal, that was good enough for me. It sounded like they knew what they wanted. My kind of buyer.

I opened a few windows to let in some fresh air and placed the bunch of flowers I'd bought at the hospital in a vase and sat it on the kitchen table. When I unlocked the French doors leading onto the deck, the ocean looked almost turquoise, reflecting the cloudless blue sky. Perfect conditions for a viewing. Whatever it took, this house was going to be sold today.

At ten to two, I heard a car come through the open gates and pull onto the driveway. Seconds later, the doorbell rang. *Ten minutes early. These people are eager.* Quickly, I finished raising the blinds to maximize the water view, then I raced to the front door.

Fear and loathing consumed me the moment I opened it. Standing in front of me was Ali, her face beaming.

"Remember me?" she asked, stepping into the house and walking right past me.

"I'm calling the police," I said, leaving the door wide open. I followed her into the living room on the ocean side of the house. "Did you hear me? I'm calling the police."

Ali sat on one of the large, white leather sofas, revealing her long, tanned legs under another short skirt. "Go ahead. I seem to remember that didn't work out too well last time."

I stood over her. "I want you out of here now."

"You know if you agreed to see me, I wouldn't have to play these stupid games."

I took my phone out of my pocket. "You have thirty seconds before I—"

"Don't be upset with me, Tom. I've forgiven you. Can't you forgive me?"

"You are trespassing. You won't be able to lie your way out

of this one."

"Come on, Tom. We both know you're not going to call them. Come and sit next to me." She patted the sofa. "You really should be thanking me. We have this whole house to ourselves. Are you really going to waste the opportunity?" When she uncrossed her legs, it was obvious she was wearing no underwear. "All those times we were alone together, I saw the way you looked at me. I knew what you wanted. I wanted it, too. Well, now's your chance. We can stay here all afternoon and fuck our brains out." She lifted her skirt. "Come and get what you deserve, Tom."

"You make me sick. I've never looked at you the way you suggest. It's all in your head."

"We'll see how long you can keep up the pretense. Where do you want me first? Would you like me to lean over the arm of this sofa, so you can ass-fuck me? I bet Marie doesn't let you do anything like that. I bet she's a boring fuck. Always with the lights off. Am I right, Tommo? Just tell me what you want. I'll do whatever you need me to do." She started unbuttoning her blouse.

"Don't ever compare yourself to Marie. You're not half the woman she is. You're a pathetic, screwed-up little girl who needs help. You disgust me."

The smile slid off Ali's face. "You don't mean that."

"Yes, I do. In your twisted little mind, you've convinced yourself we have some sort of relationship. We don't. The only emotion I feel for you is pity. You're a sad, lonely individual with a warped mind."

"I know you don't mean it—"

I hauled her off the sofa by her arm and dragged her into the hallway. "Now get the hell out of this house. If you come near me again, I'll go straight to your parents and tell them what a sick fuck they've raised."

She scratched my face just below the chin as I pushed her out of the front door. I slammed it shut then leaned back against the frame to calm my nerves. Inside my chest, my heart felt as if it were about to explode.

Moments later, I heard her drive away.

Chapter 17

Brett Mahoney was proud of his digital creation. The glitzy web-site for BM Self-Defense offered classes for groups, individuals, and women-only. There were separate pages on each of the various martial arts—ju-jitsu, karate, judo, you name it—most of which he'd lifted word-for-word from Wikipedia. A few parts of the site had not been plagiarized, where Mahoney talked about the use of skill rather than strength, a point rammed home by copious images of stick-thin female models dressed in Lycra disarming male attackers. BM Self-Defense promised anyone signing up for classes that they'd quickly learn how to fend off an attacker using the company's proprietary techniques. The team of expert instructors, led by "owner and martial arts guru" Mahoney, would teach pupils how to master a series of expert grabs, chokes, holds, and takedowns developed by Mahoney throughout his twenty-plus years' experience in self-defense. On the home page were lengthy testimonials from former students referred to by first name only: Britney, Lori, Savannah. The about us section made no mention of other team members. There was just a large photo of forty-nine years old Mahoney, a smiling, perma-tanned walking muscle, described as a God-loving family man with deep roots in the Victoria area. As well as referring to countless satisfied clients, his profile mentioned he'd worked closely with security and law enforcement personnel throughout British Columbia.

The photo was a portrait. Mahoney had cropped it halfway down his neck, so as not to show the razor wire tattoo under his Adam's apple. What his bio failed to reveal was his complete absence of professional training in self-defense. As for his dealings with law enforcement, these had nothing to do with training police officers, as implied by the slick marketing-speak. They came from a string of violent offenses, for which Mahoney had served many years in prison. While he knew how to look after himself, his street-smart methods of self-defense had all been learned while he was incarcerated.

His latest four-year prison sentence had ended a few months earlier. Right after he was released, Mahoney applied for a few menial jobs, even managed to get a couple of interviews, but he'd stormed out of both. It was bad enough having to swallow minimum wage for shit work, but he would never take orders from morons. What was it with their inane questions about his criminal record? He didn't owe them an explanation. He'd served his time; that ought to be enough. Long story short, he set up BM Self-Defense because there was nothing else he could do.

As far as Mahoney was concerned, that last period of imprisonment had been a flagrant miscarriage of justice; he'd done nothing wrong. Sure, he broke another man's neck, leaving him paralyzed for the rest of his life, but the sucker had it coming to him. Given the same circumstances, Mahoney would do it all again, only next time he'd finish the job properly.

No woman should be treated that way.

The incident happened in the parking lot outside Mahoney's favorite Irish pub in Langford on the west side of Victoria. He'd been drinking since late afternoon and left the bar around eleven. As he walked to his pickup, a few yards away, a young couple got into a heated argument. Mahoney had seen them going at it in the bar earlier. From what he could tell, it all seemed to have started after the woman—a good-looking chick so long as you ignored the tramp-stamps all down her arms and legs—said something to another man. Her partner hadn't liked that and wouldn't let it drop.

As Mahoney was about to climb into his F-150, he heard the woman scream. He turned and saw her partner laying into her face and chest with his fists. She had her hands and arms wrapped around her head to protect herself, but some of the punches were landing hard.

"You're a fucking whore," the man kept shouting. He looked like he was enjoying meting out her punishment.

Mahoney walked over to them. "Hey," he said, "leave her alone."

The young man stopped and turned to Mahoney. "What the fuck's it got to do with you?"

"You don't treat a woman that way. It ain't right."

The man cocked his head to one side.

"Only a pussy beats on a woman," Mahoney continued.

"Please mister," the woman said, fear writ large across her swollen face. "I'm okay." She tugged on her partner's shoulder. "Let's go, honey."

The man swung around and struck her in the jaw, knocking her to the ground. She rolled into the fetal position, screaming in pain from the kicking he began to give her.

"I told you to leave her alone," Mahoney shouted. "I won't tell you again."

A small group of onlookers began to circle, mostly patrons exiting the bar. Word must have got out there was a fight outside.

The young man stopped kicking and glared at Mahoney. "You want some of this?"

Mahoney walked right up to him until their faces were only a few inches apart. "Let's see you try and do that to me," he said, jabbing the bully's chest with the knuckles of one hand. "Come on, big man."

The man grinned and shook his head. Then, without warning, he swung his right arm in a wide arc, aiming to sucker punch Mahoney in the head.

Even after eight pints—could have been more since he hadn't been counting—Mahoney's reactions were razor sharp. He stepped back. The punch missed, but momentum spun the man around.

Mahoney spotted his chance and quickly powered two punches into his kidneys. Winded and stunned, the man fell to the ground.

The woman shrieked. "Please, leave him alone."

"I told you to shut the fuck up," the man shouted at his partner before he climbed back onto his feet. He lunged at Mahoney, missing him again. Then he pulled a knife from his coat pocket. "Who's the pussy now?" he asked, waving the blade in front of Mahoney's face.

Standing his ground, Mahoney didn't flinch. He waited for his moment, grabbing the man's arm when the blade thrust forward. Mahoney pushed the knife arm down with one hand, pulled his assailant in close with the other, and then head-butted him across the bridge of his nose.

The weapon fell to the ground. Its disoriented owner dropped to his knees, one hand clasping his broken nose, the other feeling along the ground to locate the knife. Mahoney saw his opportunity. He took a step back then kicked the woman beater in the head, sending him hurtling across the street. For a few seconds, the injured man lay still on the ground, bleeding from his nose.

The woman ran over to check on her partner, then screamed at Mahoney, "You've hurt him."

Mahoney turned away and started walking toward his truck. "You're very welcome."

"You fucking moron," the woman shouted. Suddenly, she didn't seem so attractive.

"He had it coming."

Mahoney reached for his keys, then felt a hand on his shoulder pulling him around. Instinctively, he ducked. It was the young man, swinging at him like a wild animal. Mahoney grabbed him by the shirt and slammed his face into the truck door before kicking the back of his legs. His dazed attacker fell forward onto his knees, facing away from Mahoney.

"Some people don't learn," Mahoney said.

Calmly, he held the man's head with both hands and twisted it as far as it would go until his neck popped. His limp body fell to the ground.

Mahoney couldn't make out what the woman was shouting as he started up the pickup and drove away. Unfortunately for him, his license plate and most of the fight were captured on smartphones held by what had become a crowd of onlookers.

When the case went to trial, Mahoney's lawyer argued in his opening statement that his client had acted to protect the woman. He'd only intervened when he saw her being brutally attacked. What was he supposed to do? He couldn't just stand there and allow that to happen. At first, the jury seemed sympathetic. Mahoney was no vigilante; he'd come to the rescue of a defenseless member of the public. He should be applauded.

But when the prosecution showed the smartphone evidence, the defendant was done for. The jury could see Mahoney had an opportunity to drive away when the man was on his knees, no longer representing a threat to anyone. In the words of the prosecutor, "But Mr. Mahoney didn't do that. Instead, this violent thug deliberately and casually broke the victim's neck."

Because of the video footage, the case made headline news on the island's TV channels. Even some of the mainland news reports picked it up. The investigating officer, and the RCMP's spokesman in front of the cameras immediately after the guilty verdict was announced, was then-inspector Bob Page.

Chapter 18

Bekah was a gem while Mom was in hospital. I couldn't have gotten through it all without her help. She took care of Mom's place, dealing with the mail and keeping neighbors up to speed on her progress, and by alternating our visits to Vic General, my sister freed me up so I could still spend some time each day at the office. While Brenda did more than anyone could ask from an assistant, I didn't want to take advantage of her good nature. There was simply too much work at the office for one person to handle.

Two weeks after her surgery, Mom moved into our spare room. "It's only until I have my strength back," she said. "Owen Bay is lovely, but it isn't Sidney."

I understood her desire to regain her independence. It must have been frustrating for her suddenly having to rely on us for everything. Mom was such a social animal, and all her friends were in Sidney. Although she had a car, the consultant advised against driving for a while, so unless we took her on the thirty-mile roundtrip every time she wanted to go see one of them, she was stuck. While I wanted her to stay for as long as she needed to get well, for her sake, I hoped she would be able to go back to her place soon.

My sister stayed for another day or two, long enough to satisfy herself that our mother was comfortable. Then Bekah had to return to West Vancouver. Her life was on the mainland; her own family was there. She couldn't be expected to put everything on hold forever. I was sad to see her go, more than she realized. While the frostiness between me and Marie had melted a little while my sister was around, I wasn't sure the détente would continue when she was gone.

Fortunately, I was worrying over nothing. Marie kept any negative feelings she had toward me hidden from my mother. In fact, both of us worked hard not to let the cracks in our relationship show when she was around. That said, with the spare room now occupied, we were sharing our bed again, and right down the middle ran the Berlin Wall.

In the days since I'd thrown Ali out of my client's house on Ocean Drive, she'd sent countless texts to me, all containing the same unhinged content as before: she needed to see me; she was sorry; she was prepared to give me more time; she hated me acting like she wasn't there. I was so busy at work and focused on the preparations for Mom coming out of hospital that I paid them little attention. As far as I was concerned, Ali didn't exist. And while there were more important things on my mind, I felt less suffocated by her unwanted attention. It helped she was no longer calling our landline, nor parking her car outside our home. If I kept ignoring her texts, I hoped she would eventually fade away. By now, I'd made it patently clear how I felt about her. Even she had to realize nothing would ever happen between us.

Even though I'd sold many homes to buyers visiting one of our open houses, I was starting to hate holding them and not just because of the tire-kickers—nosy neighbors and countless other people out for a weekend drive with nothing better to do than stop by to devour the free nibbles and wander off with copies of our expensive brochures. No, the main reason was they swallowed up most of my weekends, precious time I could be spending with Freya and working on my relationship with Marie. If the market continued its buoyant run, I decided I would need to hire a couple of weekend staff to spread the workload.

The open house for my new listing on Clayton Avenue attracted a lot of attention. In Owen Bay, there wasn't a whole bunch of new construction around. Empty lots were scarce, and it had become costly for developers to buy an existing property and tear it down. So, soon after I opened the doors to the new-build duplex, it was heaving with people, some of whom looked to be real buyers. With little inventory available in the area, my developer client had been greedy with his pricing, far beyond the level I'd advised. And judging by the initial interest we were seeing, I realized I might be wrong this time.

Forty-five minutes in, I was locked in serious conversation with a German couple from Hamburg. The husband's company had transferred him to British Columbia to open a subsidiary, and he and his family were looking to find a place before the schools started the new academic year, which didn't leave them long. They told me they'd narrowed their focus on Owen Bay because of the strong reputation of its schools. Problem for them, and my opportunity, was they were insistent on purchasing a new home.

All the omens were good; I was convinced these people were my buyers.

Then I spotted her in the corner of the room. Ali standing there, staring right at me. She looked pale, her expression empty. I tried to pretend I hadn't seen her and continued chatting with my German buyers, but my concentration had gone. They were talking, but I was no longer hearing what they were saying. My mind was elsewhere. I knew it was rude, but I couldn't stop glimpsing over their shoulders. What was she doing here? Was she about to make a scene in front of all these people? How could I get rid of her?

My gut twisted when Ali walked toward me.

"I won't be ignored, Tom," she shouted from behind the German couple, their faces filling with alarm.

I peered at her. "I can't talk with you right now." I kept

telling myself to remain calm and polite. "I'm dealing with these people. If you wait outside for me, I'll be out shortly."

"I'm not going anywhere." Ali's raised voice drew the attention of everyone else in the room. I collected their shocked glares.

"I'm sorry," I said to the couple. "Could you please give me a moment to deal with this?" I didn't wait for them to agree. I grabbed one of Ali's arms and marched her out of the room. My cheeks burned as I man-handled her to the exit. It was either that or allow her to broadcast her vitriol to a house full of onlookers. That was a risk I couldn't take, not in her state of mind.

Outside the garage, I finally let go of her arm. "I want you to stay away from me," I said, standing between her and the path to the front door. "You have no business being here. You're trespassing."

"What was I supposed to do?" she asked. "I kept sending you messages apologizing, but you wouldn't reply. I know I went too far pretending to be a client and wasting your time. I shouldn't have done it."

A group of people came out of the house, looked at us, and shook their heads. I turned my back to them, so they couldn't hear what I was about to say.

"I didn't read your messages. I deleted them because they don't matter to me. You don't matter to me. Don't you get it?"

"You didn't read any of them?"

"As far as I'm concerned, you don't exist."

"Look, I know I scared you by turning up and behaving the way I did. I get that, but can't you forgive me, Tom?"

Two more people left the house and threw me a dirty look.

"You need to leave now," I said when I turned back to Ali.

"Please don't be like that, Tom. I forgave you for calling the police, remember? I didn't hold a grudge. I let it go. That's what people do when they love each other. They don't ignore each other."

Ali tried to put her arms around me.

I stepped back.

"Okay, okay," she said. "I'll give you some more time. I know I was too fast. I can see that now."

"I don't need time. I need you out of my life."

"Don't say that when you don't mean—"

"Listen, I've been to the police and I've hired a lawyer. The legal process has already started to make sure you stay away from me and my family. They've got a record of your harassment, every single detail. If you know what's good for you, you'll stop this madness. It ends here. Do you understand?"

Ali's eyes were watery as I spoke. I'd never talked to anyone like that before, but she needed to understand that any feelings she had for me weren't reciprocated. She kept watching me as if searching for some hint I might not mean what I was saying, but I stared her down because I meant every word. And if it came to it, I was prepared to be a lot more cruel to get my message across. After a few moments, her expression turned from sad to empty and then stone-faced. Maybe she was beginning to comprehend how I felt about her. I wanted her out of my life, and she now knew I'd been to the authorities and commenced legal proceedings.

"Okay, Tom. You have a nice life," she said before walking away.

I watched her cross the street and get into her car. Only when I saw it disappear around the corner did I feel safe to go back inside the open house.

The German couple had gone.

Chapter 19

Mahoney's self-defense business was much slower getting off the ground than he'd anticipated. New client inquiries were few and far between, which was frustrating since he spent hours most mornings pimping his website in martial arts groups on Facebook and hashtagging the hell out of his tweets on Twitter. His efforts made no difference. The website had been a major investment, setting him back nearly three grand, money he'd had to "borrow" from his ever-patient mother. Fortunately, his regular business costs were low since he ran the nascent company from his home. At eleven hundred a month, his one-bedroom rental suite was the budding entrepreneur's single-largest ongoing commitment. Provided he scraped together enough revenue to cover that, Mahoney figured he could keep his head above water a while longer.

Luckily for him, rent for the hall he used for his weekly group lessons was payable on the night. In theory, so long as at least six students signed up, he wouldn't be out of pocket. That's only if they showed up. Already, he'd had to cancel the class a handful of times at the last minute when the turnout was low. Word of Mahoney's unreliable business practices and disdain for the customer was starting to spread, so much so that he'd recently disarmed the customer comments section on his website.

Because they represented repeat purchases, his most reliable source of income came from private clients where he could hold lessons in their own homes. No rent, turn up for an hour, take the money, and go. Sweet, but he needed a lot more if the business was going to take survive.

So, it was welcome news when Mahoney received a call from a prospective client, inquiring about one-on-one training. He was sitting in his basement suite watching a rerun of *Judge Judy* when the call came in.

"This is BM Self-Defense," he said, quickly muting the TV.

"Hi," the woman caller said, "do you offer individual classes? I haven't done anything like this before, so I'm not excited about joining a group of other people."

"Sure, we do," Mahoney said, unable to conceal his excitement. "A beginner's course normally runs to ten lessons. That way, we get time to show you the full range of techniques."

"I'm not sure I wanted to commit to ten. I'd need to think about that."

He'd never tried the "ten lessons" line before. Most folks decided as they went along whether they wanted another session. Maybe he'd been too heavy. Time to backtrack before he lost her.

"Is there a discount if I commit to ten?" the caller continued before Mahoney could say anything.

"Twenty percent, but you can always try one at a time and see how you do."

"Twenty percent. I think I'll go for the ten."

Mahoney punched the air. She hadn't yet asked about the price, so he'd just inflate it before knocking off the discount. "Now, what we usually do is send one of our trainers to your home at a regular time to suit you. That way, we get to keep the costs down."

"That wasn't clear from your website. I was hoping I'd be able to come to you."

"See, the venue we use for our group classes is far too big for our one-on-one sessions. I'd need to find somewhere else we could use." The glossy corporate veil was beginning to slip. "I'm sure we can work something out."

"How about if you came to my offices? We have a gym here. I'm sure they wouldn't mind if we used that. A few of my co-workers already have personal trainers come in, so it shouldn't be an issue."

"That's it then. Problem solved." Another air punch.

"I'm assuming it's the same instructor throughout? I don't really want to have different people each week."

"Of course. Continuity is important to us, too." Since Mahoney was the only person on the payroll, that was one promise he knew he could keep.

"Okay. I'd like to go ahead and schedule my first lesson."

"Let me grab the calendar." Mahoney shuffled the free version of the *Times Colonist* newspaper sitting on his coffee table. "Okay, I have it in front of me. When would suit you?"

"I'd like to start as soon as possible. Could you make six o'clock on Thursday evening? My offices are downtown."

"Let me see." Mahoney moved the newspaper again. "You're in luck. Our principal instructor, Brett Mahoney, is available at that time on a Thursday."

"Great. I'll send you send you the address. Is the email on your website the best one to use?"

"That'll work. Just mark it for Brett's attention. If he's out seeing clients, his PA will get a copy to him."

"Thanks. Please let Brett know I'll meet him in reception."

"He'll be there. Could I please take a name, so I can mark you on his calendar?"

"Sure. It's Ali."

"Once we get your email, Ali, we'll send you some more background on Brett—his qualifications and some client testimonials. I know you'll be happy with him. We'll also send you a note on how you can pay for the lessons."

"Thanks for your help."

"You're all set."

Unbelievable. The woman still didn't ask about the price. This was going to be the easiest money in a long time—well, legal, anyway. Mahoney turned up the TV volume, walked to the fridge, and grabbed a bottle of Peroni to celebrate.

Ali had known about Mahoney for years, as he was the subject of one of her father's most high-profile investigations. She immediately recognized the ex-con when he entered the reception area at her law firm dressed in a light gray Lycra tracksuit. Most people staring at the muscle-head strutting up to the security desk probably assumed he was there to see his criminal defense attorney.

"Brett?" she asked, extending her hand. Close up, he hadn't changed much from his mugshot taken right after her father arrested him.

"You must be Ali," Mahoney said, crunching her fingers.

She picked up her sports bag and led him down one floor to the basement gym. Other than a couple of people using the treadmills, the place was quiet. Mahoney pointed to some soft mats laid out for floor exercises at one end of the room and suggested the space would be ideal for their lesson.

Throughout the hour-long session, she came across as an enthusiastic student, seemingly in awe of Mahoney's depth of expertise. He felt flattered by her attention and bathed in all the compliments she sent his way.

"Have you got time for a quick drink?" Ali asked as they were wrapping up.

"Sure," he said. "I have a heavy client schedule tomorrow, but I don't have any more this evening." Even if he did have client appointments that night, he would have canceled them, anyway. She was a looker—well beyond his league, but who cared?

They left the building, found a table in the corner of a bar two blocks from her office, and ordered drinks.

"I can't tell you how much better I feel already," Ali said after their drinks came.

Mahoney ogled at her. Throughout the lesson, he'd been perving over Ali's perfect body in her skin-tight yoga gear. It left very little to the imagination. Wonderful. Sitting close to her, his knee rubbing against hers, he wondered if he'd ever seen a more stunning woman in the flesh. This one had brains, too. What would she be like in the sack? What he wouldn't give for the chance. He'd once heard these professional types liked to mix things up with a bit of rough now and then. For a few seconds, he let that delicious thought meld with the alcohol.

"I won't feel so helpless next time," she continued.

"What do you mean? Has someone threatened you?"

Ali looked down at the table. "I don't like to talk about it."

"Is that why you wanted self-defense lessons?"

"Talking about it stresses me out. Let's just say, I need to know how to protect myself if it ever happens again."

"Listen, you ought to tell someone if you're in some sort of danger. The techniques we've been going over this evening should be your last resort. The first step in self-defense is knowing how to disarm the threat before it gets physical."

"You're right, although it's too late for that in my case. Maybe I should have come to you earlier."

Mahoney felt a twinge of guilt. He'd ripped her off with the price he was charging and hoodwinked her into committing to ten lessons. Unlike most of the losers he'd taught so far, this vulnerable woman really needed his help, and he'd taken advantage of her.

"Isn't there anyone you can speak to?" he asked.

"It's difficult. I haven't been with the firm long. The last thing I want to do is cause a problem."

"I don't mean anyone at your firm. It's not something your employer would normally deal with, anyway. I meant a family member or boyfriend, perhaps." Subtle as a brick to the head.

Ali finished her wine then pointed at Mahoney's empty beer glass. "Would you like another? I know I could use one."

113

"Yes, but only if these drinks are on me, okay?"

She smiled at him. Perfect teeth. Beauty and vulnerability.

"Sure," she said. "I'll get them next week."

Interesting. So, there would be a next time. And there didn't seem to be a boyfriend in the picture. Mahoney waved at the server. He came over and they ordered the same again.

"I still don't get what your firm has to do with your private life," Mahoney said, leaning back into his leather armchair when the drinks came.

Ali exhaled loudly. "This is in confidence, right?"

"I'm not going to tell anyone."

"I was assaulted." She lowered her voice. "And the man who attacked me is a client of the firm."

"Wow." Mahoney's guilt came flooding back. "What happened?"

"I did some legal work for his company. They were going through a leveraged buy-out."

Mahoney nodded slowly. "I've heard of them." He had no idea what she was talking about, although it sure sounded important.

"The transaction involved a lot of late nights at his office." She paused. It looked like she wasn't sure whether to continue. "Well, one thing led to another and we...well, you know what I mean."

"You said he attacked you." Mahoney already hated the man. No real man assaults a woman, particularly not someone as gorgeous as this.

"At first, he was really nice. That's until I discovered he was married. As soon as I found out, I told him we couldn't go on. It had to end." Ali reached into her purse to get a Kleenex and used it to dab her eyes. "But he wouldn't listen. He kept texting me, over and over. Then he'd call me at home late at night, begging me not to end it. I told him I wanted nothing more to do with him, but he wouldn't listen."

Anger boiled inside Mahoney. He shook his head. "Some

men don't know what no means."

"One night, a couple of weeks back," Ali's lower lip was quivering as she spoke, "he turned up at my home. He kept hammering on my door, demanding I let him in. I know it was stupid of me, but I didn't want to create a scene with my neighbors, so I opened the door." She lowered her head and closed her eyes. It appeared the memory was too much. "Once he was inside, he started getting violent, slapping me around the face. I felt so helpless." She looked up at Mahoney. "Then he forced himself on me. He..."

"Did he...did..." Mahoney couldn't bring himself to use the word. The bastard didn't deserve to live.

Ali peered into his eyes. "Yes. He raped me."

The knuckles on Mahoney's clenched fists turned white. "Animal."

"Before he left, he told me if I said anything, he'd speak to my senior partner. He'd have me thrown out of the firm for coming on to him. Like I'd been the instigator. Like it was all my fault."

"I'm so sorry, Ali."

More dabs of her eyes. "Now you know why I needed to learn how to protect myself. He knows where I live. I can't sleep at night. I'm always listening out for him, fearing he's going to break-in. Next time, I'll be able to defend myself, because I'm certain he's not going to go away."

Mahoney emptied his glass and rubbed a hand over the stubble of his goatee. "You know, there may be something else we could do."

"I've thought about it," Ali said before he could continue. "I can't go to the police. I'd lose my job. The truth is, I slept with the man. I had an affair with him. If my firm got involved, he'd twist everything. They'd believe him. His company is one of our largest clients."

"I wasn't talking about the police. I'm no fan of them, believe me."

Ali frowned. "What else do you mean?"

Mahoney looked over his shoulder to make sure no one was listening then leaned forward and lowered his voice. "Maybe I can help."

Ali cocked her head to one side. "Like have a word with him, you mean?"

"Men like that don't respond well to reason. He's used to getting his own way. Bullies like him need...something clear-cut... something more direct...so they get it first time around."

"I'm still not sure what you mean."

"The man needs to learn a lesson. Needs to know it's not okay to assault a woman."

"I wouldn't want to hurt him."

"I know you wouldn't. I can see it's not the sort of person you are. But that's exactly why he feels he can get away with what he did to you. Don't you see?"

Ali covered her mouth with one hand. "Do you think he might listen to you?"

Mahoney nodded. "Oh yeah. He'll pay attention to me all right. I'll make sure of it."

"But you wouldn't hurt him? Physically, I mean."

"No more than was needed for him to get the message."

Ali sat back in her seat. "I don't think I can do it."

"How else is he going to learn? What's preventing him from coming to your home tonight?"

"I can't ask you to fight my battles. I should be able to look after myself."

"You're wasting your time. You won't get through to him."

"What if I had two classes a week, so I can—"

"Listen, with men like him, that's not going to work. I've met many of these losers. They have no respect for women. They get off on beating them. A short, sharp shock is what he needs. I guarantee he'll leave you well alone after that."

"You'd really be prepared to do that for me?"

"Um-hmm."

"I can't tell you what that means to me. Already I can feel the worry of it all disappearing. I don't know how to thank you."

Mahoney could think of one or two ways. If she was this grateful now, think how much more she'd be once he'd dealt with her piece-of-shit client. He looked into her eyes. "Let me get some more drinks," he said. "I'm going to need a few details from you."

Chapter 20

According to my lawyer, we were at least a month away before we'd learn if we were successful in our peace bond application. I hadn't told Collins about the scene at the open house, nor about the time Ali had exposed herself to me at my listing on Ocean Drive. What was the point? I already knew what she'd say: don't react, stay out of her way, and record it. All it would do is add to my rapidly mounting legal bill. Besides, long since had my blind faith in Collins as the legal cavalry evaporated. There are some threats in life, even in a so-called civilized society operating under the rule of law, which each of us must face on our own. The ugly truth was there was little my lawyer could do for me. At least, that's how it felt. Either I learned to suck it up or else I'd end up doing something I might regret for the rest of my life.

While Mom was staying with us, it was hard to tell how my home life was going. With our only spare room occupied, a new bedtime protocol had evolved between me and Marie. We'd wait until Mom and Freya had gone to bed, then Marie would go up, and I would remain downstairs watching recordings of my favorite TV shows or doing some work for an hour or so— long enough, anyway, for Marie to fall asleep, or at least pretend she had. Eventually, with the lights off, I would slip into the bedroom, climb into our king-size bed, and keep strictly to my side. We weren't allowed to touch or talk, although I sorely wished we could.

I remember that night like it was yesterday. I was watching *Breaking Bad* on Netflix after everyone else had gone to bed when I heard a car pull up. By now, my hearing had become so attuned to movements outside our property I could distinguish the regular sounds of our neighbors from those that required investigation. I went to the living room window to check who it was. It had been a week since Ali turned up at my open house, and I'd heard nothing more from her. Given her previous on/off pattern, I knew it was only a matter of time before she would be back terrorizing us.

Thankfully, while I didn't recognize it, it wasn't Ali's car parking up further down the street; we were going to be spared the hassle for another night. I closed the blind and returned to the den to see how Walter White was getting on.

Minutes later, I heard a tapping sound on the front door. *Please, not again.* That time of night, there was no way I was going to open the door. It had to be her. Who else could it be this late? I ran to the living room again and looked out the window. From the side, I could see a tall man standing outside. He had a bicycle next to him. It looked like Freya's, the one that had gone missing from our garage only a couple of days earlier. He must have seen me moving at the window because he turned and smiled, then pointed to the bike.

"Is this yours?" he asked.

Finally, a decent citizen. He'd found our daughter's bike and was doing the honorable thing, although, at the time, I didn't think to ask how he knew it belonged to us. It's not like there were identifying marks on the frame.

Funny the things we do on the spur of the moment. I went and opened the front door.

"Sorry to trouble you," he said before pointing to the bicycle. "I found this in the middle of the street and I've been knocking on doors trying to find who it belongs to."

Up close, there was a lot about him that made me suspicious.

As he spoke, his eyes darted around, looking over my shoulder into our home, and one of his boots was lodged against the door. When his coat fell open, I spotted a large tattoo just above the neckline of his T-shirt. It looked like razor wire. What kind of man has that around his neck? Not the kind I should be opening our front door to late at night, that's for sure.

"Thanks," I said, pushing the door closed a fraction until it met with his boot. "I think it might be my daughter's." I knew full well it was Freya's, but I wasn't going to step outside with him there. For all I knew, it could have been some sort of scam. He may have taken the bike from our garage in the first place. "Please just leave it there, and I'll take care of it in the morning."

"You sure?" he asked. "It's likely to get stolen left out here."

"Really, it'll be fine. She leaves it outside all the time." Again, I tried to close the door, but he made no attempt to move his boot.

We stared at each other, and in that moment, I knew I was in a lot of trouble. This was no scam. It was something much worse.

He threw the bike to the ground and charged at the door, propelling me backward into the hallway. A second later, we had an intruder inside our home. I tried to block him. Only then did I realize how big Razor Wire was; my eyes were level with his broad shoulders and bull-neck. The man looked like a serious bodybuilder.

When I tried to shout, he thrust his right arm out and wrapped his giant fingers around most of my neck. With little apparent effort, he pushed my head back against the wall and lifted me off my feet. At the same time, he kicked the front door closed.

As I struggled to breathe, a million thoughts entered my mind. What did he want? Was this a violent robbery, or something much worse? Did he know my family was in the house? I lashed out at his arm, seemingly making no impact. He slid me further up the wall, squeezing the air out of me until I stopped hitting him. My head felt dizzy; I was close to blacking out. All I could think about were the most precious people to me asleep upstairs and what this animal might do to them. Seconds later, he removed his hand, and I collapsed onto the floor.

"What do you want?" I asked, gasping. My lungs were on fire.

"You'll know soon enough." He grabbed me with both hands, hauled me off the floor, and carried me into the living room.

I managed to scramble onto my hands and knees. When I tried to stand, he kicked me in the stomach. Shock rippled through me, then piercing waves of pain deep inside my ribcage. I curled up on the carpet, bracing for the next strike.

"I didn't tell you to get up," Razor Wire said, standing over me.

He grabbed my hair and dragged me into the far corner of the room, furthest away from the staircase. From that distance, I hoped my family wouldn't be able to hear what was happening. Maybe there was a chance I could reason with this man, find out what he wanted, and get him out of the house before anyone woke up. If any of them came downstairs, there was no telling what he might do to them. I couldn't let that happen.

"Please, I'll give you whatever you want," I said, pushing myself up against the wall so I was sitting upright on the floor and able to see him.

He jabbed the sole of his heavy boot into my face, and my vision went black. On the second blow, I felt the cartilage in my nose crunching, followed by the metallic taste of blood at the back of my throat. I thought he was going to kill me.

"Did I say you could speak?"

I wrapped my arms around my head, dreading the next strike. I knew I wouldn't be able to withstand the punishment much longer. *Think.* If I rushed at him, there was a chance I could knock him off his feet maybe long enough for me to escape and raise the alarm. But if I failed, the noise was bound to wake someone upstairs. At that time, he didn't know it wasn't just me at home. I needed to try and keep it that way. The best thing would be to try and placate him somehow. Give him whatever he wanted and hope he would leave.

"Take your hands down," Razor Wire said, standing right over me. "I want to see the piece of shit in front of me."

I did what I was told. My sight was blurred in one eye, but I could still make out fresh blood on one of his boots. They looked like those work boots people use on construction sites, the ones with steel toecaps.

Razor Wire crouched down so he could look at me. "I'm here for a friend," he said, his breath reeking of beer and tobacco. "Any guess who that might be?"

I didn't say anything. Two reasons. First, I had no idea who he was talking about. Second, I didn't want to give him another excuse to beat me to a pulp.

"It's okay. You can answer me."

"I...I don't know who you mean."

It was so fast, I didn't even see movement when his fist flew into my face, crunching my cheekbone and throwing my head back into the wall.

"Wrong answer, Tom."

For a few seconds, the shock of hearing him say my name delayed the pain surging through my skull. How did he know who I was?

"Try another," he said.

What the hell did he want me to say? I was a small-town realtor, not some drug dealer or gang leader. I didn't know anyone who would want to send a hired muscle to my home. Whatever I said next, I knew I was in for more torture, so I kept quiet.

"Maybe a clue would help," Razor Wire continued. "My friend is a woman, a lawyer."

Ali sent this monster. That evil maniac was far more dangerous than I ever imagined. A sociopath.

122

"Ali?" I asked.

Razor Wire tapped me on the shoulder as though we were buddies. "Hey, you're getting good at this."

"Why would she want—"

"Come on, Tom. Don't spoil it now. Take a guess."

"She has no reason to hurt me. I've done nothing to her."

The smirk on Razor Wire's face vanished. Wrong answer. Every single fiber in my body prepared for the next torrent of blows.

"She says you've been up to a little extra-curricular activity," he said, jabbing me in my bruised ribs with his clenched fist with each word. "Funny thing is, I could forgive you for that, Tom. Who could blame you for trying your luck? After all, she's a good-looking woman."

"I haven't been—"

Razor-wire punched me in the face. "I haven't finished."

My nose felt like it was broken. I had to breathe through my mouth. I wanted to explain he'd been lied to, that Ali was using him, but I couldn't risk speaking again.

He waited for me to regain my composure before he continued. "What kind of sick fuck goes to a woman's home and rapes her?" Another punch, much harder this time.

I was drifting in and out of consciousness. *Rape?* Did he say rape? What twisted story had she told this man? There was no point trying to persuade him he had it wrong; he wouldn't listen. It would only prolong the torture. I knew for certain now he'd been sent to kill me. All I could do was pray it would be quick before my family woke up.

"Nothing to say, Tom?" Razor Wire throttled me with one hand again, forcing my head back against the wall. As I fought for air, accepting I was about to die, all I could think of was Freya being left without her father.

Razor Wire released his grip. "Do you know what they do to rapists in prison?" He jumped to his feet, his crotch directly in line with my face. "Well, I'm gonna show you how they treat those pieces of shit." He unclipped his belt and began to undo the buttons on the front of his pants.

"Please, not this," I mumbled through my swollen lips. "Just kill me." I closed my eyes.

"Hell, I'm not gonna kill you. Where's the fun in that?" I heard him pulling down the elasticated waist of his underpants. "Better make it—"

A gunshot rang out. Had he shot me? But I felt no pain. When I opened my eyes, I could make out Marie standing at the door, my pistol in her hand.

"Get the fuck away from my husband," she shouted, "or the next one will in your balls."

"Hey," Razor Wire said, one hand holding up his jeans, the other raised in the air. "I wasn't really gonna hurt him."

Mom and Freya appeared behind Marie. An ice-cold tremor passed through my body. *Please tell me they didn't witness any of this.*

"Get out of our house," Marie said, the gun trained on Razor Wire as he edged around the room, taking baby steps.

"Listen, I'm going," he said. "Don't shoot."

We stood at the front door and watched him run to his vehicle and drive away.

"Call the police," I said before collapsing to the floor.

Chapter 21

After five grueling hours in the emergency department at Vic General, finally they let me go home. The X-rays showed three broken ribs with most of the damage close to my sternum. While I had a broken nose and a rainbow of contusions all over my face and scalp, thankfully, there was no apparent damage inside my head. I counted myself lucky. The doctor, a British man in his early thirties, said he'd like to make sure there wasn't a latent bleed inside my skull. He wanted to keep me in for another day or so for observation. In normal circumstances, I would have listened to his advice, but I insisted on leaving. Marie and I had left Mom and Freya at home, and I was more concerned about their safety than my own. Though I kept telling myself it was unlikely, there was a chance Razor Wire would return to our house while I wasn't there. I couldn't bear the thought of them facing that monster on their own.

Marie drove us home from the hospital. Throughout the night, we'd been surrounded by doctors, nurses, and other patients, so the journey back in the car was the first time we had on our own. Marie reached across with her right hand and squeezed my arm.

"I thought he was going to kill you," she said.

"How much of it did you hear?" I asked, praying she hadn't caught any of the outrageous claims made by Ali's hired muscle.

I'd put my wife through enough. She didn't need to hear the sick lies Ali had told Razor Wire to get him to do her dirty work.

"Not that much. I woke up and there was all this noise coming from downstairs. At first, I thought you had the TV up loud. When I reached the landing, I heard voices, male voices, but they didn't sound like they were coming from the television. I heard you talking to another man. I couldn't make out what you were saying. Then I heard you screaming in pain. It was terrifying, realizing someone must have got into the house and was attacking you. I know I've always been against it but thank God you keep that gun in the bedroom safe. I loaded it and ran downstairs."

"I'm so glad you did. I think he was going to kill me."

Another squeeze. "I thought I'd lost you. Those few seconds while I was loading the pistol seemed like an eternity. I could hear you suffering. I kept thinking how much I love you. I kept praying you would live."

I held Marie's hand. "I love you, too. I'm so sorry you had to witness that." My ribs hurt every time we took a corner. "It must have been awful."

"Who was he? The way he beat you. It was brutal, like he was enjoying it. What did he want?"

I stared out of the window, wondering what to say. I couldn't avoid the truth because she'd find out soon enough, anyway. "I'll be giving the police a detailed statement when we see them later today, so I should tell you now."

Marie threw me a quizzical glance. "Did you know him?"

"No. But that man was sent to hurt me, maybe much worse if you hadn't stopped him."

Marie tensed and pulled her hand away. "I thought he'd broken into the house and you'd disturbed him."

"I'm afraid this was no random home invasion. It was much more personal." I winced as we took another bend at speed. "He came looking for me."

"Why?" Marie looked confused. "How do you know that?"

"Because he told me." I hesitated. "Ali sent him."

Marie's hand shot to her mouth, her scalp recoiled. "Oh my—"

"He told me she sent him. I guess he figured it was okay to tell me since he had no intention of letting me live."

"Why would she do such an evil thing?"

"I never used to think people are born wicked, but in her case...Either that or she has some serious mental illness going on, one that allows her to pass as a normal human being for much of the time."

Marie kept shaking her head. "You hear of these people, serial killers and such like, who appear perfectly normal, respectable even. Then their friends and neighbors end up being completely shocked when the truth comes out. Do you think she's like that?"

"I think it's possible. Certainly, she's much more dangerous than we first imagined."

It was just beginning to get light when we pulled onto our driveway a little after five. Marie killed the engine and turned to face me. She looked exhausted, drained of all color.

"I'm sorry I didn't believe you," she said, her eyes teary. "I should have trusted you. I hate myself for thinking the worst."

I tried to lean across the gear lever to give her a hug, but a sharp pain in the middle of my chest stopped me in my tracks. Instead, I lifted her hand to my lips and kissed it. "You don't have to explain. I've only got myself to blame for giving you a reason to mistrust me in the first place. I swear on Freya's life, apart from that one mad moment years ago, I have never cheated on you and I never will. Ali doesn't even begin to compare with you. There's only one woman in my life, and she's sitting in this car with me right now."

Marie leaned over to me and we kissed. It felt so good, I didn't want to stop. "I love you, Tom. Please forgive me."

"There's nothing to forgive," I said, holding both of her

hands. "Let's promise we'll never let anything split us apart again. Deal?"

"Deal."

I opened the car door and felt another jolt of electricity in my chest. "I need some of those painkillers the doctor prescribed for me. The pain is killing me."

When we walked through the front door, I could hear the TV on in the den, so I knew Mom and Freya had stayed up all night waiting for us. Marie and I went to the kitchen where she poured me a glass of water. I swallowed two of the codeine tablets we'd picked up at the hospital pharmacy then we walked through to the den. Mom and Freya were asleep, lying together on the sofa. I was grateful and not just because I could see they were safe. Knowing what they'd seen, it was going to be difficult looking them both in the eye again. Even if it was only for a split second, they would have witnessed what that man was about to do to me before Marie intervened. No daughter, no mother should ever have to see something so monstrous as that. At that moment, hatred was not too strong a word for the way I felt toward Ali for visiting such malevolence on our family.

"Let's not disturb them," I said, quietly.

Marie and I went to bed. Although I had to be careful not to pull on my ribs, we hugged and for the next hour we made love, the first time in many weeks we had been intimate. Afterward, lying in my wife's arms, for a short while the world felt like it had returned to its normal orbit.

Two officers from OBPD, Inspector Yvonne Butler and Detective Constable James Heinicke, arrived as arranged at two o'clock that afternoon to take my statement. Marie and I met them on our own. At lunchtime, we'd dropped Mom and Freya off at Mayfair Mall to do some shopping. We wanted to spare them from hearing the ugly details of last night's horrific events.

We sat in the living room, Marie and I holding hands on the

sofa, and the two officers in the armchairs facing us. Every now and then, as I described what had happened, my eyes would drift to the far corner of the room, where, hours earlier, I'd been beaten to within an inch of my life. Fear had long since given way to another emotion: anger—no, rage—that a stranger could breeze into our home and wreak such chaos and violence.

"We'll need you to identify him once we pick him up," Butler said once I'd recounted my story and we'd given them a detailed description of Razor Wire. "Then, if it goes to trial, you'll be a key witness."

"If it goes to trial?" Marie asked, her voice full of indignation.

"Someone like him," Butler said, "is bound to have a record. He'll know how to play the system; he'll plead guilty once he sees the evidence we'll have."

"If you have his photo on file, I'd be able to recognize him," I said. "His face is imprinted on my brain."

Butler nodded her approval. "You said he told you who sent him to attack you. What name did he give you?"

"Ali Page." Just saying those two words made me want to gag. "She's the daughter of some friends who live locally."

Butler flinched. "Friends? Can you think of any reason she'd want to hurt you?"

"I've been asking myself the same question for weeks."

"Weeks?" Butler looked confused. "You mean she's tried to hurt you before?"

"Nothing physical." I glanced at Marie and then turned to the officers. "It's a long story."

I spent the next few minutes sharing the background leading up to last night's assault. I explained how it all started and showed them the texts on my phone. I told them about the time Ali tricked her way into seeing me at my listing on Ocean Drive, and about the embarrassing scene at my recent open house. I held nothing back. If they were going to arrest Razor Wire and, hopefully, Ali, they needed to know every detail. DC Heinicke wrote it all down. While I was describing what Ali had done, I remembered Marie was hearing much of it for the first time. She kept looking at me, her face turning increasingly pale, her jaw half-open.

"If you speak to Sergeant Manning at your station," I said, "he'll confirm I came in and reported her not long after the harassment started. If only something could have been done about her then."

Dismay clouded Inspector Butler's face. She didn't say it, but I could tell she was shocked when I told her what Manning had said to me. Given what subsequently transpired, her reaction was no surprise. The police had let me down, big time, and she knew it.

"I want to give you my personal assurance," Butler said, "we will not let this drop. We will be interviewing Ali Page as soon as possible. I guarantee, once we lean on her, she'll point us to the man who attacked you."

"What about her?" I asked. "She can't be allowed to get away with this. I wouldn't have been attacked if it wasn't for her."

"I didn't mean to imply we'll go lightly on her. Far from it. We'll have a case against her for conspiracy."

Marie sat upright. "She needs to be stopped before someone gets killed."

Butler looked at Marie. "No one should have to put up with the criminal harassment your husband has had to endure. Leave it with us."

I was beginning to have some faith in this officer. For the first time, someone in authority understood the agony Ali had put us through. This time, I believed OBPD were going to do something about her. Though it had taken my near death, the police had finally woken up to what was going on.

"Do you know where Page lives?" Butler asked.

"I should. As I said, I found her the condo." I gave Butler the address and Heinicke added it to his pages of notes. "Be careful when you interview her," I continued. "She's very clever. She'll try and spin things."

Butler smiled at me in a patronizing manner. "Don't worry. We're quite good at spotting when someone's lying to us."

"Believe me. You won't have met anyone as devious as her."

Chapter 22

Mahoney was first to arrive at the bar near Ali's office building. He sat in the same corner as they had a few days earlier. Drinking a Kilkenny's Irish cream ale, he inspected the cuts and bruises on the knuckles of his right hand. Tom Harper hadn't put up much of a fight. Men like him never did. Chicken-shit pussies, who get off beating on women. He didn't have the guts to stand up to another man. They were all the same. One thing was for sure: that would be the last time Harper would force himself on another woman.

The speaker above Mahoney's head was pumping out 'Everything I Do, I Do It For You' by Bryan Adams. In his head, he sang along to the tune, word perfect. He and his first wife had danced to that very song on their wedding night. Man, how he missed her. She'd been the love of his life, but he was too stupid or too drunk to see that at the time. Latest he heard, she was married to some accountant up in Nanaimo and had three kids. That could have been Mahoney's life if he'd made different choices.

He kept an eye on the entrance, so he could see when Ali arrived. He couldn't wait to tell her. She was going to be relieved to hear the threat hanging over her had been exorcized. Hopefully, now the need for them had gone, she'd still stick with his self-defense classes. The young lawyer was a real cutie. He'd miss her if she quit now. It wasn't often he got to spend time with a woman like her. Truth was, he didn't get to entertain many women anymore. Sure, he'd had a few dates here and there, but once they learned of his three failed marriages and his spotty employment record, not to mention far too many years in prison, the women soon evaporated.

"I'm sorry I'm late," Ali said when she finally got there some twenty-five minutes after their arranged time. "My meeting at the office ran over."

By now almost through his third beer, Mahoney was mellow. "It's nothing," he said. "It's not like I have to be some place in a hurry." Killing time in a decent bar serving Irish beer sure beat sitting alone in his one-bedroom rental suite watching *The Bachelor*. He ordered drinks for both of them.

"When you called, you mentioned you had some good news for me," Ali said.

Mahoney puffed out his chest. The hero had come to the rescue and was ready to receive praise from his damsel in distress. "I'd call it very good news. You won't have to worry about Harper no more. Let's just say, he and I had a little chat last night." He deliberately rubbed his bruised hand as he spoke.

Ali looked at it then quickly turned away. "That was quick."

"Couldn't see the point in wasting time. Who knows when he might've come knocking on your door again?"

"What did he say?"

"Not much, really. The sucker made out he didn't know what I was talking about. Nothing unusual about that. These men are all the same. Cowards, the lot of them. He knew why I was there all right. As soon as I told him you'd sent me, his face gave it away. He looked real guilty, I can tell you."

"You told him I sent you?"

"Sure."

"Why did you do that?"

"I wanted to see the look in his eyes when I said your name. I wish you'd been there to see it. Man, it was priceless."

Ali's expression turned to stone. "I didn't expect you to be so…explicit."

"Say what?"

"I can't see why you had to mention my name. You could have referred to a friend of yours without naming me."

"Why would I do that?"

"It would have been just as effective."

"The man needed to understand why I was there. How else would he get the message to leave you alone? I thought that was the whole point."

"He'd have gotten it."

Mahoney waved his hand toward her. "Don't worry about it. He won't be talking to anyone. The man will be afraid of his own shadow after the punishment I gave him."

"You hurt him?"

"You bet I did. And he would've had a lot more if his wife hadn't burst into the room, firing a gun at me."

"A gun?" Ali looked around the bar then leaned in toward Mahoney. "Listen, I agreed for you to go see him. I never said I wanted him hurt. It sounds like you went way too far."

What's wrong with this chick? "I thought you wanted me to warn him off. Make sure he never came near you again. Did I misunderstand something?"

"How badly was he hurt?"

"Hard to tell. My guess is he'll be okay once a doctor has looked at him. Don't tell me you're feeling sorry for him now. Not after what he did to you."

"If he calls the police and they come sniffing around, I want you to know this is all on you. I never asked you to do anything physical. I would never have agreed if I'd known you'd go this far."

"Relax. He doesn't have the balls to call the police. Think about it. If he did, he'd have to explain to his wife why I was there. What's he gonna say to her? Trust me. A man like him would rather keep quiet."

"I wish I'd never told you. I knew it was a mistake."

"You worry too much." Mahoney emptied his beer glass and held it up toward Ali. "Are we having another?"

"No. I have to get going. I've got work to do."

"Listen, I thought you'd be happy. Harper won't ever hurt you again. In my book, that calls for a bit of gratitude."

"Gratitude? You've made things a thousand times worse."

"What is this? I thought you understood I'd have to rough him up a little."

"That was never my understanding. I expected you to warn him off; tell him there would be consequences if he continued harassing me. Whatever you did went well beyond that. That was all your own making, not mine."

"Fine. I'm sorry, okay? It's all my fault. Next time I'll know to spell it out."

Ali grabbed her purse and stood. "There won't be a next time."

"It's a figure of speech. I didn't mean—"

Ali turned and began to walk away.

"I'll see you Thursday evening," Mahoney shouted, "for your next lesson. Shall I meet you at your offices like last time?"

Ali returned to the table and stood over him. "Let me spell this out. I don't want to ever see you again, you fucking imbecile."

Chapter 23

When the call came in from OBPD the day after her meeting with Mahoney, Ali was sitting in her office, marking up a sale and purchase agreement for one of the firm's corporate clients. All the police officer would tell her on the phone was that OBPD believed she was a potential witness involving a major crime and they needed to talk to her urgently. The officer offered to come to her office to do the interview or else she could go to them. She opted for the latter and arrived at the police station at four p.m. later that same day.

Detective Constable Heinicke collected Ali from the reception area and led her to a cramped, windowless interview room. Inspector Butler was seated at the square table, tapping on her smartphone. She stood and shook Ali's hand.

"Thanks for coming in," Butler said, slipping the phone into her pocket. She pointed to the chair directly across the table. "Please, take a seat."

"What's this about?" Ali asked, making eye contact with both officers.

They ignored the question. Heinicke opened his notepad. "I'll be taking notes," he said, "plus we will be video recording this interview."

"What's going on? Am I a suspect?"

"We record all interviews held here at the station," Butler said. "Suspects and witnesses."

"And which one am I?"

As she paused to consider the question, the look on Butler's face gave nothing away. "You really have no idea why you're here?"

"All I was told is I might be a witness. I haven't a clue what this is about."

"That surprises me." Butler's voice was laced with contempt.

"I don't see why it should. Are you going to tell me?"

"We're investigating an aggravated assault that took place earlier this week, here in Owen Bay. We believe you can help us."

Ali frowned. "There must be a mistake; I haven't witnessed any assault. I don't even live in Owen Bay."

"I didn't say you'd seen the assault."

"So what are you saying?"

"We think you know the man who did it."

Ali leaned back in her seat. "I very much doubt that. I don't know anyone who'd go around attacking other people. As I say, I think you must be mixing me up with someone else."

"There's no mistake; we know exactly who you are."

"Then you know I'm a lawyer. What makes you think I associate with violent people? I can't understand—"

"What kind of law do you practice?"

"What does that matter?"

"I'm curious. Humor me."

"Corporate. Not criminal, if that's what you're thinking. My clients are large companies. To the best of my knowledge, their executives don't make a habit of attacking people. What's the name of this person I'm supposed to know, anyway?"

Butler nodded to Heinicke, and he opened the large brown envelope in front of him. He retrieved a photo and slid it in front of Ali. "Do you recognize this man?" he asked.

Ali looked down at the photo and flinched. "Is that Tom Harper?"

"That's right," Butler said. "That was taken when he was in

the hospital two days ago. As you can see, his face is a mess. The photo doesn't begin to show the extent of his other injuries. He's very lucky to be alive. So, you can understand why we want to find the man who did this."

Ali was holding her hand over her mouth. "What happened to him?"

"We were hoping you could tell us."

"Me? I don't know anything about this. Tom and his wife are friends with my mom and dad. I have no idea why anyone would want to do that to him."

"Let me get this right, for the record," Butler said, leaning both elbows on the table, steepling her hands. "You're telling us you don't know who assaulted him?"

"Absolutely. No one I know would be capable of doing such a vile thing to another human being. Any form of violence makes me sick."

"That's interesting."

"What is?"

"That you deny knowing who attacked Mr. Harper."

"I don't. This has nothing to do with me."

Butler smirked. "Yesterday we took a statement from Mr. Harper, and he says you sent the man who beat him to within an inch of his life. He was quite certain about that."

Ali shook her head. "That's just not true. I didn't send anyone. What reason would I have to harm him?"

Butler waited while Heinicke wrote down Ali's denial before continuing with her questions. "Mr. Harper appeared to be a rational person when we met him. As far as I'm aware, none of the painkillers he's on affect his cognitive capacity. Why would he make up such an accusation?"

"I'm asking myself the same thing."

"Really? According to Mr. Harper, you've been harassing him for weeks. He says you've made his life hell."

Ali made a face. "I'm sorry, but I don't know where any of this is coming from. None of it is true."

"Listen, we've seen your text messages, so cut the crap and stop insulting our intelligence."

Ali stared at the table, deep in thought.

"They don't exactly seem the kind of messages you'd send to a family friend," Butler continued. "They're persistent and personal. What are we missing here?"

Ali's cheeks were flushed when she raised her head. "If you have read them, then you will know we were having an affair."

"According to Mr. Harper, there is no relationship and there never was. He says all the communication was from you. And from what I read, it looks a pretty one-sided affair to me."

Ali exhaled loudly through her nose. "Tom and I started seeing each other when he was helping me find a condo. I'm not proud of it. He's a married man. I know his wife. Plus, he's around the same age as my father. But the truth is, he made me feel special. I was flattered. I liked the attention."

"So why are all the texts from you?"

"Tom would always call me, either from his office or cell. He kept telling me not to text, in case Marie ever found his phone and read them. He was always much more cautious than me. I think, deep down, part of me wanted her to find the texts, so they'd split and we could be together. He kept telling me that was something he wanted, but he needed time."

"You said you were having an affair. What caused it to end?"

Ali's fingers were shaking as she clasped her hands together on the table. "He started to get creepy. At first, he was gentle, but soon he wanted to tie me up when we had sex. He'd put his hands around my neck, so I couldn't breathe. He got me to do things to him, sick things that became more and more violent. It freaked me out. I didn't know what to do. I felt trapped. Once I realized the kind of person he really was, I felt frightened, worried what he might do if I walked away. I wanted to speak to my parents about him. My father is a superintendent with the RCMP, but he's also friends with Tom. Eventually, when I summoned up the courage and broke off the relationship, he wouldn't accept it. He kept calling my phone and, night after night, he'd turn up at my condo at all hours, demanding to be let in. I couldn't get rid of him." Ali paused to sip some water. "A couple of weeks ago, I was staying at my parents' home in Owen Bay. I was out running at night, and Tom saw me. I'm assuming he'd been looking out for me. He stopped me in the middle of the street near his home. Said Marie was away. He tried to persuade me to go into his house. That was the last thing I wanted. When I refused, he became angry. I thought he was going to hit me." Ali wiped her eyes. "I managed to run away. I reported the incident to one of your officers that night. You can check with him. Tom Harper is dangerous."

Butler and Heinicke exchanged glances.

"Why would Harper claim you sent the man who assaulted him?" Butler asked. Her questioning tone had become a little softer.

"I really don't know. Maybe it's his way of hitting back at me for ending the relationship. He can be quite scheming."

"I don't buy that. No one arranges to be beaten so they can blame someone else for the crime. That makes no sense."

"I'm sorry. I can't explain it."

"Did you tell anyone about the affair?"

Ali shook her head. "As I said, I wanted to tell my parents, but I was too embarrassed. I felt so alone, terrified what he might do to me."

"So no one knows about it?"

Ali peered at Butler. "Wait a minute. There is someone. I told him how scared I am of Tom. Could...no, that doesn't make sense."

"Who did you tell?"

"It's probably nothing."

"We'll decide that."

"Last week I started taking self-defense classes. I was worried Tom would...if he came to my condo and got in...I wanted to learn how to defend myself. I guess the instructor could see how desperate I was. After the class, he asked what was troubling me. I explained how I felt threatened and that I wanted the lessons in case Tom attacked me."

"And that's all you told him?"

Ali narrowed her eyes. "What do you mean?"

Butler leaned into the table. "Did you send him to assault Harper?"

"No, absolutely not. I told you, I abhor violence. The instructor said the best form of defense is to avoid any chance of conflict. That made sense to me. When he offered to go see Tom and to explain how he was making me feel, I agreed. I thought it might defuse some of the tension. That it would put an end to the harassment." Ali's face went white as she pointed to the photo lying on the table. "My God. You don't think my instructor did this, do you?"

"What's the name of this instructor?"

"Mahoney. Brett Mahoney."

Chapter 24

Most of the country's captains of industry and members of the political elite make their money back east in cities like Toronto and Ottawa. But when it comes to retirement, many of them take their savings and fat pensions and move west, attracted by the milder climate and the relaxed west coast culture. The greater Victoria area has always drawn more than its fair share of these domestic migrants as well as affluent foreigners from Europe and China.

The Peninsula community center was a shining testament to the area's wealth. Built out of steel and concrete a couple of years earlier, the three-story municipally funded, state-of-the-art facility had a library, IT rooms, swimming pool, two restaurants, a well-equipped gym, and various workout areas and meeting rooms. Basking in its reflected glory, Mahoney ran his group self-defense classes there every Wednesday evening—well, every Wednesday he had enough students to cover the one-hour rental charge for the space, anyway.

The class was coming to an end that night, and Mahoney was doing his best to hype the advanced techniques he planned to cover at next week's session, hoping they'd all choose to come back, when the double doors at the front of the room flew open. Mahoney had his back to the entrance, but he could tell from his students' shocked expressions something was wrong. He turned and saw three burly, uniformed police officers approaching him. Instinctively, he ran toward the rear fire exit. He reached it, only to discover two more officers right in front of him.

"Brett Mahoney," Detective Constable Heinicke said as Mahoney was about to be cuffed, "I am arresting you for aggravated assault." Mahoney resisted when they tried to force his arms behind his back. It took three of them to make him comply. "You have the right to retain and instruct counsel without delay. You have the right..." Mahoney wasn't listening; he'd heard it so many times before he knew it by heart.

With an officer gripping each of his arms, Mahoney collected the horrified stares from his class members as he was perp-walked out of the room. Things like this didn't happen in the leafy suburbs of Victoria. "I'll see you all next week," he said, head held high. "Don't be late."

They processed their suspect at OBPD, reading out his charter rights again and offering him the chance to speak to a lawyer. Mahoney declined. The truth was he couldn't afford one, not anyone decent, anyway. His mother had "loaned" him the money for an attorney last time he was arrested. Since he'd not paid her back, she was unlikely to be duped this time around. When the officers advised him of his right to call the free twenty-four-hour duty counsel, he dismissed that, too.

"Why would I want their help?" he asked the booking sergeant. "We both know those jerks are in your pocket. Just show me to my suite and leave the room-service menu."

It was a little after nine p.m. when they placed him in a holding cell. Next morning, he was taken to an interview room where Inspector Butler and DC Heinicke joined him a few minutes later.

"This interview is being video-recorded," Heinicke said, his tone on automatic pilot.

"Be sure to make a copy for my mom," Mahoney said, grinning and cracking his knuckles.

The two officers ignored him as they took their seats and

placed the papers they'd brought with them on the table.

"Where were you on the night of August twenty-third?" Butler asked.

"Good morning to you, too," Mahoney said. "I see someone's overdue their customer service refresher course."

"Just answer my question, smart-ass."

Mahoney pretended to think about the question for a few seconds before answering. "What day of the week was that?"

"Tuesday."

"Oh, that's easy then. I was at home. Tuesdays I stay in to wash my hair."

Butler stared at the thin mop behind the badly receding hairline on Mahoney's head. "What did you for the other ninety-nine percent of your time?"

"You're good, Columbo. Keep demonstrating those detective skills and they'll soon give you your own patrol car."

Butler stared right through him. "I take it from your answer you can't explain where you were that night."

Mahoney shrugged. "Take it how you like."

Butler nodded at her colleague. Heinicke turned over a photo of Tom Harper and slid it in front of their suspect; it was the one taken of Harper in hospital.

"Do you recognize the man in the photo?" Butler asked.

Mahoney glanced at it for a nanosecond. "Not much of a looker, is he?"

"Take a closer look."

Mahoney scratched the stubble on his chin while he examined the photo. "No, I can't say I recognize him."

"That's funny, because he recognized you."

"And how's that possible when I've never met the man?"

Heinicke slid two photos of Mahoney across the table. "One of the benefits of having a record as long as yours," Butler said, "is we always have recent mugshots we can use. He identified you immediately."

"I get it," Mahoney said, tapping Harper's photo. "Some guy

gets attacked, so you send officer Dibble here," he was looking toward Heinicke, "to round up any local sucker with a record to pin it on him. Now that's what I call real detective work. Forget what I said about the patrol car. You people are amateurs."

"His name is Tom Harper," Butler said, "the man you beat to a pulp. But you knew that anyway, right?"

"I didn't touch him. I told you I was pampering myself at home." More knuckle-cracks.

"Mr. Harper says you forced your way into his property and assaulted him. When we showed him your mugshot, he had no doubt it was you. Can you think of any reason he'd identify you as his assailant if you didn't do it?"

Mahoney threw open his hands. "Beats me."

"It doesn't make sense to blame you if you're innocent. You'd think he'd want to see the man who nearly killed him held responsible."

"You know better than I do there are some weird folks out there."

Butler nodded at Heinicke again. The junior officer opened the envelope in front of him and retrieved a typed report. He handed it to Butler.

"You're telling us you've never met Tom Harper, right?" Butler asked.

"Never seen him before in my life."

"And you have never been to his home here in Owen Bay?"

"I think I'd remember if I had."

"That's funny," Butler said, as she started reading the report in her hands. "Says here your fingerprints were all over the Harper residence. Now we don't have the DNA report back just yet, but I think we all know what it's going to say."

The smirk slid off Mahoney's face.

"You know what else we have?" Butler continued. "In addition to Mr. Harper's statement, we have eyewitness confirmation from his wife, his mother, and his daughter that you were in their home that night. Mrs. Harper was very specific. She said if she hadn't threatened you with their pistol, you would have killed her husband."

Mahoney said nothing. He was in trouble and he knew it. He probably had left traces of his DNA at Harper's house. But after the pasting he'd given him, it was surprising Harper had had the balls to call the police.

Butler looked at Heinicke. "What are we looking at for aggravated assault?"

Heinicke pondered the question before answering. "This one's at the most serious end of the spectrum," he said. "I'd be amazed if it wasn't the maximum sentence."

Butler stared at Mahoney. "That's fourteen years," she said.

The officers remained silent, allowing Mahoney to marinate in the bad news. Fourteen years.

"By my reckoning, that'll make you almost a pensioner by the time you get out," Butler continued.

Mahoney was stroking his stubble again. Fourteen years was a hell of a long time, more than twice his longest previous sentence. And for what? To protect Ali Page, a woman he hardly knew. And what thanks did it get him? None. The ungrateful tramp had thrown it back in his face. She'd set him up from the beginning. Come to think of it, she had to be the one who fingered him to the police. How else could they have identified him so quickly? Harper didn't know his name. That bitch had turned on him.

"Speaking hypothetically, how would someone go about reducing a sentence like that?" Mahoney asked, with none of the earlier bravado in his voice.

Butler exchanged glances with Heinicke. "When this goes to trial," she said, "the evidence will be so overwhelming, putting up a defense will be futile. The courts always look favorably on those people who choose not to waste their time. Then, of course, there's any mitigating circumstances to take into consideration."

"Such as?" Mahoney's tone revealed a little too much excitement. If there was a possibility of cutting the years he'd have to spend in prison, he'd jump through whatever hoops were needed.

"Maybe you had a good reason for going to the Harper residence. I don't know. You'd have to tell us."

Now he was about to come clean, Mahoney's throat suddenly felt dry. What he wouldn't give for another Kilkenny right now. "I didn't mean to hurt him—not that much, anyway." He swallowed and stared into space.

"Go on," Butler said.

"I only went to see him to warn him off. Tell him to stop."

"Why did he need a warning?"

Mahoney sighed. That dumb hoe lawyer had used him, then turned on him. She had this coming. "One of my students, a woman, told me she was terrified of Harper. She said she'd had an affair with him, and how he's a married man and all. When she finished it, he started harassing her, threatening her with violence. Anyway, things got worse and then, one day, he went to her home and raped her."

Butler took a quick look at her colleague then turned back to Mahoney. "What's the name of this student?" she asked.

"Ali Page."

"And she told you Harper raped her?"

"That's right."

"You're certain that's what she said?"

"One hundred percent. I tell you, when I first met her, the woman was desperate. Of course, I offered to help her. I couldn't just leave her, not in the state she was in. She was vulnerable and didn't know what to do. I suggested I could go and see Harper. Give him a warning, tell him if he went near her again, there'd be consequences."

"But you did more than that."

"I know." Mahoney blew air out through his teeth. "I didn't want to do it, but she insisted. She kept saying how speaking to him wouldn't work, that Harper wouldn't listen to reason. She told me if he didn't get the message, he would attack her again. It was only a matter of time. I've never seen a woman that scared of anyone. I promise you, if it was down to me, I would have tried a simple warning first."

Chapter 25

Butler and Heinicke wasted no time summoning Ali back to the station for another interview. There were too many inconsistencies between her story and Mahoney's. Was Page the victim she was making out to be, or had she conspired with Mahoney to assault Harper? Harper had warned them she was devious, but then, of course, he was the one who'd had an affair he was trying to hide from his wife.

The officers began the interview by reading out the statement Ali had given days earlier. "Is there anything in your statement you now wish to change?" Butler asked.

Ali paused before answering. "On reflection, I could have gone into more detail about Tom's behavior and why it made me feel so scared of him. Other than that, no. I think it's accurate."

"We can add to it, if you like."

"That's okay. It's not like he's the one who's being investigated."

"No, that would be Brett Mahoney." Butler picked up a document that had been face down on the table in front of her and began to read it. "This is a statement we took from Mahoney, and there are some things in here that don't exactly tie in with your version of events."

Ali tilted her head to one side. "Such as?"

"In here, Mahoney says he only wanted to go see Harper to give him a warning, to tell him to stay away from you."

"That's exactly what I said. He offered to go and see him. To explain how his harassment was making me feel and tell him it had to stop."

"But he did a lot more than that."

"I know that now. With the benefit of hindsight, I realize I know nothing about Mahoney other than he's a self-defense instructor. I don't know what possessed me to confide in a total stranger. All I can say is, with all the stress I was under, I wasn't thinking straight. Believe me, I had no idea he was going to attack Tom. If I had thought for one moment there was the slightest risk of that, I would have stopped him from going."

"You sure about that?"

"Absolutely. Since we last talked, I've done a little research on Mahoney. The man is a violent criminal with multiple convictions. I'm amazed he could set himself up as a self-defense instructor. I feel duped by him."

Butler read some more of Mahoney's statement. "He said it was your idea to assault Harper, and that he resisted it at first."

"That's just not true."

"He said you told him Harper wasn't the kind of man who would listen to reason and that he needed to be taught a lesson. Did you encourage Mahoney to assault Harper?"

"No. It was all Mahoney's idea. He was the one who first suggested going to see Tom. Not me. Okay, I know I agreed to it, but I only wanted Mahoney to warn him off. Nothing more. Now I know about his criminal record, I'm not at all surprised he was violent. But that was his decision, not mine."

"Why would he lie about that when he's already confessed to the assault?"

"I don't know. Maybe he's angling after a deal over his sentence by pointing the finger at me. He's clearly a good liar. He fooled me and a whole bunch of other clients into thinking he was legitimate. I feel so stupid."

Butler placed Mahoney's statement back down on the table. "Did you tell Mahoney Harper raped you?"

Ali flinched. "What? No. Is that what he said? He's unbelievable. The man has no—"

"Did Harper rape you?"

"No. But is he capable of something like that? Yes, I think he is. He scares me."

"Why do you think Mahoney said that if it isn't true? It's not the sort of thing you'd make up."

"You'll have to ask him. I can't explain it. If I had been raped, he'd be the last person I'd tell. Don't you think I'd report it to the police, so you could arrest him?"

"Maybe." Butler leaned back in her chair and crossed her arms. "Given the kind of man Mahoney is, telling him Harper raped you would be a good way to motivate him."

"I don't follow you. Motivate him in what way?"

"It would be like loading the gun for him. If you wanted Mahoney to really do Harper some harm, what better way than making up something like that?"

"That's not what happened at all. I told you Harper scares me—no, he terrifies me. But I'm not going to say he raped me when he didn't. Mahoney is a liar. He knows he went too far. Maybe he feels the need to justify his own violence."

"How do we know Mahoney is the one lying to us?"

"I'm not sure why you would choose to believe someone like him over me."

Butler uncrossed her arms and relaxed her shoulders. "We're not saying we believe everything Mahoney has told us, but we wouldn't be doing our job if we didn't challenge you where your statement differs from his. For what it's worth, I don't believe you would make up something like that. You'd have to be crazy or evil, or maybe both."

"I wish I'd come to you in the first place, the moment Tom began to harass me after I ended our affair."

"Would have been a lot simpler."

"What should I do if he continues to contact me? I dread him turning up at my door again one night."

"I suspect he won't be doing that again. Mahoney is likely to have put an end to all that. Besides, by now Harper has probably had to tell his wife about the affair. How else would he explain away Mahoney's visit? He'd be a fool to risk contacting you in those circumstances."

"I hope you're right."

"Listen, if he starts harassing you again, you must come back and see us. We've got a record of his prior history now. It wouldn't take much for us to obtain a court order preventing him from contacting you. If he broke that, you'll understand he'd be committing a criminal offense."

"Would it be okay to speak to you, personally, if he does come back?"

"Sure." Butler slid her card across the table. "That's my number. Call me anytime."

"Thanks. I know I could always speak to my dad about it, but I don't feel comfortable admitting I had an affair with one of his friends."

"I get that."

Chapter 26

Bekah came over to help me and Marie settle Mom back into her Sidney condo. All of us had tried to persuade her to stay at our place a little longer, but she wouldn't have it. Mom had always valued her independence, so none of us was that surprised she wanted to go home once she was back on her feet. Part of me did wonder whether she thought she was being an extra burden on us while I was recovering from my injuries. If that was the case, she was wrong; I liked having her around. We all did.

Marie and Freya stayed with Mom for her first two nights in Sidney. Since we never did learn how she came to fall and injure herself that night—Mom couldn't remember—we wanted to make sure she was able to get around her home without difficulty. I would have stayed, too, but the way my ribs felt, I needed the comfort of my own firm mattress.

Bekah came back with me to Owen Bay after we said good-bye to Mom. That night, the two of us walked to a local Italian restaurant for dinner. Now the police were taking an active role, I was starting to feel confident the worst was over, so I took the opportunity to open up a little more. I told my sister everything Ali had been doing prior to my assault.

"I just assumed it had all stopped," Bekah said. "After my car was damaged, you never mentioned any more trouble from her."

"That was because I didn't want to worry you," I said. "It

was my problem to deal with, not yours."

"I'd much rather have known. It must have been a nightmare. The police had better lock her up for what she and that man did to you. She deserves what's coming. You're lucky to be alive."

"I don't think we'll hear much from Ali again. They will have hauled her in for questioning by now. Even she wouldn't be stupid enough to continue harassing us with the spotlight on her."

"She's one evil witch. I hope she rots in hell."

I picked up my glass of wine and tapped it against Bekah's. "I'll drink to that."

"What sentence do you think she'll get?" Bekah asked.

"I'm not convinced it'll get that far."

"You think she'll try and do a deal?"

"No. I have this nagging doubt she'll wriggle off the hook entirely. Somehow, she'll try and place the blame on that muscle-head she sent to our home."

"It would be awful if she got away with it. What she did was every bit as bad as the man who assaulted you. Probably worse."

"I know, but nothing would surprise me with her. I'm just grateful we won't have to put up with her any longer. If she gets a prison sentence, that'll be a bonus."

Bekah shook her head. "I can't be that forgiving. I'm sorry."

"It's not that. More relief it's all over, apart from the trial. If there is one, the police said I'll have to testify as I'm the main witness."

We sat in silence for a few moments, then Bekah said, "It's good to see you and Marie getting along better. I know how difficult things were between you."

"I think we'll be okay. If there's a silver lining to the beating I took, it was that Marie could see what I was dealing with. She finally saw for herself what that deranged woman is like."

"Must have been hard for her."

"It was. All the evidence pointed to me having an affair with

Ali. She played us well. I couldn't blame Marie for thinking what she did. We're good now, though. This will make us stronger."

After the meal, we walked back to our house, hand-in-hand.

Next morning, we were both up early as Bekah had reserved a spot on the first ferry from Swartz Bay which meant she'd have to leave our place by six. Over a quick breakfast of toast and coffee, we chatted about all of us taking a trip up to Tofino in October. As kids, our parents had taken us there every year to walk the endless miles of sandy beaches and to watch the surfers riding the huge waves coming in from the Pacific. It felt good to be focusing on the fun things in life. Such a contrast to the past few months.

I carried Bekah's overnight bag downstairs and left it near the front door. "Thanks for all your help with Mom," I said, hugging her goodbye. "I hope she'll be okay on her own."

"You make sure you look after yourself for a change," Bekah said. "Next time I see you, you need to have put some weight back on."

My sister was right. I figured I'd shed almost twenty pounds since the last time I saw her. "Don't worry." I tapped my stomach. "A few more bowls of pasta like last night will take care of that."

Bekah walked in front of me as we left the house. She pressed her key fob and released the lock on the trunk. While I was loading her bag, Bekah walked around to the driver side of her car.

"Oh my God," she shouted.

"What is it?"

"Look at this," Bekah was pointing to the car door.

I felt a dead weight in my gut when I rushed to her side. There it was, scratched into the paintwork:

I told you to keep away from him
WHORE

"This is her again," I said, unable to take my eyes off the door. "This is never going to end."

"I just had it repaired," Bekah said. "I'm calling the police."

Bekah missed her ferry that morning. Instead, she and I went into OBPD and reported the vandalism to her car. We requested to see Inspector Butler, but we were told she wasn't in. Detective Constable Heinicke was available, so we met with him and explained what had happened. While he recorded everything we said, I was left with the distinct feeling he was going through the motions. We all knew this was no random damage to a vehicle, that it had to be Ali, but Heinicke wasn't listening. Something had changed from OBPD's more sympathetic posture only a few days earlier. Suddenly, Heinicke seemed detached, as if he thought we were wasting his time. I tried to explain the significance of the message scratched into Bekah's door. I kept saying it had to be Ali, but my words went over his head.

What's wrong with this man?

I asked him to get Inspector Butler to call me when she returned, and Heinicke assured me he would pass on the message. If he wasn't concerned, surely, his superior would take the necessary action?

For whatever reason, Butler never called me.

Chapter 27

It was two fifteen in the morning when Ali approached Tom's house on foot, a half-filled plastic garbage bag in her right hand. She waited by the curb, looking up at the bedroom windows. They were dark, like those on the rest of the street. A vehicle approached, thumping bass music escaping through the young driver's open window. Ali crouched behind Tom's car until it drove by. She stood and walked toward the house. As she reached the corner of the garage, a motion detector triggered outside lights, instantly flooding the front of the property. They were new. They hadn't been there when she vandalized that woman's car—the whore Tom was seeing when Marie was away—nor during the eight nights Ali had been back since. Quickly, she ran into the yard of a neighboring property and watched. Nothing. Moments later, the lights went out.

For fifteen minutes, Ali waited, ducked behind a row of bushes along the property line, scanning and listening. Other than the odd car passing by, the only sound came from a couple of raccoons, scratching themselves on the rough stucco siding of a house across the street. After a while, they moved on. She could hear them calling each other as they waddled down the middle of the road.

She grabbed the plastic bag and walked slowly toward the side of Tom's detached garage. Although the Harpers had installed new security lighting, the motion detector appeared to point only in the direction of the driveway. Ali took baby steps around the back of the garage to the same spot she'd visited on those previous nights: where the Harpers kept their the two-wheeled trash can. She opened it, reached inside, and retrieved the garbage bag lying on the top, replacing it with the one she'd brought with her. Before she left, she used the small flashlight on her smartphone to examine the area next to the bag's red tie-strings. The small pen mark she'd left on the one she returned the previous night wasn't there, so this had to be a freshly filled bag and one she'd not yet inspected.

Five minutes later, she was back inside her VW Golf, the plastic bag sitting on the floor in front of the passenger seat. Despite her efforts to avoid drawing attention, flashing blue lights appeared in her rear-view mirror shortly after she set off.

She pulled over, and the police vehicle stopped behind her, headlights on. There was no time to hide the bag before the patrolman walked up to her car and tapped on her window.

"Good evening, ma'am," he said when she lowered it.

"Is there a problem?" Ali asked.

"Can I see your license and registration?"

"Sure." Ali reached across to the glove box. The officer used his flashlight to follow what she was doing. "Here they are," she said, handing over some papers and her BC license.

"Wait here." The patrolman returned to his vehicle to run her name and registration through the onboard computer. Minutes later, he returned and handed back the documents.

"Is everything okay?" Ali asked.

He kept his flashlight on when he leaned into the window. "I stopped you because you failed to come to a halt at the stop sign back there."

"I'm sorry. I didn't realize."

"What's in the bag?" the officer asked, jutting his chin toward the passenger seat.

"Nothing. I just haven't had time to throw it into the trash at home."

The officer threw her a quizzical look, as if to say, that doesn't make much sense.

"Wait until I tell my dad I was stopped for a stop sign violation," she continued. "He'll kill me. He's a superintendent with the RCMP. He's always going on at me about my driving."

The patrolman tapped his hand on the window-frame and stood upright. "I'm going to let you off with a warning this time, since you're my first catch of the night."

Ali smiled at him. "I really appreciate that. Thanks."

"You drive carefully," he said as he walked away.

Once back inside her condo, Ali put on rubber gloves then emptied the contents of the garbage bag onto a tarp she had already spread out on her living room floor. Immediately, the smell of dog faeces wafted into the air. She found the torn doggy-poop container and held her breath while she wrapped it in a plastic shopping bag. Carefully, she picked through the food debris, wastepaper, take-out containers, and paper coffee cups, placing everything she'd inspected to one side.

She had almost completed her search when a clump of Kleenex tissues caught her eye. She picked them up and slowly unwrapped them. A wide grin lit up her face when she saw what was in her hand. Nine straight nights in a row she'd visited Tom's house and finally she had what she was looking for: a used condom. She sat cross-legged on the floor and removed her gloves, so she had better control of her fingers. She used them to tie a knot in the open end of the condom, thus sealing in the contents and preventing contamination. From one of her kitchen cupboards, she took out a small airtight Tupperware container and placed the condom inside. She hid it at the back of her fridge behind two bottles of wine.

Next morning, leaving for the office, she took the rolled-up tarp, together with the Harpers' garbage bag, and dropped them into the large dumpster in her building's basement parking lot.

Chapter 28

Dine-out Wednesday was back for the first time in weeks. As usual, we invited Freya to join us, but she said she'd invited some friends over to the house and so couldn't come. At least she had the good grace to feign disappointment. In truth, I welcomed the opportunity to have a quiet moment one-on-one with Marie. To celebrate, I booked a table at The Empress hotel on the waterfront in Victoria's inner harbor. Local history buffs always liked to mention to tourists that Rudyard Kipling once stayed there in the early 1900s. For Vancouver Island, the place was an institution. It had a special significance for us, too: it was where we held our wedding reception almost two decades earlier. While a night out at The Empress wouldn't begin to make up for what she'd been through, I was hoping Marie would appreciate the gesture. It was time I treated my wife.

We enjoyed pre-dinner cocktails at the bar then took our seats for dinner. We hadn't been there in ages, and since our last visit they'd carried out a complete refurb of the place. Marie was delighted they kept the traditional colonial feel of the old Bengal Lounge, now with new oversized portraits of Queen Victoria hanging on the walls. When we were dating, we'd enjoyed many great curries there. Fond memories. Sadly, Indian food was no longer the focus of the updated high-end restaurant. I guess they weren't targeting people like us anymore. Victoria was fast becoming a hub for tech companies, and many of the downtown restaurants were adapting their offerings to the younger, higher-spending crowd. We weren't hip enough. Nonetheless, we were both impressed by the place, though the new prices meant it was unlikely we'd be back in a hurry. I'm old enough to remember when twenty dollars was enough to last the night. Somehow, spending that much on a single gin cocktail seemed a little extravagant to me.

We were tired of talking about Ali, what she'd done, and what she might do in future. It was emotionally exhausting and depressing. Marie and I adopted a new rule that night: we agreed we wouldn't mention her name on Dine-out Wednesdays. She was off-limits.

Not talking about her was one thing; not thinking about her was another challenge altogether. Earlier that week, OBPD had informed me that the man who assaulted me was called Brett Mahoney, a local slimeball with a long list of violent convictions. Apparently, when confronted with the evidence, he'd confessed to assaulting me and was already in prison awaiting sentencing. Thankfully, because of his prior history, the judge denied him bail—a massive relief for all of us. As our statements made up the key evidence against him, the thought of Mahoney turning up at our home seeking retribution was terrifying. It was a relief, too, to learn that I wouldn't have to appear in court to testify against the man, though I would still have to if and when Ali was hauled up in front of the bench. Sadly, that was rapidly becoming a diminishing prospect.

Despite our earlier faith in the law, I was fast losing hope Ali would be made to answer for her actions. Even though Inspector Butler had virtually promised to bring a conspiracy charge against Ali for her part in orchestrating my assault, recently OBPD had been noticeably silent on the subject. I didn't get it. It was obvious to everyone she was behind Mahoney's savagery. She'd been pulling his strings. Hell, the man even admitted it to me the night I became his punchbag.

Although she never said as much, I suspected Marie was feeling the same gnawing uncertainty as to how everything was going to end. If Ali got away with this, there was no telling what she might do to us. Enjoying a full night's sleep had become impossible for both of us. Whenever I woke in the middle of the night, I'd check if Marie was awake. Nine times out of ten, she was and, like me, turns out she'd been lying there thinking about our tormentor, dreading what she might do next. My draining sense of inadequacy was wearing me down. I should have been able to protect my family, but there was nothing I could do.

After dinner, although it was early September, it was still warm enough for us to enjoy a stroll around the inner harbor. The moored yellow whale-watching boats bobbed in the water alongside expensive yachts, many of which were registered in exotic-sounding tax havens. Every now and then, we'd stop and stare at the lights of the Parliament buildings reflecting off the sea. They always reminded me of Christmas illuminations. As we turned north, we admired the blue lights of the recently replaced Johnson Street Bridge, separating downtown from the residential towers dotted along the Songhees walkway to the west.

We loved living in this part of the world. Neither of us could imagine anywhere else we'd rather be. Standing arm-in-arm, we gazed at the seaplanes at the floating terminal, quiet now, but tomorrow they'd be buzzing in and out of the harbor several times an hour, almost touching the surrounding buildings as they came in to land on the water.

When I spotted Ali's condo in the background, my stomach muscles tensed. In the space of a few weeks, she had ruined our lives. *No more.* Right then, I vowed to myself I'd do whatever it took to prevent her from destroying our future. It had taken Marie and I twenty years to build what we had. It wasn't a glamorous life—many would call it mundane—but it was precious to us. I was not going to allow that woman to steal it away from us.

The following day, I had a busy schedule packed full of listing appointments. Unusually, all of them were with out-of-province or foreign owners—mainly people from Calgary, who'd bought a place in Owen Bay to escape the worst of Alberta's winters, or Americans from places like Arizona and New Mexico, who spent the milder summers on the island to avoid the stifling heat back home. The BC government had recently introduced a "speculation" tax, levying an additional two percent annual charge on the assessed value of second homes. I thought it was a crazy idea; for most of these folks, for many months every year, this was their home. They were anything but speculators. How many people can afford that kind of additional annual tax bill? I suspected my listing appointments that day had been booked by those owners thinking of selling to avoid the heavy cost. While in the short term a flurry of selling instructions would be good business for my firm, I feared the new tax might trigger a tsunami of sales and crater the entire market. Politicians and the law of unintended consequences.

Marie was working from home that day, preparing for the start of her school's new semester the following week. When I mentioned I had a full day ahead of me, she said she was glad to have me out of the way; she could get her work done without interruption. Normally, if I knew she was working from home, I'd pop back for lunch when things were quiet. But I got the message: don't even think about it today.

"I should be back around eight this evening," I said, kissing her goodbye. "Make sure you miss me."

"What would you like for dinner?" she asked.

"Since we're both busy, why don't I pick up a Thai take-out on the way home?"

"That would be nice. Don't forget, Freya doesn't like it as hot as you."

Marie went straight upstairs to the study and turned on her laptop. While she was waiting for it to boot up, she heard something come through the letterbox. It was too early for the regular mail delivery, so she carried on working, assuming it was junk or one of the free local newspapers.

Mid-morning, she went downstairs to make a drink. Passing the front door, she spotted an envelope lying on the hallway floor. She picked it up and inspected it. The label on the outside was addressed to her and it had the full mailing address, but no stamp. It had to have been hand-delivered.

Sitting on the bottom two stairs, she opened it. Inside was a two-page printed letter:

Dear Marie,

I have been wanting to contact you for some considerable time, but guilt and the fear of upsetting you have held me back. Please believe me when I tell you how difficult this is for me, but as hard as it is, you need to know. It's important you understand the kind of man Tom really is.

Marie's fingers trembled as she quickly turned to the end of the second page to see who had sent it. As she suspected, the letter was from Ali. Part of her wanted to tear it up without reading any further. Nothing that woman said could be trusted. She was a manipulative and dangerous bitch.

But she read on.

First, let me say I am not proud of my behavior. I must take much of the blame for how things started. When Tom was helping me look for my condo, you will remember how long it took to find one I liked. The truth is there were many I could have bought, but he and I wanted to drag the process out for as long as we could. You see, searching for a property gave us the cover we needed, allowing us to spend whole days together without raising your suspicion.

I am sorry, but you need to know, for most of that time, Tom and I were sleeping together. Often, we'd use properties he was selling when the owners were away. Sometimes, we stayed at hotels downtown. I don't know if it has any significance, but Tom's favorite was always The Empress. We became quite the regulars there. After I bought my condo, we would meet at my place. Tom told me he could always get away on Saturdays and Sundays if he used his open houses as an excuse. During the week, when he didn't have to take Freya with him, he would make out he had something on at the air cadets in the evenings, so we could meet. He said you never suspected anything. He used to laugh about that and how gullible you were.

I am telling you these details, not to be cruel, but to illustrate the true character of the man you call your husband and to show you how calculating he has been. Lying comes naturally to him. Only when you know this, will you believe what I am about to share with you.

About a month ago, I realized our relationship had to end. Of course, I always knew he was a married man. But, as time went on, I found it more and more difficult knowing we were both deceiving you. You have always been kind to me and my family. You didn't deserve to be treated like this. Strange thing was, it didn't appear to affect Tom in the same way. Not once did he seem concerned about your feelings.

It is important to me that you understand it was my decision to end the affair, not his. In fact, Tom would not accept it when I told him it was over. He wanted us to continue. He kept calling me at work and coming to my condo, begging me to reconsider. He promised he would leave you and Freya, if that's what it would take. I wasn't interested. To be honest, while I liked the attention at first, in my heart I always knew it was nothing serious. The moment had passed, and I wanted to move on before anyone got hurt. The more I spelled things out to him, the more persistent he became. He just wouldn't listen to reason. He talked of marriage and how we would have beautiful kids together. His mental state began to worry me.

Then he became violent. One night, he turned up at my door at home. He said you and Freya were away and that we could spend the whole night together. When I tried to close the door on him, he kicked at it and forced his way in. I tried to call the police, but he ripped the phone cable out of the wall. He kept begging me to take him back. It was like he was having some *sort of breakdown. When I told him that I never wanted to see him again, he grabbed me and forced me to the ground. I kept screaming at him to stop, but he wouldn't.*

Your husband raped me.

The man you live with is a monster.

That night has been a nightmare replaying over and over in my mind. It won't go away. I didn't go to the police. I was too frightened. Knowing what he is really like, I thought he would kill me if I reported him. I guess part of me also thought it was karma. I'd betrayed you, so his violence against me was my punishment. Somehow, I thought I deserved it.

Living with the dread of what he might do next was suffocating. I had to tell someone. In the end, I shared my fears with the man who was teaching me self-defense. I wanted to know how to protect myself from Tom if he tried to hurt me again. My instructor is called Brett Mahoney. You will know him as the person who came into your home and attacked Tom.

Hurting Tom, physically, went against everything I believe in. I was horrified when I found out. Mahoney promised me he would only speak to Tom and try to reason with him, so he wouldn't come near me again. Please understand I didn't know Mahoney was a violent criminal when I confided in him. As soon as I found out what he had done, I told the police everything about him. I wanted him caught. I believe he has now confessed to assaulting Tom. I am so sorry he intruded into your home.

If you have read this far, I hope you will understand how guilty I am feeling and how desperate I must be reaching out to you, the woman I betrayed. But I need your help. If you choose to ignore my plea, that is something I must accept. You owe me nothing. I respect that.

While Tom hasn't threatened me with violence again, he continues to harass me. He calls me at work every day and when my home phone rings late at night, I know it's him. Earlier this week, he called my office direct line. He told me if I didn't give him another chance, he would ruin my life. You see, he has pho-

tos of me, taken on his phone when we were having sex in my condo weeks ago. He's threatening to send them to my firm and to upload the images onto my social media pages. He told me he even had some printed out and will mail them to my parents if I don't do what he wants. The thought makes me sick. Who does this to another human being?

I don't know what else to do other than ask for your help, please. I am begging you to delete the photos from his phone. If you can find them, I am pleading with you to destroy the hard copies, so that he cannot use them. My parents would be devastated. Please do it for them if not for me.

I never wanted any of this. I feel stupid and ashamed.

I hope one day you will find it in your heart to forgive me.

Yours

Ali Page

Chapter 29

Lucy stood at the bottom of the stairs and leaned her head on Marie's knee. Marie stroked the dog's head and stared into space. Everything now began to make sense: the extraordinary amount of time it had taken Tom to find Ali's condo; Tom's recently increased workload with open houses eating up most weekends; his reticence to share many of the details of the apparent harassment he was suffering; and the reluctance of OBPD to take any action. What did the police know about her husband that Marie didn't? Though it turned her stomach, the letter rang true. Even allowing for Ali's spin on things, it provided an explanation for Tom's bizarre behavior these past few months.

He had cheated before. Why not again with a much younger and attractive woman? But rape? Could that be true? Tom had never been a violent person. He wasn't aggressive. He didn't even have much of a temper. Tom was a conciliator, the first to back down, always seeking ways to avoid confrontation. Surely, the man Marie knew—Freya's loving, caring father—wasn't capable of such a heinous act?

But something must have happened to make Ali feel so frightened she had to confide in a total stranger like Mahoney. And for him to have attacked Tom so viciously, Mahoney must have been convinced Ali was genuinely terrified. What Tom told the two officers from OBPD, that Ali had sent Mahoney for no reason, never did make sense. But Mahoney beating Tom to guarantee he would never touch Ali again was, at least, a rational explanation.

The thought that she might not know the man she'd lived with for the past twenty years sent a shiver through Marie. Were she and Freya safe? Could they stay in the house with him around?

She stopped stroking Lucy and read Ali's letter again. Images of Tom with Ali flooded her mind; they'd been laughing at her. The betrayal hurt almost as much as the fear she may be living with a rapist. After reading it three more times, the thought entered her head. There was one way she could prove beyond all doubt whether Ali was telling the truth: if the photos were still on Tom's phone, then Marie would know. To find that out, she would have to wait for him to come home. For now, at least, she could try to find the hard copies, if they really existed.

Where would he hide something like that? Unlikely to be at home where she or Freya might stumble across them. The obvious place was Tom's office. Marie folded the letter, placed it into her purse, and grabbed her car keys. Minutes later, she drove around the back of Tom's brokerage and parked. His car wasn't there.

"Tom's out all day," Brenda said when Marie came through the door.

I bet he is, Marie thought. *Probably screwing some other slut.* "That's okay, Brenda. I don't need him. I just need to find a document I'm hoping he's filed in his office."

"Would you like me to help?"

"No. It shouldn't take me long."

Marie walked into Tom's office and closed the door. Inside were two large filing cabinets crammed with real estate contracts, property descriptions, and brochures. She took them out and waded through every piece of paper, in case he'd hidden the photos in among them. Nothing.

The three desk drawers were locked. She opened the door

and asked Brenda if she had a key. Tom trusted his assistant with everything. If Brenda didn't have access to Tom's desk, then that's where the photos would be. If she had to, Marie decided she would break into the damn thing.

"Here it is," Brenda said, handing over the key. "I don't know why he locks it. There's never anything in there."

Marie took the key, shut the door again, and sat at the desk. On the corner stood a large, framed photo of her, Tom and Freya, taken on their vacation to BC's Okanagan wine region two years earlier. Tom's beaming smile—the honest, loving family man—made her want to gag. She turned the frame away, so she didn't have to look at him.

Inside the drawers were a few stationery supplies, a phone charger, and an open bag of peanut M&Ms, Tom's favorite candy. No sign of the photos. Was it possible they didn't exist? Was Ali playing mind games?

"Did you find what you were looking for?" Brenda asked when Marie handed back the key.

"No. I think it must be at home."

"I can give Tom a call, if you want. He won't mind."

"Don't worry. I already did that. He thought it might be in his office."

When she arrived home, Marie started searching in their bedroom and then moved on to the walk-in closet where she rifled through all Tom's clothes. Again, nothing. An hour and a half later, she had been through all the cabinets and drawers in the study, looked in every kitchen cupboard, and even checked the boxes in the crawlspace, but to no avail.

Maybe there really were no photos. If she couldn't find them, and if there was nothing on his phone, what would that prove? That he'd destroyed them? That they'd never existed? That Ali was making it all up? All she wanted was the truth.

A little before two o'clock, Freya came home from visiting one of her friends, so Marie suspended the search long enough to have a sandwich with her. Over their late lunch, she suggested to Freya she might want to visit Tom's mom given she'd be back at school the following week and wouldn't have as much time to see her. If Marie was going to confront Tom and demand to see his phone that evening, she didn't want their daughter around to witness what could turn into a nasty scene. Luckily, Freya didn't take much persuading; she enjoyed stopping over at her grandmother's. Tom's mom always treated her to dinner at the Beacon Inn on the Sidney waterfront, Freya's favorite place to eat.

By the time she'd taken Freya to Sidney, chatted with Tom's mom over cake and tea, and driven back to Owen Bay, it was almost five o'clock when Marie pulled into the driveway. All afternoon, she'd been racking her brain, trying to work out where Tom would hide the photos. The moment she opened the car door, the thought struck her. The garage. That was Tom's domain; he never liked anyone touching things in his man-cave. Other than parking her car inside when it was raining, Marie spent little time in that part of their property. If Tom was going to hide something at home, the garage would be the obvious place. Why hadn't she thought of that earlier?

Marie raised the garage door and left it open, so she had good light to see what was inside. Immediately, her eyes were drawn to the two gray metal storage cabinets along the back wall. One of them was locked. Strange. Why would one be open and the other locked? She looked around for something to prise it open. On top of the bench above the cabinets, was a long, flat-head screwdriver. The perfect implement to force the lock.

Marie's heart raced when the cabinet door sprang open at the first attempt. She hesitated before looking inside. It was full of chemical containers and boxes: lawn feed, weed killer, plant fertilizer, lawnmower oil. She took everything out. No sign of the photos. The other cabinet looked unpromising. Inside was a bunch of things Tom used in his business, mainly open-house signage and old for-sale signs with his former logo, the one they'd designed together when he started the brokerage. When she pulled them all out, something fell forward from the back.

A sealed, brown envelope.

Marie stopped breathing. Why would Tom keep something like this in their damp garage? She stood and stared at it in her hands. While the for-sale signs that had hidden it were covered in dust and cobwebs, the envelope was different. It was clean, as if it hadn't been there long. Maybe she was imagining things, but from its weight she thought there could be photos inside. Her gut twisted.

She left everything else on the garage floor, ran into the house, and ripped open the envelope on the kitchen counter. A handful of images spilled out, face down.

A block of ice formed in the pit of Marie's stomach when she turned them over. She choked back the reflux. These weren't innocent keepsakes. No, the photos were explicit, hard-core, color shots of Ali. And they left nothing to the imagination.

Marie closed her eyes. *Everything that woman said is true.*

Chapter 30

I was right; all the out-of-province owners with whom I met that day had been spooked by BC's new speculation tax. I picked up three new sale instructions—a one-day record for my small firm—and I was confident there'd be more in the weeks to come. A silver lining for me, but I was still worried about the tax's long-term impact on the market. It didn't seem right so many long-term owners and occupiers of property were being labeled as speculators and forced to sell because of punitive tax rates simply because they had a main home elsewhere.

By the time I left the Royal Orchid Thai restaurant with our take-out dinner, it was a quarter to eight. No wonder I was starving; I hadn't eaten since breakfast. I called home to let Marie know I was on my way and to ask her to warm the plates up, but there was no answer. Ten minutes later, I pulled up behind Marie's car and noticed the garage door was wide open. Marie had to be home, because her car was there, but the lights in the rooms on the front of the house were off. Call me paranoid, but considering the weird couple of months we'd had, my first thought was something bad had happened. Since Mahoney's visit, it didn't take much to make me jumpy.

Quickly, I grabbed the take-out and ran to the front door. Inside the place was dark and eerily quiet. With a teenage daughter, silence was a rare commodity at our house.

"Marie," I shouted, turning on some lights. "Are you here?"

No answer.

A crack of light escaped under the closed door when I walked toward the kitchen. Panic barreled through me. I knew Mahoney was behind bars, but had Ali sent someone else to attack my family? Opening the door, I braced myself for the worst.

"Sit down. I need to talk to you," Marie said in a monotone voice. She was sitting at the kitchen table facing me. Her eyes looked glassy and bloodshot.

"Thank God you're okay," I said, my heart still redlining. "Did something happen? The garage door is open. I thought—"

"Sit down, Tom." Marie sounded weird, almost robotic.

My mind turned to our daughter. "Where's Freya?"

"She's staying over at your mom's."

"Ugh? I got her favorite sweet and spicy red snapper." I placed the take-out bag on the table, and that's when I first noticed the brown envelope in front of Marie.

"I'm not hungry."

I sat at the table and pushed the food bag to one side. "Something's happened. What is it?"

Marie looked like she wanted to spit. "Let me see your phone."

"My phone? What for?"

Marie's open right hand thrust toward me. "Just give me the damn phone."

I reached into my coat pocket and handed it to her. "Here. What's going on?"

"What's the passcode?"

I told her the four-digit number and watched as Marie punched it in. She opened the photos app and began thumbing through the images.

"You know, if you tell me what you're looking for, I might be able to help."

Marie ignored me and kept scrolling. After a couple of minutes, she slid the phone across the table to me. "When did you delete them?"

"Delete what?"

"Come on, Tom, you know exactly what I'm talking about."

"Listen, I've had a really hard day. I'm tired and hungry. Can we please stop playing games? Just tell me what you're looking for."

Marie clapped her hands slowly. "You're good. All this time, you've been making out you're the victim. You even managed to make me feel sorry for you. I bet it gave you a real kick to—"

"Marie, Marie. I have no idea what you are talking about. Please, tell me what happened. Has Ali been here? Has she done something? I can see you're upset. Please tell me what it is, darling."

"Don't you darling me. Don't you dare..." Marie's voice was raised, her face bright red. "All this time playing happy families with me and Freya, you were fucking that woman—our friends' daughter. What kind of man are you?"

I had no idea where any of this was coming from. In all our years of marriage, I had never seen Marie like this. Such deep-seated anger directed at me. I thought we'd been over all this. I thought we were getting back on track. Obviously, something had happened since that morning and whatever it was, it had caused a one-hundred-and-eighty-degree shift in our relationship. Marie's mind had been turned against me. What could I say to persuade her she had it all wrong?

"I swear on Freya's life, I haven't slept with Ali. I haven't been anywhere near her. You have to believe that. The woman has a warped mind. You know it's all in her head." I could tell my words were bouncing off Marie, like I was speaking a foreign language. "Has she been here today? Is that what this is about? Has she said I touched her? You know you cannot rely on anything that comes out of her mouth. I don't know how many times I need to say that."

Marie shook her head. "Still you deny it. You sit there and lie to my face." I reached across the table to squeeze her hand. Marie pulled it away. "Don't you touch me," she said, her tone laden with acid. "Don't you ever touch me again. You make my skin crawl."

"Please, what is this about, Marie? Has she been feeding you a bunch of crap about me? Just tell me. What has she said?"

"You can drop the pathetic little act. I know everything. Every single lie that came out of your mouth. How for weeks the two of you pretended to be looking at condos. You're good; deceiving me seemed easy for you. You certainly had me convinced she couldn't find anything she liked. Meanwhile, you were screwing her all day. In your clients' homes and hotels downtown." Marie chuckled. "Last night, when we were at The Empress, I bet you had a good laugh at my expense. While we were having dinner, all the while you were replaying the times the two of you shared a room there. How sick is that?"

I kept shaking my head no. "Is that what she told you?"

"Oh, there's much more than that, Tom. You worthless piece of shit."

"None of it is true. Not a word. What do I need to do to convince you?"

"Tell me you didn't go to her condo on the weekends when you said you were holding open houses, I dare you."

"I didn't. I've never been to her condo, other than the one time when we first viewed it."

"See how easy it is for you to lie. You're incredible."

"It's the truth."

"I know you've been there."

"Listen, if she's said these things to you, it's because she's trying to drive a wedge between us. Don't you see? First, she sent Mahoney to attack me, and now she's trying to destroy our marriage. Don't let her do this to us. It's exactly what she wants."

"You deserved everything Mahoney did to you. I wish I'd never stopped him. I should have let him do what you did to her."

"What exactly is that supposed to mean?"

"I know what you put her through. She told me everything. How she tried to end your sordid affair and how you wouldn't accept it."

"None of this makes sense, Marie. She's been lying to you. This is exactly what she wants."

"Are you telling me she didn't try to end your relationship?"

"There never was a relationship. That's what I'm trying—"

"Save it, Tom. I know how you begged her not to leave you. You're pathetic." Marie looked like she was about to vomit. "And when you couldn't get what you wanted, you broke into her home and raped her."

The word was like a jolt of electricity. "Rape? This is madness."

"No wonder she wanted Mahoney to kill you. I don't know who you are. Did I ever know the real Tom Harper?"

I held my head in my hands. "Please, Marie. You must believe me. Not a single word of this is true. She's playing with us. Don't you see? The woman is sick, perverted."

"Then what the hell are these?"

When I looked up, my heart jammed my throat. Marie had opened the envelope in front of her. Spread out on the table were photos of Ali. Naked, repulsive images. "What are they?" I asked, my words struggling to get out.

Marie stood. Her expression was a mix of disgust and loathing. "I found them hidden in *your* garage."

"You don't think…" I couldn't process my thoughts. "I've never seen them before."

"I want you out of this house. I don't want our daughter anywhere near you."

Chapter 31

Now that the new school semester had started, Vancouver Island's tourist season was drawing to a close. As usual, there had been far fewer visitors around since Labor Day, and the roads were suddenly much quieter. Fortunately for me, that meant I only had to spend three days in a local hotel before I was able to find a vacation rental property in Owen Bay. I hated hotels at the best of times. Too many people about and there's always someone in a room nearby with the TV turned up loud when I'm trying to sleep. The rental was available for the next month, if I needed it. More than enough time, I prayed, to straighten things out at home.

For now, at least, I'd have some cooking facilities of my own—there was only so much take-out pizza even I could eat—and, most important, a spare bedroom for Freya to sleep in when she came to visit. Though I wasn't sure when that would be. Since Marie had put me out, I'd tried to call home several times a day, but on the rare occasions she answered, Marie wouldn't let me speak with our daughter. She said I wasn't fit to be her father. On those few instances when Marie didn't slam the phone down on me right away, I begged her to let me come over to the house and talk things through, explain how I'd done nothing wrong and didn't deserve her contempt. She wouldn't entertain the idea. With Marie the way she was, my biggest fear was losing my relationship with Freya. I kept telling Marie she was going to alienate our daughter from me and how that wasn't fair to either of us. She wouldn't listen. Sure, I could have turned up on the doorstep and demanded to see Freya, but there would have been an embarrassing scene. Not something I wanted Freya to witness. I wasn't sure what to do for the best.

How do you prove something you haven't done? We were being played. This was exactly what Ali wanted to happen. Why couldn't Marie see that? As hard as it was, I decided to give it some time, hoping Marie would eventually realize I couldn't have done the things Ali told her. When her rage had subsided, I was confident my wife would remember the kind of man I am. For now, she needed some distance from me, space to think things through on her own. We would get through this.

The temptation to go see Ali and to shake some sense into her was overwhelming. I had to fight back the urge every waking hour. But I knew that would make matters even worse.

That said, I couldn't just sit there feeling sorry for myself. That would have driven me crazy. I had to do something to wrestle back an element of control over my life. So, the day after moving my stuff into the rental unit, I called my lawyer. Apart from emails, attaching her regular legal fee invoices, I'd heard very little from Collins. For someone so expensive, she seemed remarkably uncommunicative. I was beginning to question what I was getting for my money. Maybe I was projecting my anger onto the wrong person, but I decided if I didn't get much satisfaction from Collins, I was going to terminate her engagement and look elsewhere. Find someone more proactive.

"I've been meaning to call you," Collins said when I finally reached her on my third attempt that day. I didn't believe her for one moment. That was another thing that wound me up. She never returned calls when I left a message.

"There have been some developments," I said. "But first, what news on the peace bond application?"

"That's what I wanted to speak to you about. Seems the police have considered everything I sent them and they're refusing to apply."

"Ugh? Why not?"

"Don't worry about it. Sometimes happens."

"I am worried." It was easy for her to be relaxed, sitting in her plush Vancouver office building billing me at several hundred an hour. This was my life we were talking about. "Did they say why they won't do it?"

"Some garbage you don't want to hear."

"Try me."

"Seems someone's fed them a completely different story. For some reason, they now suspect you've been the one harassing Page."

"Are they for real? Nothing could be further from the truth. I hope you put them right?"

"Of course, but they weren't interested."

"She was the one who sent Mahoney to my house, not the other way around. What more do they need?"

"Apparently, she's saying she only confided in Mahoney. Told him you'd been harassing her for ages and that she felt threatened by you. She told the police she had no idea he would get violent. They believe he acted on his own, in some misguided attempt to protect her from you. Off the record, they told me he'd done this kind of thing before. Served some time for it."

"And she just happened to chance across a man like that? That's convenient."

"Mahoney has his own business, offering classes on self-defense. I'm told that's how she met him. The police are asking why she felt the need to learn how to defend herself. Looks like they're joining up the dots and drawing their own, wrong, conclusions."

"She's not the one who needs protection. That man almost killed me. And she sent him."

"Listen, not all is lost."

"It certainly feels like it to me."

"I can apply to the court directly on your behalf. It would

have been better had the police made the application, but we can still do it."

"Okay, let's do it. I can't believe we're having to do the police's job for them."

Collins paused. "Word of warning, though. Now Page is claiming she's the one being harassed, the police might apply for a court order against you."

"Are you serious?" A cloud of despair settled over me. Could things get any worse? I exhaled loudly through my teeth. "Look, it's best you hear this from me." I found it hard to get the words out. "She's also claiming I raped her."

"Whoa...that's a whole different..." Collins remained silent for a few seconds. I must have caught her off-guard. "Has she said that to the police?"

"I don't know. I heard it second-hand. She told Marie."

"It would certainly help explain their sudden change in attitude. When is this supposed to have happened?"

"I'm not entirely sure. Some weeks ago, I think."

"She couldn't have reported it; you would have heard from them by now."

"There was nothing to report. None of it is true."

There was another pause. Did Collins think I'd done it? "This is a game-changer," she said, a sudden urgency in her voice. "I need to speak with Marie to find out exactly what was said. Even if she hasn't reported it, if Page is going around making accusations like this, no wonder the police have become unsympathetic toward us. We need to be very careful."

I gave Collins Marie's cell number. "Listen, there's something else you need to know."

I heard a loud sigh down the phone. "Go on," Collins said.

"Marie and I have separated."

"When did that happen?"

"A few days ago. After she found..." I was going to tell Collins about the photos, but something stopped me. I could sense she was already having doubts about me. With precious few allies right now, I needed her on my side more than ever. "After Ali claimed I raped her, Marie put me out. I'm hoping it's not for long."

"You realize this won't look good to a court? Does Marie believe her?"

"Right now, it seems that way. She's still in shock. I'm sure she'll feel differently in a day or so. At least, I hope she will. I don't know what I'd do if I lost her. I can't let that happen."

"You need to stay strong, Tom. I'm going to apply to the court immediately, but it'll be some time before we hear back with a decision. In the meantime, I want you to stay away from Page. I can't stress that enough."

"Please do whatever you can. I don't know how much more of this I can take."

Far from regaining control over my life, things were spiraling down fast. It was as if a vise was crushing my chest, a little more each hour. Not only had the police abandoned me, but it was clear they were also taking Ali's side. Although Collins hadn't said anything specific during our conversation, I sensed from her tone an element of panic. For such an experienced lawyer to be spooked, it had to mean I was in a ton of trouble.

The vise tightened some more with my next thought. What would Marie say to Collins? With my wife's current frame of mind, there was a risk she might alarm my lawyer even more, especially if she mentioned the photos.

Chapter 32

Costco opened at nine on Saturdays. To avoid the weekend crowd, Marie and Freya arrived as the doors were being unlocked. Marie had her regular list and her plan was to zoom around, pay, and get out of there within half an hour. But that was never going to happen. Freya liked to wander up and down all the aisles, checking out the deals, particularly on training gear and running shoes. If she found anything interesting, she'd always find a way to persuade her mom to buy it. Today, whenever Freya sniffed out a bargain, Marie just told her to place it in the cart; she was in no mood to put up even a cursory fight. Her mind was elsewhere. This was the first time they'd done the Costco run without Tom, and it felt weird walking past his favorite items: cinnamon bread, Balderson's mature cheese, and multi-packs of batteries. Tom liked his batteries.

The lines at the checkouts were already growing when they finished. Minutes later, Marie presented her membership card, paid, and then rushed toward the exit. Freya held back. Even though it was mid-morning, there was one more area she needed to visit.

"You know Dad always stops for a hot dog," she said when Marie turned to see what was delaying her daughter.

Marie caved. She stood at the counter and watched Freya devour her second breakfast.

When they left the building ten minutes later, Ali's mother, Sonya, was approaching from the parking lot. Marie pretended not to see her by looking in her purse to find her car keys. The last thing she needed was to get drawn into a conversation. She hadn't seen Sonya since that night Ali fawned all over Tom at the dinner table.

"Look, there's Simon's mom," Freya said, waving at Sonya.

"Hi Freya," Sonya said, wheeling an empty cart toward them. "I didn't see you."

Marie looked up. *Shit.* "Hi Sonya. You just arriving? Better hurry; it's getting really busy in there."

Sonya stopped. "You guys must have arrived early," she said, pointing at their shopping.

"Mom wanted to come early," Freya said. "She can't stand it when its crowded." She picked up the till receipt from the top of one the bags. "Can you believe we spent over three hundred dollars?" She rolled her eyes. "And Mom thought with Dad no longer at home, we'd save some money. Wrong."

Sonya threw Marie a quizzical glance.

"Yes...Tom's not..." Struggling over how much to say, Marie could feel the warmth in her cheeks. She hadn't told anyone about their separation. It was nobody else's business.

"Dad moved out a couple of weeks ago," Freya said in a matter-of-fact voice. "He's renting a place in Owen Bay, but I haven't seen it yet."

"I hadn't realized," Sonya said. "I'm sorry to hear—"

Marie tapped Freya on the shoulder and handed the car keys to her. "Would you do Mom a favor? Can you take the shopping and start loading it in the car for me?"

Freya took the hint; it wasn't a request. She grabbed the cart and walked toward the parking lot. "Bye, Mrs. Page. Say hello to Simon for me."

"I had no idea," Sonya said once Freya was out of earshot. "You and Tom have the strongest relationship of all the couples we know. I'm stunned. Is there anything we can do to help?"

"It's too late for that," Marie said. Her words sounded like an accusation.

Sonya looked confused. "You know we'd do anything to see you and Tom back together again. Have you got time to talk about it? We could grab a coffee, if you like."

"I can't do this now. Not with Freya here. There are things you need to know that I don't want my daughter to hear."

Sonya's confused expression turned to worry. "Things I need to know? What sort of things?"

Resentment welled up inside Marie. Why hold it in? Sonya needed to learn who her daughter really was. She'd find out sooner or later. "Maybe you should ask Ali."

"Ali? What does she have to do with anything?"

"I've said more than I should." Marie started to walk away. If she stayed, she knew she would say something she'd regret. Her issue was with Ali, not her parents. They'd always been decent enough.

"I want to hear it," Sonya said, catching up with her. "Why would Ali know anything about you and Tom?"

Marie stopped and turned to face her friend. "Because your precious daughter isn't as sweet and innocent as she makes out to be."

Sonya recoiled. "What are you saying?"

Marie checked to see that Freya was far enough away not to hear. "Ali has been having an affair with Tom. It's been going on for weeks."

Sonya stepped back, her mouth half-open. "Ali...and Tom? That's ridiculous. Tom's almost twice her age."

"Don't take my word for it. Go ask her."

Marie stormed away, leaving Sonya in the middle of the road, staring into space.

They didn't call ahead. That was deliberate so as not to give Ali any warning they were coming. Her parents just turned up at the condo that evening. Sonya wanted to look their daughter in the eyes and demand an explanation, without allowing her time to plan her answers. Bob went along with it, convinced that his wife or Marie, probably both, had it all wrong. When she could attract any man she wanted, why would his princess have an affair with Tom? The idea was crazy, and he'd told Marie as much, many times over.

Loud music boomed from inside the condo when they approached Ali's front door. After a few knocks with no response, a neighbor from across the hallway came out. He was a man in his seventies.

"It's no good," he said, continually shaking his head. "It's like this every weekend. I've tried banging on her door, but she never answers. Is she disturbing you, too?"

Sonya frowned at the man. "This is our daughter's place."

"Well, maybe you can talk some sense into her," the neighbor said. "It's not right. The music goes on well past midnight, even during the week. I've already reported her to the residents' council." He waved his hand down through the air at them then returned to his unit and closed the door.

Sonya looked at Tom. "What's going on? Is she having a party in there?"

Bob shrugged then knocked louder and tried the bell. "At least we know she's in."

They tried two more times before Sonya grabbed the phone from her purse. "I'm going to call her. This is ridiculous."

On Sonya's third attempt, the music died down and then Ali answered the call. "Hi, Mom. Sorry, I didn't hear my phone."

"I'm not surprised given the racket going on in there."

"What do you mean?"

"I could hear it from here."

"Yeah, right."

"I'm serious, Alison. Your father and I are standing outside your door right now."

There was a pause. "You're here?" The music stopped completely. "I didn't know you were coming. What are you doing here?"

"Well, if you open the door, maybe we could tell you."

When the door opened, they stormed in. No smiles, no hellos. Immediately, Bob recognized the smell of marijuana. His daughter's shiny eyes and spaced-out expression confirmed it. What was she doing alone on a Saturday night, taking recreational drugs?

"What's going on?" he asked, his eyes dancing around the room. After almost thirty years with the RCMP, it was second nature for him to search for drug paraphernalia.

"Nothing's going on," Ali said, avoiding eye contact.

"I can smell it, Ali. Don't lie to me."

"Oh, that. It's nothing. You guys do know it's legal here now?"

"Don't get smart. I don't care that it's legal. How many times have I told you what that stuff can lead to?"

"Relax, Dad. It's safer than alcohol."

Sonya took a seat on the couch. "We just met your neighbor," she said. "He wasn't very happy about the noise coming from here. I can hardly blame him."

"That old fart. He's always complaining."

"You seem to think it's amusing. Your father and I could hear it outside. What's got into you, Alison?"

Ali sat in an armchair, while Bob joined Sonya on the couch. "I'm sorry, Mom. I'm under a lot of stress at work right now. I like to let loose on the weekends."

"And you think taking drugs is the answer?" Bob asked. "When did that start?"

"It's not what you think it is, Dad. It's not like it's a regular habit or anything. It's just to take the edge off."

"It has to stop, Ali. Do you hear me?"

Ali adopted her reprimanded little girl face. "I won't do it again."

Bob melted. Maybe his daughter was under too much pressure at work. Certainly, this was out of character; the Ali he knew would never resort to chemicals as a way of coping. "If they're pushing you too hard at work, you need to say something."

"I will. I promise. What are you doing here anyway?"

Bob leaned back into the couch, partly hiding behind his wife. "I'm sure it's nothing," he said. "I'll let your mom explain."

Sonya remained sitting forward on the edge of the cushion. "I bumped into Marie at Costco this morning. What she told me was shocking."

In less than a second, Ali's face morphed from happily intoxicated to cold-stone sober.

"She said," Sonya continued, "she and Tom had split up." She paused and observed their daughter.

Ali's face was impassive. "I'm sorry to hear that."

"Is that all you have to say?"

"What do you want me to say? They're your friends. I don't really know them like you do. I know they've been married a long time."

Bob rested his hand on Sonya's shoulder. "See," he said, "I told you there was nothing in it. I told your mom it was a waste of time coming over here."

"That's not all Marie told me," Sonya said, her eyes locked onto Ali.

"What else did she say?"

"That you and Tom are having an affair."

Ali snorted. "Me and Tom? Are you serious?"

"There you have it," Bob said. "I told you it was all wrong. I'm sure Marie has misunderstood something."

"Do you deny it?" Sonya asked.

"Of course, I do." Ali made a face. "He's Dad's age."

"Hold on," Bob said. "I'm not that old."

When she turned to look at her husband, Sonya looked like she was chewing on a lemon. "This is not funny, Bob."

"What made her say something like that?" Ali asked.

Sonya looked at Ali. "We couldn't really talk. Freya was there, so she couldn't go into any details. But she was adamant you're having an affair with her husband."

Ali raised her palms. "For the record, there is no affair going on between me and Tom Harper. Okay?"

Sonya was sucking on the lemon again. "It's not something a woman makes up."

"What do I need to do to convince you? There's nothing going on. I find it kind of offensive, if I'm honest."

Sonya appeared unconvinced. "Seems Marie has made a mistake, then."

Bob leaned forward. "Okay, that's an end to this. Have you eaten, Ali? Why don't I go get us a take-out? Is that pizza place in Cook Street Village still open? It used to be your favorite before you moved to Vancouver."

Ali stood. "I am hungry. Why don't I come with you, Dad?"

Minutes later, Ali and her father were in his car. Sonya stayed behind to prepare the table.

"I get why you came with me," Bob said. "You wanted to avoid being on your own with Mom. Don't worry. She'll be alright. She just needed to vent. What Marie said this morning really upset her. I kept telling her you wouldn't do anything like that, but you know your mom; she had to hear it from you directly."

Ali kept focused on the road ahead while her father drove. "I can't blame Mom. Actually, I can't blame Marie for saying it, either."

"Ugh? Why would Marie say something like that?"

Ali sighed. "You remember Tom spent a lot of time with me in the early part of summer helping me find the condo?"

"Sure. He was doing his job. Doesn't explain why Marie would think you were having an affair with him."

"I wish that were true. That he was just doing his job."

Bob took his eyes off the road and glanced at his daughter. "Please don't tell me there's some truth in what Marie said."

"No. I'm not saying that, Dad. Not at all."

"So, what are you saying?"

Ali waited a while before answering. "I wasn't entirely truthful with you and Mom earlier."

Bob could feel his blood pressure rising. "About what?"

"I told you I was under a lot of pressure at work. Well, that isn't exactly true; work is fine. I love my new job. But I have been under a tremendous amount of stress these past few weeks. I've been wanting to talk to you about it, but I didn't know how to."

Bob reached over and squeezed his daughter's arm. "You know you can tell me anything, Princess."

"Tom is fixated on me. He won't leave me alone."

Bob stood on the brakes and swung the car into the curb. The vehicle behind them swerved and the driver flipped the finger as he sped past. When they stopped, Bob stared at Ali. "Has he hurt you?"

Ali ran her front teeth along her lower lip. "I'm scared, Dad. At first, he was really nice to me. He reminded me a lot of you. Caring, supportive, a gentleman. When we were searching for my place, he was always so patient. He seemed interested in me and what I had to say. I assumed it was because he didn't want me to make a mistake. It was a huge financial commitment. But once I found the condo, things changed. He wouldn't stop contacting me, calling me at all hours, saying he wanted to see me again. He kept telling me how much he enjoyed being with me and that he didn't want to give that up. It was creepy. I told him I didn't see him that way. At first, I tried to ignore him, but then he started turning up at my place at night."

Bob's hands were clenched around the steering wheel. "Did he touch you?"

"No. He frightens me. I'm always worried what he might do. Sometimes, I look out of my window at night, and he's standing outside on the street looking up at me. I even spoke to the police about it."

"You should have come to me."

"But he's your friend. How could I tell you someone we all trusted was stalking me? I know how much you hate drugs,

Dad, but that's been the only way I can get to sleep at night. I'm not proud of it. I was desperate."

"Listen to me. You have nothing to be ashamed of, Ali. Nothing."

"No wonder Marie thinks something is going on between us. I can't blame her. But I swear I've done nothing to encourage him. It's like he's obsessed with me or something."

Bob grabbed Ali's hands. "Listen, Princess. You've done the right thing telling me. I promise you he will never trouble you again."

Ali's eyes were teary. "Thanks, Dad."

"Would you like to come and stay at home for a while?"

"I should be okay. He hasn't done anything for a couple of weeks. Marie must have thrown him out. I'm hoping he's learned his lesson."

"You sure you don't want to stay?"

"I'll be fine. It feels so much better getting this off my chest. I've been carrying it around for weeks, not knowing whether I should tell you."

Bob started the engine. "Come on, let's go get some pizza, before your mom starts worrying where we've got to." He made a conscious effort to sound normal but, inside, he was ready to explode. Nobody gets away with treating his daughter that way. Tom Harper was going to pay for the hell he'd put Ali through. How dare he? *I'll show him what frightened feels like.*

"Will you tell Mom for me?"

"Of course. Don't you worry. I'll take care of everything. She'll understand."

Chapter 33

Collins called me at the office in the middle of the afternoon to say she'd finally gotten a hold of Marie. It had taken several days to make contact, and I knew right away from her tone it wasn't a good news phone call. She told me Marie had been aggressive and refused point blank to discuss anything to do with Ali. Before she slammed the phone down on Collins, my wife's exact words were: "Tom can go to hell for all I care."

I had hoped Marie would help if only for our daughter's sake. Her attitude toward me was deeply disappointing. Eighteen years of marriage seemingly counted for nothing. Suddenly, I was the enemy.

"You're certain you've told me everything?" Collins asked as our short telephone conversation ended. She sounded skeptical. I wondered whether Marie had told her about the photos.

"What's that supposed to mean?"

"Look, if Page seeks a court order keeping you away, the fact that Marie believes—"

"Not you as well. When is someone going to realize I'm the victim here? Not her."

"I'm your lawyer, Tom. I wouldn't be doing my job if I didn't make sure I had all the facts. How else am I supposed to protect you, otherwise? If you've done something you shouldn't have, you can tell me. It will remain confidential. But I can't defend you if I don't know exactly what went on between you and Page."

The police thought I was harassing Ali, clearly my wife had given up on me, writing me off as a rapist, and now my own lawyer was openly questioning my version of the truth. I'd had enough. "Well, you won't have to worry about it any longer," I said. "I'm terminating our relationship."

"You misunderstood me. All I'm trying to do—"

"Save your energy. Just send me your final bill, and then we'll be done." I smashed the phone down on my desk. *Damn you all.*

Afterward, when I'd calmed down, I wasn't proud I lost my temper with Collins. My real anger was toward Marie for not standing by me. I felt let down. Collins was simply collateral damage. No doubt, she would have continued to act for me, whether she believed my story or not. Professionals do that all the time. But that wasn't good enough; it was important to me that she trusted what I was saying. When precious few others did, I needed her to have faith in me.

Anyway, from what Collins had said, I was unlikely to get a court order of my own, so why did I need a lawyer? And if Ali sought an injunction preventing me from going near her, a lawyer would be redundant since I had no intention of going anywhere near that woman. Period.

With my mind distracted by Marie's attitude toward me, I could no longer concentrate on work, so I left the office early. Desperate to see Freya, if only for a few minutes, I toyed with the idea of meeting her from school. In the three weeks since I'd moved out, not once had I been allowed to see her, and I could count on the fingers of one hand the times I'd been able to talk with her on the phone. During those short conversations, I could tell she knew more than she was letting on. Throughout the calls, Freya seemed distant, almost distrusting. Given Marie's hostility, I was worried she was feeding Ali's poisonous lies to our daughter. The thought of losing my entire family ate me up inside. Soon, the only lawyer I would need was a good practitioner in family law. If it came to divorce, and I had to accept that was looking increasingly likely, I was not going to give up on our daughter without a fight.

I drove past the school without stopping and went straight back to my rental unit. Five minutes later, I heard a knock at the door. Other than Marie and Freya, no one had my temporary address. Naïvely, I hadn't planned on being there that long, so I couldn't see the point in giving it to anyone else. Not even Brenda had it, so I assumed it was someone trying to sell me something.

"Bob," I said, surprised to see Ali's father standing at the door. My brain went into overdrive. What was he doing there? How much did he know? Who gave him my address?

"Can I come in?" he asked. The impatient look on his face told me he was coming in no matter what I said.

"Sure." I opened the door, and he marched in. "How did you know where to find me?"

"I followed you."

Before I could respond, Bob sucker punched me in the stomach. A searing pain tore through my damaged ribs. I fell to the floor, winded and coughing.

He slammed the door closed then dragged me by my shoulders into the living room, throwing me against the wall. I pushed myself up to a sitting position with my back to the wall, bracing for another beating. The pounding Mahoney had meted out flashed through my mind.

"What kind of sick bastard are you?" Bob was standing over me, fists clenched.

Suddenly I knew exactly why he was there. Ali must have told him the same lies she'd fed Marie and Mahoney. Or else Marie had betrayed me, but I found that hard to accept. What difference did it make? I couldn't change the fact that the man hovering over me probably believed I raped his daughter.

"Listen," I said, mentally preparing for the onslaught, "whatever you've been told, it isn't true."

Bob kicked the drywall next to me, his boot leaving a massive hole in the surface. "I can't tell you how close I am to squeezing the life out of you right now." Spittle sprayed from his mouth as he spoke. He kicked the wall several times again, only much harder. As his boot flew past me, he kept shouting something, but I couldn't make out what he was saying.

He stopped, and I raised my hands. "I know this is about Ali. I swear on Freya's life, I didn't go anywhere near her."

His breathing was heavy. "That makes sense," he said. "A chicken-shit coward like you would hide behind his own daughter."

"I'm telling you the truth, Bob. I don't know why, but Ali has been obsessed with me ever since she found her condo. I would have come to you about it, but I knew how you'd react."

Bob pulled his fist back. I was convinced he was about to punch me in the head. "What kind of grown man follows a young woman around?"

"Go ahead. Hit me if you want. There's nothing I can say to make you believe my word over hers. Whatever you do to me won't alter the truth. Ali is the one you should be talking to, not me. She's been harassing me for months. I reported her to the police. I even sought legal advice to stop her."

Bob made a deep guttural sound then pounded his fist into the drywall. "You stay away from her. Do you hear me?"

"I have never been near her."

He took a couple of steps back. I thought he was going to kick me, so I wrapped my arms around my head.

"Even your own wife doesn't believe you," Bob said. "Why else would you be living in this shithole? The moment she discovered the lowlife she's married to, she threw you out."

"You're wrong. Ali lied to her, too. She wanted to split us up. Your daughter needs help. There's something badly wrong with her, but you refuse to see it. She—"

"You don't get it, do you?" Bob's face was deep crimson, his eyes rolled back in their sockets. "If I hear you've been within a mile of my daughter…" He punched the wall again and again.

"I won't. I have no reason to. But you need to make sure she stays away from me and my family."

He shook his head. "I know people. For a thousand dollars, they'd break both of your legs. Just give me one more reason and I'll have them come here. That's a promise."

Chapter 34

I hadn't heard directly from Ali since she vandalized Bekah's car the day we took Mom back to Sidney. And then, a week after her father attacked me, it all began again. Texts started hitting my phone. At first, only a couple of messages a day. Soon after, it became a torrent. Some days I'd receive twenty or thirty of them, at all hours of the day and night.

I don't mind admitting, I was terrified. Either I was reading the ramblings of a seriously deranged mind or else, much worse, she was laying a written trail, making me out to be the perpetrator.

Please don't keep calling me.

I'm sorry if I gave you mixed signals. I was only being friendly. Nothing more.

I saw you again outside my building last night. This has to stop. You're scaring me.

Was that you just now hammering on my door?

I know you are looking at me now.

You leave me with no choice. I'm going back to the police.

Stay away from me.

Threaten me again and I'll report you.

I'm begging you. Please don't use the photos.

My father now knows about you. I've told him everything.

I wrote to your wife telling her what you did to me.

She knows everything.

As far as I could see, my options were thin: either I could try and ignore her texts, or I could go back to the police. The prospect of speaking to OBPD again was daunting. Collins had already warned me they believed Ali's story, and given how incriminating her latest texts looked, I was concerned the police would use them as evidence against me. Doing nothing was not much better. I had no idea how long this torment would last or what she might do to me or my family.

It felt like I'd been dropped in the middle of hell and there was no way out.

Countless nights, I lay in bed unable to sleep, searching for answers. What caused her fixation with me in the first place? There had to be something I did or said that triggered her obsession. What was it about our time together that made Ali think I had any feelings for her?

All that time we spent searching for properties, she hardly said a word to me. I'd been the one doing most of the talking. And whenever I asked her questions, it's not as though they were personal or particularly probing. They were polite, ordinary inquiries about her work, her family, where she'd been on vacation, the kinds of food she liked, what she thought about living in Vancouver or Victoria. The same things I discussed with most of my clients. Innocuous day-to-day stuff to pass the time of day. Sometimes, when things were really quiet, in order to punctuate the long uncomfortable silences, I talked about my family, how Freya was doing, what Marie liked to do, the vacations we'd been on, and places I'd still like to see. I didn't share anything confidential about my marriage, despite what Ali said that time. And, certainly, I said nothing that could possibly be construed as intimate or suggestive.

Looking back, there was only one occasion that stood out. At the time, it didn't seem that significant. I had gone to collect Ali from her parents' home one Saturday morning. It was early because we had a lot of viewings to get through that day. Up until then, she had always dressed conservatively. If you didn't know her, you probably would have guessed she was a lawyer by her choice of conventional attire, even on the weekends. But that day, when she jumped into my car, it was different. She had on what I considered to be an ultra-short skirt, revealing almost her entire legs when she was sitting in my passenger seat. On top, she wore a thin T-shirt and obviously no bra, leaving very little to the imagination. The car filled with a strong scent of perfume the moment she closed the door. It was as if a completely different client had joined me that day.

I said something like, "You look nice today." An innocent enough comment. Given that she'd obviously made a special effort, I thought it churlish not to register it. I swear I meant nothing by it. I was only being polite.

"Thank you," Ali said.

"What's the occasion?" I expected her to say she had a date later that day or that it was her birthday or something.

She turned and smiled at me. "I did it for you."

At first, I thought I'd misheard her. I didn't really know what to say. "That's nice of you." Inside, as her comment sunk in, my overwhelming feeling was one of embarrassment. From the warmth in my cheeks, I suspected it showed.

What she said next was, I thought at the time, an attempt to change the subject, but now I'm not so sure. "You ran past our house again this morning."

I started the engine and pulled away from the curb. "Yes, I jog past most days."

"You saw me at my bedroom window."

"I would have been too busy fighting for breath. By the time I get to your place, I'm usually too tired to notice anything."

"I know you saw me, Tom. I waved back when you looked up."

I hadn't seen her at the window, of that I was one hundred percent certain. The truth is I hadn't even glanced at their house. Whenever I was out running, my focus was on the exercise and getting it over with. But given the strange thing Ali said in one of her texts many weeks later, about dropping her towel when she thought she saw me looking up at her window again, this non-event for me seemed to have much more significance in her mind.

Was this the trigger I was looking for? Had she always been watching me run past each morning, waiting for me to look at her? Weird thing was, she never dressed like that again and, until that text, she never mentioned my running.

Chapter 35

Sidney's Thursday evening street market was heaving with people—mainly locals, but also a few visitors to the seaside town making the most of the September warm weather. After today, the market would close and wouldn't start up again until next May. All along Beacon Avenue, the sugary smell of doughnuts clung to the air, melding with the unmistakable aroma of fried onions. As usual, the lines at the food stands were long, wrapping around the corner into Fourth Street. In the middle of one of them, Ali waited patiently for her wild salmon burger. When she was growing up on the island, her parents would often bring her here just for the salmon burgers. Along with camping trips to Sooke every summer, driving up to Sidney on a Thursday evening during the summer was a Page family tradition.

It was getting dark when Ali left the market and walked the two blocks north to where she had parked her Golf. She sat inside and cleaned her fingers with wet wipes she kept in the glove compartment. Moments later, she picked up the white envelope sitting on the back seat then stepped out of the car.

Like many others dotted around the central core of this popular retirement town, the blue-and-white, four-story condo building next to where she was parked had a sign on the front: *A Fifty-Five Plus Community*. Ali looked over her shoulder before she walked in.

Unit 106 was on the first floor at the end of a corridor. She stood outside the front door, staring at the envelope in her hands. The sound of a TV came from inside the unit. Ali knocked. No answer. She waited a few seconds then tried again, only this time much harder. The TV sound stopped, and moments later there was movement. The door opened.

Standing in the doorway, the old lady who lived there was leaning on a walking frame. "Yes, dear?" she asked, with a quizzical expression.

"I hope I've come to the right place," Ali said, a friendly smile lighting up her face. "I'm looking for Mrs. Harper."

The woman looked more confused. "That's me. Who are you?" She stepped back and closed the door a little.

"I'm sorry to turn up like this, especially at this time of the evening, but Tom sent me."

Mrs. Harper opened the door wide. "Tom. I see."

"Didn't he call to let you know I might be coming?"

"No. Why are you here?"

"I'm sorry. When I mentioned I might be going to the last Sidney market, he asked if I would stop by to check up on you."

"I can cope perfectly well. He's such a worrier."

"You know Tom."

"He didn't mention anything to me about you visiting."

Ali rolled her eyes. "He's crazy busy right now. I suspect he forgot. Anyway, I can see you are alright, so I'll be heading back to Victoria. I'll let him know you're okay. Sorry I disturbed you."

"Don't be silly, dear. If you've come all this way to see me, the least I can do is offer you a drink. Come in."

"Only if you're sure I'm not intruding."

"Not at all." Mrs. Harper stood aside and waved in her visitor.

Ali stepped inside and walked into the living room. Through the window, there were glimpses of Sidney marina and beyond the water glimmering in the full moonlight, the silhouette of the Gulf Islands.

"What a wonderful view," Ali said, pointing toward the ocean.

"Yes, it is," Mrs. Harper said. "Tom found the place for us. His father and I bought it almost ten years ago when we moved from Owen Bay."

"So, you used to live near Tom and Marie? He didn't tell me that."

"Oh, yes. We were there for many years." Mrs. Harper tapped the top of an armchair. "Do take a seat. I have just made some tea. Would you like some?"

"That would be lovely." Ali sat, resting the envelope on her lap and scanning the room. "Do you need a hand?"

"That's very kind." Mrs. Harper stared at the walking frame. "I can't carry anything while I'm still using this infuriating thing."

They went to the kitchen, and Ali carried the drinks through on a silver tray. "Tom never mentions his father," she said, taking her seat again.

"I'm afraid he passed two years ago. He was a realtor, too." Mrs. Harper sat in the armchair on the other side of the coffee table.

"I'm sorry. So, you live here on your own now?"

"That's right. My granddaughter stays over now and again."

"That would be Freya."

Mrs. Harper's face softened. "She's a lovely girl."

"She is," Ali said, before taking a sip of the herbal tea. "She's in the same year as my brother at Owen Bay High."

"How do you know Tom?"

"Well, my family has known them all for many years. My parents live in Owen Bay, too. Years ago, before I moved Vancouver, I used to babysit for Tom and Marie. Their house is only five minutes away from ours."

"Do you still live on the mainland?"

Ali shook her head. "I moved back a few months ago to join a firm in Victoria. Tom helped me find a place in town."

"Your parents must like having you back," Mrs. Harper said, picking up her teacup.

Ali slid forward to the edge of her seat. "Look, I know I said

Tom asked me to check up on you, but that's not the only reason I came to see you."

Mrs. Harper wrinkled her nose. "Okay."

"Tom's too embarrassed to say anything. He wants you to know, but he doesn't want to upset you either. I told him you'd understand."

"What on earth are you talking about, dear?"

"There's no nice way to say this. I wish there was." Ali paused. "Tom and Marie have separated."

"Don't be silly. I saw Marie only a few days ago, and she never mentioned anything about it. I'm sure you've misunderstood something. Tom would never leave his family." Red blotches appeared on Mrs. Harper's neck. "Never."

"Tom said you would find it difficult."

"Why are you here telling me this?" Mrs. Harper's face had hardened. "What does it have to do with you, anyway?"

Ali looked down at the carpet. "Tom and I are in a relationship."

Mrs. Harper spilled some of her tea. She put the cup down on the coffee table. "Don't be…you're…you can't be that much older than Freya."

"I'm afraid it's true. We've been seeing each other since I came back from Vancouver. In fact, Tom's planning on moving into my place soon."

"I don't believe you."

"I don't wish to upset you, but Tom and I plan to marry, eventually."

Mrs. Harper pursed her lips. "I'd like you to leave."

Ali stood. "Of course. I'm sorry this is so distressing. It must be a shock. That's exactly what Tom wanted to avoid, but I told him we couldn't hide it from you much longer." Ali patted her stomach. "Not now we're having a baby."

"A baby. That's impossible."

"Tom's always wanted another child. He says Marie was unable to conceive after Freya. I think, over the years, that became an issue between them."

"I want you to go now."

Ali raised a palm. "I'm leaving, I promise. Here." She handed over the envelope she'd been holding. "Tom wanted you to have this."

"What is it?"

"Open it. You'll see."

Mrs. Harper's fingers had a slight tremble as she opened the envelope and retrieved what was inside. "What is this?"

Ali beamed from ear to ear. "It's the first ultrasound image of our baby. Tom's so proud."

Chapter 36

Mom sounded hysterical when she phoned me. My first thought was she'd had another fall, but I soon discovered it was something much worse.

She kept repeating: "Tell me it's not true." Between her tears, she was saying something about Marie and I splitting up. I assumed Marie or Freya had mentioned what was going on at home. I knew it was bound to happen sooner or later. Maybe I ought to have told her, but I'd been shielding her from things ever since Mahoney's visit. After the loss of my father, and Mom's recent falls, she'd already been through a lot. The last thing I wanted was to pile on more pressure. Besides, a small part of me still clung to the hope Marie and I would patch things up before Mom had to find out.

Now I had to explain why my marriage had fallen apart and why I hadn't said anything to her about it. I owed her a face-to-face explanation, so I drove over there that night.

Mom's eyes were puffy when she came to the door. "Just tell me it's not true," she said.

I hugged her. Gut-wrenching guilt coursed through me; I was to blame for her distress. "Let's go sit down," I said. "I'll explain everything."

After I made us both a cup of tea, we sat together on the couch. "What exactly did Marie tell you?" I asked, figuring it had to have been Marie who'd shared our news.

Mom cocked her head. "Marie? I haven't spoken with Marie."

"Then how do you know about our separation? Did Freya tell you?"

Mom looked like she had a bitter taste in her mouth. "I had a visit this evening…from your new…friend. She told me."

"What new friend?"

Mom hesitated. She seemed lost. "Do you know something, she never told me her name?"

"What did she look like?"

"Young. She was very young, and pretty, too. She said she works in Victoria and that you and Marie are friends with her parents."

A dead weight formed in the pit of my stomach. Ali had been here. To my mom's home. Playing evil mind games with this innocent, frail woman. Even for her, this was a new low. This time, she had crossed the line. How dare she use my mother to get at me?

"I think I know who you mean," I said, trying to sound calm while fighting to contain my emotions.

"I should hope so. She said you'd left Marie because you're planning on marrying her. Please tell me that's not going to happen."

Every fiber in my body was taut with fury. Now I understood why Mom was so upset. This was unforgiveable. One way or another, Ali would pay for this.

"I have moved out of our home. That much is true."

Mom raised a hand to her mouth. "Oh, please don't tell me—"

"It's not what you think. I didn't tell you because I thought it would all blow over quickly. Our marriage is strong. I believe we will get through this."

"Then who is this woman? Why does she think you're going to marry her? I don't understand."

What could I say to my mother without sharing with her the turmoil of the past few months? She knew nothing of the harassment we'd been through. As far as Mahoney was concerned, Marie and I had told both Mom and Freya it was a burglary gone wrong.

"She's a confused young woman," I said. "I can't explain it, mainly because I don't understand her behavior myself. For some reason or other, she's been making our lives hell. Stalking, harassment, you name it."

"Why didn't you tell me this was going on?"

"I didn't want to worry you. I'm sorry she's brought you into this mess. That's the last thing I wanted."

"So, you're not going to marry her?"

"Absolutely not."

I could see the relief on Mom's face. "Thank God."

"She needs help, professional, psychological help. If she comes anywhere near you again, I want you to call me. She's dangerous."

"Have you spoken to the police?"

I sighed. "I've tried. Several times, in fact. They won't take it seriously. Seems the system has a hard time accepting that men can be the victim of stalking."

Mom reached out and grabbed my hand. "I still don't understand why you and Marie have separated. Wouldn't something like this bring you closer together?"

"It's a long story. In the same way this woman lied to you, she lied to Marie. She made things up to drive us apart. None of it is true."

"And Marie believes her?"

"I'm afraid so. At some point, she'll realize we've all been manipulated. She just needs time to get there. I'm confident we'll be okay."

The truth was, my confidence had ebbed away weeks ago. I was saying the words, not because I believed them any longer, but because I wanted to put Mom's mind at rest.

"It must be awful living like this, Tom, not knowing what she will do next. Without the support of your family…"

"I can't begin to describe how hard it's been. I can't get on with my life. There's this constant fear she is up to something. It's always at the back of my mind. I just want it to stop. I never thought I would say this about anyone, but the woman is evil."

"I got a taste of it tonight."

"I know. I'm desperately sorry you were brought into this."

"She didn't just tell me you were going to marry her."

"She didn't harm you?"

"No. Nothing like that. Wait here." Mom stood and hobbled through to the kitchen. When she returned, she was holding an envelope in her hand. "Before she left, she gave me this."

I took the envelope. "What is it?"

"See for yourself."

I pulled out the document, recognizing it as an ultrasound image. The last time I saw one like it was when Marie was pregnant with Freya. "Why did she give you this?"

"She said she was having a baby."

"Ugh?"

"She told me it was yours."

A jolt of electricity pierced my skull. I dropped the image on the floor. "The woman needs locking up. How could she make something up like that?"

By the time I left Mom's, it was a little after ten thirty. The Pat Bay Highway was a lot busier than I'd anticipated because I ran into traffic coming off the last ferry from the mainland. While I waited at a set of lights just outside Sidney, my thoughts kept turning to Mom and her emotional state this evening. The last time I'd seen her like that was just after Dad passed. How could anyone be so wicked to a frail and defenseless old woman? Only someone with a complete lack of empathy would do such a thing. I knew for sure Ali was a sociopath.

While Mom seemed fine when I left her, I suspected she was putting on a brave face. She was bound to dwell on the poisonous lies she'd been told tonight. Apart from Bekah, we were the only family Mom had. My mother would worry about us and not until she saw Marie and I back together would she be able to relax again. The reality was that could be months away, if at all. Ali's malevolence had wrecked another life.

I despised her for what she'd done to me and my family. The rage that had been building inside me all night felt like a pressure cooker about to explode. I hadn't invited that woman into my life. She'd waded in and blown it apart, and Mom, Marie, Freya, and Bekah had been collateral damage. No, it was worse than that; the people I loved the most had been used as weapons to attack me. She was a dangerously sick individual, who, for some unfathomable reason, was not going to stop until she'd destroyed me.

Sitting in my car, I realized I'd wasted far too much time and energy searching for an explanation. What did it matter why she was obsessed with me? The only thing that counted now was what I did from here on. I'd long since exhausted the few potential legal remedies: reporting her to the police, obtaining professional advice, seeking a court order. None of them had worked. In some ways, they'd made things worse. The reality was it was down to me; if I didn't force her to stop, her persistent cruelty could go on for years, and there was no telling how it would end.

When the traffic began to flow again, I knew what had to be done. I wasn't prepared to put my family at risk a moment longer.

There was only one place I had to be.

Chapter 37

At exactly eleven fifteen, I pulled into at an empty parking bay right across the street from Ali's condo building. Through my windshield, I could see the lights were on inside her fourth-floor corner unit. She was home. I ran across the road to the main entrance and pretended to be checking my phone. Minutes later, a man holding a Jack Russell terrier on a leash walked by me and used his key fob to open the front door. He threw me a strange look as I rushed in behind him. I was in. He headed for the elevators, so I took the stairs.

When I reached Ali's condo, doubt inveigled its way into my mind. Was I right to continue? There was still time to turn around. Standing outside her door, I realized it was one thing deciding to come here, quite another now I was only moments away from confronting the woman I'd grown to despise. There were plenty of reasons to proceed: I'd been more than reasonable; there was no other way to stop her; the harassment would go on forever unless I did something; next time she might even kill someone I love.

You have to do this.

My heart pounded when I pressed the doorbell and stood back. Moments later, I saw movement at the glass peephole, and then the door opened, a security chain stopping it part-way.

"Tom," Ali said. In a split second, her expression went from shock to a broad smile. "What are you doing here?" She was wearing a white bathrobe, and I could smell nail polish remover.

Adrenaline coursed through my body. I rammed my right foot into the door, snapping the chain away from its clasp. The door burst open, striking her left shoulder.

Ali fell back but somehow managed to keep her balance. She screamed.

Automatically, my right hand gripped the front of her neck.

She stopped screaming but kept thrashing out at me with her arms.

I kicked the door closed behind me.

As she tried to wriggle free, her bathrobe fell open. Under-neath, she was naked.

For some reason, that image remained seared into my brain long after that night. It was the moment I almost stopped. Seeing her exposed and vulnerable for the first time, made me hesitate. Suddenly I was the monster, not her. I didn't recognize myself. I guess it's what people mean by an out-of-body experience. I knew it was me throttling her, but it wasn't.

The hesitation soon evaporated when Mom's face flashed into my mind. "How dare you do that to my mother?" I said, pushing her head back into the wall. "You sick bastard."

I could see panic in her eyes, and seconds later the flailing subsided. I'm not proud to admit it, but a small part of me wanted to continue applying pressure to her throat. I could end it all right now, and she'd be gone forever. But I couldn't do it. I released my grip, and she fell forward onto the floor, gasping for air.

Red blotches appeared on her white skin where my fingers had been pressed hard into her flesh. Every instinct in my body screamed at me to get out, but I had to see this through. I had to make sure she would leave us alone. I grabbed hold of Ali's arms and pulled her into the kitchen in the center of the condo, so the neighbors couldn't hear us. I threw her onto a chair at the small table and stood between her and the door. If she made a run for it, I'd be able to block her.

Eventually, her coughing stopped, and she looked up at me. "What happens now?" she asked.

"That's up to you," I said. "As I see it, you have two choices. You can either stop what you're doing, seek psychological help, and get on with your life."

"Or what?"

"I finish this now."

"What's that supposed to mean?"

"You know exactly what I mean. You've already destroyed everything precious to me. I have nothing more to lose."

"You haven't got the balls to kill me."

"Don't test me."

She was right, of course; it wasn't in me to kill anyone, not even someone I reviled as much as her. I'd already gone much further than I should. Harming a woman went against everything I believed in. In many ways, it made me as bad as her. All I could do now was leave, hoping the threat of me coming back would be enough to stop her.

Ali's defiant expression softened. "I only ever wanted you, Tom. I still do. You deny it, but I know you want the same. It's written all over your face." She stood and dropped her bathrobe to the floor. "All those mornings you looked up at my window, this is what you wanted, right? Well, now you don't have to dream. I'm all yours."

She walked toward me.

I stepped back. The rage I felt earlier was boiling inside me again. What would it take to get through to this woman? I backed up to the wall until I could go no further.

Ali slipped both arms around my waist and rubbed her body against mine. "Make love to me, Tom," she whispered in my ear. "Marie doesn't want you anymore."

Lightning surged through my body. With more strength than I knew I had, I thrust her away from me. "No!"

She flew backward through the air, bounced off the table, and crashed onto the floor.

213

At that moment, I wanted to kill her. I lunged forward and tripped on a glass bowl that had fallen from the table.

Terror written all over her face, Ali scrambled to her feet before I did. She grabbed a knife from the block on the counter-top.

I froze, my heart pulverizing the inside of my chest.

"Get out of here," she shouted, swinging the blade back and forth.

I could feel the air moving as the blade passed close to my face. "I'm going." I stepped back.

Tears welling in her eyes, she threw the knife onto the table. "I never want to see you again." She looked like a lost soul as she slumped into a chair.

"As long as you stay away from my family, you won't see me again."

I grabbed the knife to keep it out of her way then slowly backed out of the room. When I reached the front door, I threw the knife on the floor and left.

Chapter 38

Next morning, after a long night spent staring at the TV because I couldn't sleep, I went into the office early. Shortly after Brenda arrived, there was a tap on my closed office door.

"Tom," she said, entering the room. "There are some people here to see you." Her expression seemed concerned and confused in equal measure.

Two uniformed police officers and a detective walked in behind her. My stomach went into spasm; I knew immediately why they were there. All night, I'd been thinking Ali might go to the police and play the victim, but I hadn't expected things to move this quickly.

I stood. "This is about last night, isn't it?" The words jumped out of my mouth without thinking.

"Mr. Harper," the detective said, "I'm arresting you for sexual assault..."

My office walls closed in around me, in an instant all oxygen was sucked out of the room, and I felt as if I was about to faint. The two uniformed officers grabbed my arms. While the detective's mouth was still moving, I heard none of his words after 'sexual assault'. Brenda stood to one side to let us through, revulsion in her eyes. She said something, but it didn't register with me.

I couldn't tell you how I got there, but the next thing I remember was having a brief meeting with the duty counsel and then being led into a grimy interview room at the police head-quarters in Victoria where they sat me on a cheap plastic chair. The cramped space, built out of cream-painted building blocks, already felt like a cell. No windows, just bare walls and a door, plus a camera screwed to a metal bracket high up in one corner. The smell of stale coffee hinted at the source of the sticky brown circles on the tiny wooden table. Sitting opposite me were two detectives, one of whom had been at my office that morning.

"I'm Detective Sergeant Hudec," he said, then glanced at his colleague. "And this is Detective Constable Epps."

Epps had dead eyes that looked right through me. She said something about the interview being recorded, but she spoke so fast, I didn't catch it all. I got the impression she'd said the words a thousand times.

"Where were you last night between eleven and midnight?" Hudec asked. He was smartly dressed in a dark gray suit and had on what looked like a tie from an expensive private school, complete with its own logo and Latin inscription. Every time he picked up his paper coffee cup, he made a loud slurping sound as he drank through the hole in the lid.

"I was in town," I said.

Earlier, the duty counsel had advised me I had the right to remain silent. That didn't feel right; I had nothing to hide. I'd always thought it was only the guilty who bit their tongues. That wasn't me. Everything I did at Ali's condo was justified. I did it to protect me or my family from further harm. If I had to, I'd do it again.

"What were you doing in town?"

"I'd been to see my mother in Sidney and I was on my way home."

Hudec frowned then took another noisy slurp. "You live in Owen Bay. Why go out of your way?"

"I had to take care of something before I went home."

"Where'd you go?"

It was obvious Hudec already knew where I'd been. Even I'd

spotted the security camera outside Ali's condo building while I was waiting for someone to open the front door. If Hudec hadn't seen the recording yet, he was bound to discover it sooner or later, so I decided to cut to the chase. "I went to see Ali Page."

Epps looked at the senior detective then wrote something down on her pad.

"Okay," Hudec said. "Thanks for leveling with us." He leaned back in his chair. That's when I noticed the two detectives had seats with cloth cushions and not the plastic type I was sticking to. "Why did you go see her at that time of night?"

"Because earlier in the evening she visited my mother and said some things that frightened her. I wanted to make sure she didn't go near my family again."

"What things?"

"A bunch of lies about being pregnant with my baby."

"So, I'm guessing you know Ali Page quite well?"

"I've known her for years, but I wouldn't say well. She's the daughter of friends."

"I don't get it," Hudec said. "Why would she lie about being pregnant?"

"For reasons I still can't comprehend, she's been harassing me and my family. What she told my mother was a classic example of the crap I've had to put up with."

"Is that right?" Another slurp.

"I'm telling you, the woman is obsessed with me."

Epps threw me a look, as if to say, "You should be so lucky." She couldn't have made it more obvious she didn't believe anything I was saying.

"You could save a whole lot of time," I continued, "by speaking to Owen Bay Police Department. They have a file on her and the trouble she's been causing. She's made our lives a living hell."

"So, you were angry with her when you went there last night," Hudec said. "You wanted to teach her a lesson."

"I didn't say that. I wanted to warn her to stay away from

me and my family. I'd had enough. What she did to my mother crossed a line." I paused to calm down. My voice was getting louder. While I was still mad at Ali, it didn't serve me well to appear aggressive in front of the police. "Listen, you really should be speaking with OBPD."

"Maybe we'll do that. Right now, I want to focus on what happened last night."

"I told you I went to give her a warning."

"Some warning. You broke into her condo."

"That's not true. I rang the doorbell."

"Then why is there a large footprint on the outside of her front door? When we've completed the search of your home, my guess is we're going to find a match with one of your shoes."

"Look, I was angry. I admit that. I rang the bell and pushed my way in when she opened the door, but it's—"

"She says you kicked the door in and then tried to strangle her."

"That's not what happened at all."

"Then why does she have bruising all around her neck? Explain that to me."

What could I say? I was responsible for those injuries. I'd snapped. I didn't want to lie, but neither was I going to make this easy for them. None of these people had any interest in the months of torture I'd been through. The police did nothing when I was asking for their help.

"I have nothing more to say to you," I said.

"Did you cause them?" Hudec asked, pushing his empty cup to one side and leaning forward.

"I have nothing to say."

"Ali Page says you tried to kill her."

I tried to avoid eye contact with the detectives, but the room was small, and they were so close, it was almost impossible.

"What do you have to say?" Hudec continued.

"No comment."

WATCH FOR ME

Hudec glanced at his colleague. "I know if I was being accused of something I didn't do, I would say as much. I'd want to clear my name."

"He's already told us he was there," Epps said, "and we know he forced his way in. If he was as angry as he says he was, it's hardly much of a leap to believe he attacked her."

They stopped talking and stared at me. I looked down at the table. I wanted to scream at them. I wanted them to understand the agony we had lived through before last night. Yes, I'd snapped, but it was only after months of provocation. I wanted them to see I was the victim, not her.

"Ali Page told us, after she got away, you grabbed a knife from her kitchen," Hudec said. "You held it to her throat and forced yourself onto her."

I looked up and peered at the detective. They had this all wrong.

"You raped her, didn't you?" Hudec continued, his head so close to mine I could smell the coffee on his breath. "You wanted to teach her a lesson, so you held her down and raped her."

I shook my head no. Where was this coming from? Yes, I had put my hands around Ali's neck, but I hadn't tried to rape her. What evil lies had she told these people? It was bad enough she'd lied to Marie, but to say something like this to the police. She really was crazy.

"You said you went there to give her a warning," Hudec said.

"The fingerprints on the knife will confirm her story," Epps said. "You might as well come clean."

"It'll be easier on you in the end," Hudec said.

My fingerprints were on the knife, but only because I moved it out of her way. What was I supposed to do? Turn my back on that woman with the knife still there? That evidence would look bad for me. There was no getting around it. But rape? I would fight that allegation to my last breath.

"I didn't go near her," I said. "Not in the way you're suggesting."

219

"We're going to need a saliva swab," Hudec said.

"Sure, I have nothing to hide."

When they released me, Hudec sidled up to me. "Next time we see you," he said, "you'll be charged. It's only a matter of time."

From the disappointment on his face, it was obvious he'd been expecting me to confess to everything. There was no doubt in his mind I'd raped Ali, and he was going to see that I paid for it. What he didn't know yet was how good she was at lying. I knew the truth, and when they'd had a chance to look at all the evidence, Hudec would come to see it, too. This time, by misleading the police, Ali had gone too far.

Chapter 39

"When are you coming home, Dad?" Freya asked as I drove the two of us up the Pat Bay Highway for her air cadets shooting practise at the rifle range near the airport.

Although Marie had made it patently clear she didn't want our daughter coming anywhere near me, fortunately for me, Freya was old enough to decide for herself what she wanted. She missed her dad as much as I missed her. The weekly sessions at the range were our one regular opportunity to spend precious time together. In truth, those moments with Freya were one of the few things keeping me sane right now.

"I'm really not sure, honey," I said. "It's not entirely my decision. You know your mom and I are going through a tough patch."

I knew Marie had shared with our daughter her version of why I'd moved out of the house because Freya told me. Apparently, I'd started seeing someone else and that meant I had no time for my 'real family'. Thankfully, Marie had spared many of the sordid details, so Freya didn't know the name of my supposed mistress. Being accused of an affair was one thing, but if Freya thought for one moment I might have been sleeping with Simon's sister, she would have given up on me weeks ago, and rightly so.

The instant we pulled into the parking lot at the range, I spotted Bob Page waiting next to his car. He'd parked it immediately outside the entrance to the building and was locked in conversation with two other men; one I recognized as the parent of another cadet and the other was Frank Holmes, who used to work with Bob in the air force and now ran the shooting facility. The last time I'd seen Bob was when he attacked me at my rental unit, although I had half-expected to run into him at the air cadets long before now. I assumed he'd been avoiding me these past couple of weeks.

With Freya there, I hoped he wasn't going to make a scene and embarrass me in front of my daughter. I killed the engine and braced myself for the verbal onslaught. Bob pointed at our vehicle, and the three of them walked toward us as we got out of the car. I could tell by their serious expressions something wasn't right.

"Listen," Holmes said when they reached us, "we don't want any trouble, Tom. It'll be best for everyone if you don't come here anymore."

I glanced at Freya, whose face took on a glaze of confusion. "I don't understand," I said. "What do you mean don't come here anymore? I bring Freya here every week."

Holmes looked at Bob for support.

Bob stood forward, fists clenched at his sides, his jaw muscle twitching. "Go home," he said. "We don't want anyone like you near the kids."

I moved slightly in front of Freya to shield her. "What's that supposed to mean?"

"We really don't want to have this conversation with your daughter here," Holmes said.

I turned to Freya. "Please go sit in the car, honey." I handed her the keys and waited until she returned to our vehicle before continuing. "What's Bob been feeding you?" I asked Holmes.

"Enough to know we can't risk you being near any of the cadets. It isn't right."

"Risk? What exactly are you getting at?"

Holmes's cheeks were flushed. The man was a long way out of his comfort zone. He glanced at Bob then looked back at me.

"Bob told us all about you and his daughter. We just can't allow a man like you near the kids."

"Someone like me? I haven't done anything wrong. His daughter's one troubled individual. Did he tell you that?"

Bob stepped forward. "You better watch your mouth."

Holmes put his hand on Bob's shoulder. "Leave this to me, Bob, please."

"You know who I am, Frank," I said. "You've known me for years. I'm no risk to anyone."

Holmes shook his head.

"Let me spell it out for you," Bob said, shifting his weight from one foot to the other, like a man bristling for a fight. "We don't want a pervert like you going anywhere near the cadets. Now get back in your car and go home before I do you some real harm."

Pervert.

A thousand thoughts ran through my mind. Bob already thought I'd been stalking is daughter. Now Ali must have told him the same poisonous lies she'd fed the police and Marie. In turn, what had Bob told the other parents? There was nothing I could say to persuade these people I was innocent. Their minds were made up. *Freya.* How much had she heard of this conversation? Was she sitting behind me right now thinking her father had sexually assaulted Ali?

"Go home, Tom," Holmes said, disgust written over his face.

As I turned and walked back to my car, I wanted to dig a hole and climb right in it. Freya had her window all the way down. From that short distance, she must have heard everything. When I looked at her, she averted her eyes. Throughout her life, I had always tried to be a role model, a man she could look up to, a man who treated others with respect and kindness, the type of man I hoped she'd marry one day. In an instant, that image of her father had been destroyed. I didn't know what was harder, being falsely accused of rape or losing the respect of my daughter.

"How much of that did you hear?" I asked when I sat in the car.

"Enough," Freya said.

"I want you to know none of what they just said is true. None of it." Freya wouldn't look at me. "That is not the man I am. No matter what you might hear said about me, I need you to know that, Freya. Okay?"

"Please. Just take me home."

During our forty-minute drive back to Owen Bay, not a single word was spoken. The moment I pulled up outside our home, Freya jumped out of the car and ran to the house, not once looking back.

That was when I knew for certain I'd lost her. Without the love of my daughter, what did I have left?

Alone in my apartment that night, for the first time in my life, I flirted with the idea of suicide. What was the point in carrying on? My life couldn't get any worse.

But then it did.

Chapter 40

My office was no longer the sanctuary it once was. Right after the police turned up to arrest me, Brenda, who for years had been more like an older sister than an employee, started behaving differently toward me. Gone were the friendly banter between us, the playful rivalry over listings, the sharing of family stories when the place was quiet. The atmosphere was frosty.

Most of the time Brenda remained hidden behind her PC, engaged in work with an intensity I'd never seen before. Even though she sat only a few feet outside my office door, she began communicating with me by email. I'd still get the occasional grunt when I bought coffee for both of us on my way into work, but that was it.

Whatever happened to innocent until proven guilty?

A week after my arrest, and two days after the ugly scene at the shooting range, Brenda surprised me by walking into my office at the end of the day.

"Now we know why we had three potential listing appointments canceled on us this afternoon," she said, throwing a copy of the *Times Colonist* on my desk.

"What's this?" I asked, picking up the local newspaper.

"Take a look at page five." Brenda looked like she wanted to spit.

Before I could say anything, she returned to her desk, picked up her purse and coat, and left the building. Not even a goodbye.

A cloud of despair descended over me as I opened the paper and turned to page five. My breathing stopped when I saw an old photo of me standing outside our offices. It was the one we'd used for marketing purposes when we opened our new premises a couple of years earlier. The headline next to the photo drove a spike through the middle of my chest: *Owen Bay Realtor Arrested for Suspected Rape.*

I tried to read the article, but my eyes wouldn't focus. I rested my palms on the desk and forced myself to take in deep breaths. *Concentrate.* Slowly, I began to make out the words on the page, and each one rammed that spike deeper into my heart.

Owen Bay realtor Tom Harper, 48, was arrested last week for suspected rape. OBPD are continuing with their investigation, but, at this time, no charges have been filed. No one from OBPD was prepared to comment, although we have learned from a source close to the case that the alleged victim is a Victoria-based corporate lawyer. She is believed to be in her twenties and is a former client of Harper's real estate brokerage, Harper Realty...

Halfway through the piece, I had to stop and run to the bathroom where I threw up. All I could think of was my family reading this and what it would do to them. How would Freya cope with the inevitable hostility at school? Kids could be so cruel, and Freya was still a sensitive child for her age. I pictured them taunting her about her "pervert" father. That sort of pressure could destroy my precious daughter. And what about Mom? How would she handle seeing her son paraded in public as a rapist? In her current state, there was no telling what it might do to her.

I left the bathroom, locked the front door to the office, and drew all the blinds. With the paper just out, I wondered how much time it would take for word to get around the community. It wouldn't be long before people came knocking on my office door for a glimpse of the Owen Bay rapist.

I didn't need to read the rest of the story. All venomous lies that had probably been leaked to the paper by Ali's father. From the way Bob acted at the shooting range, this had to be his doing. One way or another, he was out to destroy me. The strange thing was, I couldn't blame him. I understood his need to lash out at the man he believed had sexually assaulted his daughter. If someone had done that to Freya, would I have behaved so differently?

I had to fix this and quickly. Not for me, but for Freya, for Marie, and for Mom. My life was over, but I couldn't sit and watch while theirs were ruined, too. In my desperation, there was only one thing I could do: I had to speak to Ali. Try and reason with her one last time. I knew it was a long shot, but I had to get her to stop this madness.

"This is Ali Page," she said when I called her office direct line.

"It's Tom."

A few seconds of silence and then, "I can't talk to you right now."

"Please, don't hang up. I need to speak to you."

"I see. Now you want to speak to me. Let me guess. You want me to get the police to drop the case." She sounded angry, furious even. The same kind of rage I felt inside, except mine was justified.

"We both know what happened." I forced myself to stay calm. *Don't lose it*, I kept saying in my head. "I'm assuming you've seen the local paper? What they say in there isn't true. None of it. I'm asking you to stop this now, before someone gets hurt."

"Is that some sort of threat?"

"Imagine what this will do to Freya. It'll destroy her, thinking her father is a rapist. I can't let that happen. All I'm asking is you tell the police the truth. I know I put my hands on you. I accept that, and I'm prepared to answer for it. But rape? We both know that isn't true."

It took a few moments before Ali responded. I thought I might have gotten through to her, convinced her she'd gone too far this time. Maybe she would drop the rape allegation, if not for me, then for Freya.

"Is that what you've told yourself?" she asked, her tone now laden with contempt. "That nothing really happened? You're unbelievable."

"I'm not saying nothing happened. I shouldn't have come to your home that night. I was angry. I know it's no excuse. I went too far, bursting in the way I did and grabbing you around your neck. I'm sorry. I lost control."

"What about the rest of it?"

"What do you mean?"

"When you held the knife to my throat and made me undress. When you forced me to have oral sex and then lay face down while you penetrated me. What about that, Tom? Have you conveniently wiped all of that from your memory? Well, I haven't. I relive it every night."

What was going on? Did she think I was recording the conversation, trying to catch her out? "If you have any grip on reality, you'll know none of those things happened. I'm begging you to stop now."

"It's unfortunate Freya has to be dragged into this, but you only have yourself to blame. I'm not responsible for the story in the paper. Equally, I'm not concerned that it's out there. The public should know the kind of man you really are."

"Think about the impact on my family, please."

"You should have thought about them before you came to my home in the middle of the night. I want you to pay for what you did to me."

"Why are you doing this? What did I do to—"

"I have nothing more to say to you." Ali terminated the call.

I wanted to scream. I wanted to climb down the phone line and beat the truth out of her. My world was spinning out of control, and I was powerless to stop it. While I knew I hadn't done any of those things, and logic told me there was no evidence to support her malicious allegations, none of that mattered now. The story was already out there. Over the next few hours, the people I loved would be devastated and there was nothing I could do to protect them.

Those thoughts of ending my life seeped back into my brain and, this time, they wouldn't go away.

Chapter 41

That evening I called Bekah. I had to talk to someone I trusted before I did something stupid. Since the night her car had been damaged outside our home, I'd kept her out of my nightmare. I couldn't risk any harm coming to her, so it had been easier to shield my sister from the truth. Whenever we spoke on the phone, she always asked what was happening. I made light of things, making out my lawyer was handling everything; the legal process was finally taking care of Ali's harassment.

This time was different, however. I'd reached breaking point and I knew I wasn't thinking straight. I had to unload some of the stress I was under, talk to somebody on my side. Bekah was the only person I had left, who was strong enough to help me without judgment.

I told her about the rape allegation and my fears, particularly for Freya, now the story was in the public domain. Despite her initial shock upon hearing how far things had deteriorated, Bekah was a rock. She listened to me for the best part of an hour as I shared the whole sordid saga about Ali's visit to Mom, how she'd pretended to be pregnant, and how I'd gone over to her condo and physically attacked her. Not once did she question my version of the truth.

As usual, Bekah soon went into practical mode, offering to come and stay with me and promising to find me a new lawyer to "blow that bitch out of the water." While I was desperate for her support, I couldn't put her in harm's way. I persuaded her not to come over to the island, and she agreed but on one condition: she insisted we talk every afternoon, so she'd know what was going on. She made me promise not to withhold the truth from her ever again.

Speaking with my sister helped me get things into some sort of perspective. No longer did it feel it was me against the world. I wasn't alone. With her love and support, I was starting to believe I could get through this.

Next morning, I went into the office early so I didn't get seen by anyone. I kept the front door locked and the blinds drawn to keep the rubberneckers away. I expected a hard day ahead, dealing with the inevitable deluge of calls from clients understandably spooked by the story in the newspaper. I wasn't sure what I was going to say to alleviate their concerns, but I had to try if I was going to avoid my business going over the cliff edge.

Just after nine I received an email from Brenda. In it, she said she had thought long and hard about things and had decided she could no longer work with me. She was resigning immediately. I wasn't surprised by her decision, more saddened that she didn't speak to me in person. I had thought our relationship was stronger than that. In many ways, her leaving marked the end of an era. She'd been with me since the day I started the brokerage many years earlier. And throughout those early years, she had quickly become a trusted friend. At least, that's the way I saw her. Even if that sentiment was no longer reciprocated, I was going to miss her, more than she would ever know.

I had just started writing a reply to her when I heard someone knocking on the front door. There were no appointments that morning, so I assumed the worst; it was probably a local reporter looking to get me to comment on the rape allegation. When the knocking continued, I decided to peek through the slats of the window blinds.

Standing outside was a tall, bearded man around my age. He was wearing jeans and a smart corduroy jacket with leather patches at the elbows that were fashionable back in the seventies and eighties. He spotted me.

I unlocked the door, prepared to be bombarded with questions. "Can I help you?" I asked.

"I'm looking for Tom Harper," he said, "and judging from the photo in the paper, it looks like I've found him."

I was right; I was being door-stepped by a reporter looking for more dirt. The disdain must have been written all over my face because, before I could say anything, the man said, "Don't worry. I'm not here to hassle you. Quite the contrary. I'm here to help."

My next thought was he might be the new lawyer Bekah had promised to find, but that didn't make any sense. I'd only spoken with her a few hours earlier.

"Who are you?" I asked.

"John Templeton," he said, extending his right hand.

Instinctively, I shook it. "You said you're here to—"

"Help," Templeton said, releasing his grip. "Might I have a few minutes of your time? I came across from the mainland this morning. I caught the first ferry, hoping to catch you in."

Still not sure what he wanted, I blocked the door.

"Listen," he continued, "I know you probably think I'm here to cause trouble. Really, I'm not. I only need a few moments."

I figured if this man had come that far to see me, the least I could do was listen to what he had to say. I stood aside and let him in, bolting the door again. "Come through to my office," I said, leading the way.

Templeton sat on the other side of my desk while I took my seat. "What is it you want to see me about?" I asked.

Templeton suddenly looked serious. "Ali Page."

I was right the first time; he was a journalist and he'd tricked his way in. I stood. "I have nothing to say about her. Now, if you'll excuse me, I'm busy."

Templeton raised both palms. "Please, sit down. I promise you'll want to hear what I have to say."

"I doubt that." I glanced at the clock on the wall. "I'll give you two minutes," I said, sitting again.

Templeton rubbed his beard then leaned forward. "I'm a law professor at UBC. Ali Page was one of my students a few years back." Templeton looked like he had just lost a filling when he said her name. "You see, I have a Google alert set up, so I can follow what she's up to. And yesterday I was alerted to the article in the *Times Colonist*. That's how I found you. As soon as I read she'd accused you of rape, I had to come and see you."

"I'm sorry, but I don't see what this has to do with you. Just because she was one of your students—"

"I'm getting there, I promise. Trust me, I'm here to help."

"How, exactly?"

Templeton sighed. He looked troubled. "You see, she has done this before."

"Done what?"

"She accused me of rape, too."

I bolted upright in my chair. "What...When?"

"When she was my student. It's a long story. I don't know if I can cover it in a few seconds. Would it be easier if I came back later today?"

"No. I want to hear this." Nothing was more important than hearing what this man had to say. "Please continue."

"Well, she was perfectly nice when I first met her, if a little timid. Then, for no apparent reason, she became fixated with me. She'd follow me around the campus, send me hundreds of text messages, call me at all hours, day and night, even stand outside our home watching us. At one stage, my wife thought I was having an affair. Eventually, I could take no more, so I confronted her. Told her I'd have her thrown off the course if she carried on." He gazed at my desk, seemingly lost in thought.

"What happened?"

Templeton's eyes were shiny when he looked at me. "It's weird. For some reason, she thought we were in some kind of relationship. I had to spell it out. Tell her that I had no interest in her. Least, not the way she imagined."

"She didn't like being rejected, right?"

Templeton nodded. "That's when she made up the rape allegation. There was no truth in it, of course, but I was suspended while they investigated. That hateful woman nearly cost me my career and my marriage." He was clasping his hands together in a tight ball.

"I'm assuming you were cleared in the end?"

"Not before my name had been dragged through the dirt. For weeks, I couldn't sleep. She made my life hell. Fortunately, I could prove to the police she was lying. I wasn't even in Vancouver when she claimed I assaulted her. In the end, she withdrew her complaint, but not until after she'd graduated."

"And the police did nothing to her?"

"They wanted to, but I'd had enough. I told them I wanted my life back. Besides, she'd moved on by that time. The last thing I wanted was a trial stirring up all the adverse publicity around campus again. It was easier to let it go and move on. Had I known she was going to do it all again to someone else..."

While I felt for Templeton, a wave of relief washed over me. His story proved a pattern of behavior, that it wasn't just me. Ali had history. Templeton had been through the same torture and had come out the other side.

"She did exactly the same thing to me," I said. "Like you, it started with the texts and the stalking and then things became violent."

Templeton flinched. "She attacked you?"

"Not her. She had someone else do that. He came into our home and..."

"That woman is evil."

"And now she's alleging I raped her."

Templeton leaned back in his chair. "I'm sorry I didn't do anything to stop her. I should have known she'd do it again if she was allowed to get away with it."

"You couldn't have known."

"Well, I'm here now and I want to put things right. Tell me how I can help. If you need me to make a statement to the police, I'd be happy to."

I could feel my eyes watering. Thank God, there were still decent human beings around like Templeton. "I can't thank you enough. To come all this way to help me…"

"She's a very dangerous person. We have to stop her. If we don't, one day, she's going to kill somebody. I'm convinced of it."

Chapter 42

Before Professor Templeton left my office, I called Detective Sergeant Hudec. I explained there'd been a development that had a material bearing on the case and I requested a meeting as soon as possible later that day. At first, Hudec seemed reluctant to meet. The man's mind was made up. He finally caved when I suggested I'd take what I had to the press if he wasn't interested. Hudec "squeezed" me in for half an hour at Victoria police headquarters at ten the following morning.

Fortunately, the delay wasn't a problem for Templeton. He said he could remain on the island overnight. His brother lived in Cordova Bay, a few miles north of town, so he arranged to stay with him. After he left, my thoughts turned to Marie and Freya. I wanted them to hear the good news about Templeton, proof that their husband and father was not the man described in the newspaper. If they knew Ali had done the same to another innocent man, there was a chance I could save our relationship.

I left the office and drove to our home, hoping they would be there. With all the adverse publicity surrounding my arrest, I thought they might have stayed away from school that day. I was right; when I approached our house, Marie's car was in the driveway. I pulled in behind it and walked to the front door. Even though I still had a key, I rang the bell. Somehow, it didn't feel right letting myself in.

Marie's expression said it all the second she opened the door.

Repulsion mixed with panic. "What are you doing here?" She took a step back.

"Can I come in?" I asked. "We need to talk."

"I have nothing to say to you. Haven't you done enough harm?"

"Please, Marie, I only need a few minutes."

One of our neighbors came out of his house. Before he climbed into his car, he looked in our direction and shook his head in judgment. By now most people in the street probably felt the same about me. In a close community like Owen Bay, there were few secrets.

Marie had almost closed the door on me when Freya walked up behind her. "Who is it, Mom?"

"It's your father."

Freya opened the door and stood next to Marie. Our daughter's eyes were puffy. She looked exhausted. I wanted to hug her and tell her everything was going to be alright.

"Look, I'm not here to cause any trouble," I said. "All I want is five minutes. I promise, I'll leave as soon as you say the word."

Marie looked at Freya. "Let's hear what he has to say," Freya said.

They stood aside, and I walked in. The place looked familiar, but it felt different. The house lacked the warmth it once had. While it had been a little over a month since I'd last been there, already I felt like a stranger in my own home. We sat around the kitchen table, Marie and Freya close to each other on one side, me on the other. Marie crossed her arms and pursed her lips; she wasn't about to make this easy for me.

"I know how difficult it must be for both of you," I said. "The piece in the paper is embarrassing for everyone."

"Embarrassing?" Marie said. "That's one way of putting it."

"Believe me. I'd do anything to make it go away. You don't deserve any of this."

"It's too late. You should have thought about us a long time ago."

"None of what was written in the newspaper is true. I didn't touch her."

"Save the hollow words. We don't want to hear them."

I looked at Freya. Her eyes were watery. I could tell she wanted to believe her father wasn't the monster she'd heard described at the shooting range and read about in the paper. She was torn.

"If you've come here to tell us you're innocent," Marie continued, "don't waste your time. Save it for the court."

"I am innocent, but I didn't come here to tell you that."

"Then why are you here?"

"There won't be a court case. Something happened this morning that changes everything. It proves Ali's a liar and that she's done all this before."

Marie's face softened a little. "What are you talking about?"

"I had a visitor at the office, a law professor from UBC in Vancouver. He used to teach Ali." I told Marie and Freya everything I'd learned from Templeton, how he'd found me after reading the story in the paper, how Ali had stalked him for weeks, how she'd almost ruined his marriage, and, when she couldn't get her own way, how she'd made up a rape allegation.

Marie's jaw was hanging open when I finished talking. "Is this true, Tom?" she asked.

"All of it is exactly as he told it to me. I came right here as soon as he left."

"You need to go to the police and tell them about him."

"Already taken care of," I said. "Templeton has agreed to go with me to see them tomorrow morning. He's prepared to give them a formal statement. He feels terrible that she's done the same thing to someone else, and he wants to stop her. He's a decent man trying to do the right thing." I could hear my voice weakening as I struggled to hold it together. "Thank God he found me."

Freya stood, walked around the table, and hugged me. I can't tell you how good that felt, knowing I hadn't lost her. I held onto her, trying my best to contain the wall of emotion inside me. I had to stay strong for her.

Marie reached across the table and squeezed my hand. "I'm sorry," she whispered.

That day we talked for hours, as if nothing had happened, as if the past few months had never existed, as if it had all been a bad dream. With my family now behind me, and with Templeton's testimony, I knew we were going to be okay. No doubt, in the absence of DNA evidence against me, eventually, the police would have dropped the case, anyway. But Templeton made all the difference. Once his story was out there, the world would know right away that Ali's allegations were completely unfounded, and my family and I would be able to move on without any stigma left hanging in the air.

We were about to put Ali behind us once and for all. However, I wouldn't do what Templeton did; I wouldn't drop it. I'd do whatever it took to make sure she answered for the evil she'd visited upon us. She would never be allowed to do this to anyone again.

It was just after five when I stood to leave. I felt exhausted by the emotional turmoil of the past few days and exhilarated by the prospect of getting my life back.

"Where do you think you're going?" Marie asked as I reached for my car keys.

"Home," I said. "I'm planning on having an early night, so as to be fresh for my meeting in the morning."

Marie smiled at Freya and then turned to me. "You are home, Tom. You're not going anywhere."

Chapter 43

Templeton met me at my office, and we traveled together in my car to the police headquarters downtown. While I drove, he fired question after question at me, a forensic grilling that demonstrated his legal expertise. He wanted to know everything: how I'd met Ali, what I thought had triggered her interest in me, chapter and verse on the circumstances surrounding Ali's rape allegation, and what led to Marie and I separating. It felt like an interrogation, but I answered all his questions.

In his circumstances, I would have done the same. If he was about to put his reputation on the line for me, it was understandable that he wanted to cover off his due diligence first. The professor was shocked when I told him how Ali turned up at my mother's place, claiming she was pregnant with my child. I explained that was the reason I went to her condo that night, but I didn't tell him I put my hands around Ali's neck, nor how close I'd come to throttling her. I needed his help and didn't want to give him any reason to doubt me.

"So, you were there the night she claims the rape happened?" Templeton asked.

"I'd love to say I was somewhere else," I said. "You were lucky; you could prove you weren't there. I don't have that get-out in my case."

"It'll be your word against hers, then."

"That's right. Plus the absence of any physical evidence."

Templeton glanced at me. "I wouldn't worry; my statement should trounce any weight the police place on her testimony."

"I sure hope so."

Across the street from the police building, I found a place to park for two hours, and we walked in a little before ten. Detective Sergeant Hudec was accompanied by Detective Constable Epps when they came to reception. Again, Epps looked like she was chewing on a wasp while Hudec had a permanent smirk, as if he was enjoying some sort of private joke.

"Who's this?" Hudec asked, pointing at Templeton. "You didn't say anything about your lawyer coming with you."

"He's not my lawyer." I introduced the professor. "He has a lot of important information on Ali Page."

From the glances they exchanged, the officers didn't seem at all convinced. I hoped they would remain open-minded enough to hear what Templeton had to say. My life depended on it.

In the interview room, I asked the professor to share the story he'd told me the day before. He did a great job, providing a lot more detail about the weeks of harassment he'd suffered before Ali finally made the false rape allegation against him. The parallels with my situation were so similar, surely even Hudec and Epps could see a pattern. It was obvious Ali was unhinged and couldn't be relied upon as a witness.

Templeton came over as thoughtful and credible, especially when Hudec peppered him with questions at the end. Not once did the professor lose his composure and, believe me, Hudec asked some dumb questions that sure tested my patience. The detective seemed to be more interested in any connection between me and Templeton, as if I'd conjured him up to save my skin. Still, if they were reckless enough to take me to trial, I was confident Templeton's evidence would annihilate anything Ali had to say.

"If you talk to Owen Bay Police Department," I said. "They'll have a record of my complaints against Ali. What she did to me was identical to what she put Professor Templeton through.

And, just like him, it was only when I rejected her that she made up the crazy story about being raped."

Epps, who had been quiet throughout the meeting, leaned forward and peered at the professor. "I'm confused about something," she said. "Why wasn't Page charged for making a false allegation?"

"That was down to me," Templeton said. "I was just glad to have my life back. I wanted to put the whole thing behind me as quickly as possible."

"Accusing someone of rape is a serious matter," Epps said. "I can't understand why you wouldn't want her to pay for that."

"I know I'd want to," Hudec said.

Templeton blushed, shifting his weight on the seat. "As I say, I'd had enough. She'd left the university by then. For months, she'd shredded my reputation. I couldn't face this thing hanging over me, waiting who knows how long for a trial. With the benefit of hindsight, I wish I had seen it through. If I'd been stronger, maybe she wouldn't have done what she did to Tom."

"Mr. Harper's situation is entirely different," Epps said.

"How can you say that?" I asked. "The pattern is completely the same. The professor's statement proves she has a history of lying. Who knows how many other people she's done this to?"

"In Professor Templeton's case, he could prove he wasn't there at the time the alleged rape took place."

"What difference does it make? Just because I was there, doesn't mean I raped her. The history of harassment and lies means she has no credibility. You must see that?" I could no longer hide the frustration in my voice. Why weren't they listening? The truth was staring them in the face.

"As you say, you've already admitted you were at her condo that night."

"So what? For all I know, she set me up by going to see my mother. She knew I'd come after her. But I didn't rape her. That's a figment of her imagination. She's lying."

Epps leaned back in her chair. "We don't have to wait much

longer to find out. The rape kit evidence will be back from the lab next week."

I jolted forward in my seat. "Rape kit. What rape kit?"

"The night Page reported she'd been attacked, the police medical examiner obtained a sample from her. Why do you think we took a saliva swab when we arrested you? In a few days' time, we'll know if there's a match."

When I glanced at Templeton, his face was white. He averted my eyes.

"Then we'll just have to wait," I said to Epps. "Ali's going to look pretty stupid when the results come back."

"I think we're done," Hudec said. He pointed to the pad of notes Epps had been taking. "Professor Templeton, do you still wish to submit your statement at this time?"

Templeton swallowed, quickly looked at me, then turned to the officers. "I'd like a little more time to think it through, if I may?"

"Of course," Hudec said. "We'll sit on the draft for now. When you're ready, you know where to find us."

Chapter 44

There was an awkward silence as we drove back to my office where Templeton had parked his car. While it had started well enough, the meeting with Hudec and Epps turned out to be a disaster. Not only had Templeton been made to feel guilty for not pursuing Ali after she made her false allegation, but he'd also just learned about potentially incriminating DNA evidence against me. No wonder he had a troubled look on his face, the kind you see when someone is about to deliver bad news.

Before we left Victoria police headquarters, I already knew he'd lost faith in my innocence. My ally was gone. Templeton was just working out how to bow out gracefully. Once again, everything would now rest on the absence of DNA evidence to prove I'd done nothing wrong. For some reason, I no longer felt as confident as I should have about that. Hudec and Epps had been far too quick to dismiss Templeton's testimony. While it was impossible, it was as if they knew the DNA results would incriminate me. Something else was troubling me, too. Why would Ali submit herself to a medical examination and allow a sample to be taken when she knew I hadn't gone anywhere near her? I didn't get it. Even her deluded mind would realize the police would go after her once the results came back with nothing, proving she was a liar.

Templeton made some lame excuse about having to rush back to Vancouver for a meeting the moment I pulled into our

244

parking lot. Watching him drive away, I knew I'd never hear from him again. I was on my own.

Immediately, my mind turned to my family. Now that Marie had allowed me back home, what was I going to tell when I got home? She knew we were seeing the police that morning, so she was bound to ask how it went. Like me, she'd been hoping the professor's statement would show Ali for the liar she was and bring our nightmare to an end. How was I going to explain Templeton had cold feet and was no longer willing to help? For now, I decided I wouldn't tell Marie anything about his abrupt departure. To do so would mean having to tell her about the rape kit, and that would frighten her. Our relationship wasn't strong enough yet. Hopefully, I'd never have to share the news about Templeton. Once the DNA report was back from the crime lab, hopefully, it would make the professor's change of heart irrelevant.

To distract myself, I locked the office door and piled into work. With Brenda no longer around, there was more than enough for me to do on our existing listings, at least for now. However, business would soon dry up if things continued the way they were. Since the article had appeared in the *Times Colonist*, I hadn't had a single new client inquiry. It was sickening to think I might escape Ali's clutches only to have no way of supporting my family because my firm had failed.

Mid-afternoon, my cell phone pinged. It was a text from Ali.

I've been thinking about our last conversation. I'd like to meet and talk some more.

What was she up to? A couple of days earlier, she'd made it perfectly clear where she stood. Even though I'd begged her to stop, she was adamant I was going to pay for what she claimed I had done to her. She probably only wanted to meet so she could watch me squirm while she tortured me some more. I wasn't about to give her that satisfaction, so I didn't reply.

Half an hour later, another text came in. *There's a way to end this, Tom. I just need to see you.*

Was she extending me an olive branch? In my gut, I knew the chances were slim. More likely, she was getting cold feet. She'd taken me to the brink and was now realizing the risk she faced if she carried on. She knew the results were imminent and that they would show she made up the rape. Soon the tables would turn, and then she'd be the one under the police microscope.

On the other hand, if she was prepared to go to the police and withdraw the rape allegation altogether, it would look a lot better for me than the case being dismissed through a lack of evidence. I'd be exonerated, and she'd have to explain why she wasted police time. It would be a better outcome for my family, too, if Ali admitted making up the whole thing.

I had to find out. After a couple of minutes, I texted her back. *What do you want from me?*

I'll explain when we meet. Can I come to your office later today? ☺

The pathetic smiley made me want to throw up, but if I was going to find out more, I'd have to play along and agree to a meeting. Trouble was, I couldn't risk seeing her at my office. Being on my own with her would place me in a vulnerable position. It would give her another opportunity to claim I attacked her. I needed a public location, somewhere with plenty of people about, so she couldn't make up another story. But even that was risky. If someone saw me with her, and the police found out, I could be accused of interfering with a witness. I needed somewhere outside of Victoria and away from Owen Bay, where the chances of being recognized were slim.

After a few minutes' thought, I tapped out a reply. *Not at my office. I can see you at Brentwood Bay pub in an hour.*

Okay. I'll be there.

Almost immediately, I had regrets. Was I doing the right thing? What if I was wrong about her motivation? What if this was another way to trap me? If Bekah had lived close by, I would have asked her to come with me, to make sure there was a witness. On my drive over to Brentwood Bay, I can't tell you how many times I thought about turning around.

Other than a couple of guys sitting at the bar, the pub was quiet when I walked in at four thirty, almost exactly an hour after our last exchange of texts. I sat at a table on the deck overlooking the Saanich Inlet and watched the boats come and go at the nearby marina. I ordered a drink and waited. Fifteen minutes later, there was still no sign of her. I began to think I'd been right all along; this was another of her mind games. She wasn't coming.

Some of the other tables on the deck were filling up with early diners. I emptied my glass and was getting ready to leave when I felt a tap on my shoulder.

"Sorry I kept you waiting, Tom," Ali said, taking a seat next to me. She was dressed in a tight leather skirt, far too short for work, and her make-up looked fresh. My guess was she had left work right after texting me and had gone home to change. What was she up to?

"I was about to leave," I said, pointing at my empty glass.

"I couldn't get away from the office," she said, then waved down one of the servers and ordered a glass of white wine. "Would you like another, Tom?"

"No. I'm hoping this won't take long."

"I've been thinking about what you said when we spoke earlier this week," she said after the server left.

"Go on."

"You asked me what it would take to persuade me to drop the case."

"And you made it perfectly clear you intended to go on with your charade. What's changed?"

"I've thought some more about us." She reached for my hand, but I managed to pull it away. "We don't have to be enemies, you know."

"There is no us."

The server came with the glass of wine. Ali waited until he

left. "But there could be. I'm prepared to forgive you. Put everything behind us. I never wanted to hurt you."

"What are you talking about?"

"I could go to the police and withdraw my statement, tell them nothing happened."

"Nothing did happen."

"If we could put this behind us, Tom, think what could be. Marie doesn't want you. That's obvious. She never loved you. Not the way I do, anyway. You and I could find a place of our own. We could live anywhere. We don't even need to stay on the island. I've thought about it. I could get a job back in Vancouver, and you could set up a brokerage over there. Start a new life together."

The tables next to us were busy now, so I had to be careful not to raise my voice. "Is this really why we're here?" I asked. "Did you seriously think for one moment I'd consider living with you? You're crazier than I thought. The idea is repulsive. You are repulsive. I'd never leave Marie for you. Never."

As I spoke, Ali slowly leaned away from me, and her left eyelid twitched.

"I know I hurt you," she said, "but there's no reason to destroy what we could have together. You can't stay here. You know what people are like on the island. They'll always remember what was printed in the newspaper, even if I withdrew the allegation. You don't have to live that life. You and I can start again. All I want—"

"Listen, you twisted little fuck..." A woman at a nearby table stared at me, so I lowered my voice. "I'd rather kill myself than spend a moment living with you."

Ali sat, stone-faced for what seemed an eternity. "Then you give me no choice. The world's going to know Tom Harper's a rapist. Freya's going to find out who her father really is. By the time I'm finished, you'll have nothing."

"I bet you got a kick out of leaking your fairy tale to the newspaper, but that's as far as it goes. You don't get to play me anymore. I don't give a fuck whether you drop your allegation or not. I'm calling your bluff. I know all about the rape kit being processed at the lab. And I say bring it on. We both know it'll show nothing. So, I say we wait for the results to come back. At that stage, it'll be your word against mine. And if it ever gets to court, which I very much doubt, the first witness I'm going to call to show you as the lying piece of shit that you are is Professor Templeton. That's right. He and I are close friends now."

Ali cupped her hands together as I spoke, and the twitch around her eye became more pronounced. She looked like she was about to explode. Finally, she'd been caught in her own snare.

"There's going be a court case, Tom," she said, her voice much calmer than I had expected. "Trust me. There's more evidence than you think."

"Not evidence. Just your made-up lies. Templeton proves you have a history. None of it will wash in court."

"As you say, without evidence, it's just my word against yours. I'm talking about irrefutable proof. The kind you can't hide from, the kind juries love."

Where was this crazy woman going? I'd heard enough of her madness. "Full marks for trying," I said, slowly clapping my hands. "I'll give you that much. But I'm still calling your bluff. Are we done?"

Ali leaned into me and lowered her voice. "The sample that went off to the crime lab. Where do you think it came from?"

I snorted. "It doesn't exist. We both know that. Time to give it up."

She smiled, but there was no warmth in her eyes, only malice. "You ought to be careful what you throw into your garbage." She stood. "Someone might pick through it and use it."

Chapter 45

I sat in my car outside the Brentwood Bay pub, gazing toward the water, watching the tiny car ferry leave the dock on its half-hour journey across the inlet to Mill Bay. On the passenger deck, a group of kids waved back at their friends standing on the shore. I envied them their normal lives, each of them probably going home to have dinner and spend time with loved ones. Tomorrow, while they were back at school, their parents would be at work or following some other routine. My life had been like that once. Predictable, rhythmic, safe. How I longed for the luxury of my once mundane existence.

In a matter of days, maybe hours, my world would be turned upside down. I would never know the peace and stability of an ordinary family life again. Once the lab results came back, the ax would fall; Hudec and Epps would waste no time hauling me into court to face a rape charge. No wonder they'd been so unmoved by Templeton's story. It made no difference to them that Ali had lied in the past; this time, the police weren't having to rely on her statement alone. All along, they were comfortable the hard DNA evidence would be enough to support their case. Compelling proof that would seal my fate.

There was no word to describe the kind of malevolent mind that could think to go through a person's garbage to fabricate evidence. It was way beyond evil. What made it even more chilling was that Ali must have planned it all weeks ago, well before I'd moved out of our home. She knew she was going to accuse me of rape back then, just as she had with Templeton. She knew if she went to see my mother that I'd come chasing after her. She was just waiting for me to react. That had been her plan all along. How could someone do that? It was inhumane, sadistic, sick.

The ferry headed northwest and soon disappeared from my view. I remained seated, in no hurry to move. Where could I go? The thought of going home, telling Marie about Templeton, and preparing her to expect the worst filled me with dread. But what choice did I have?

Once she knew what I knew, would Marie still believe I was innocent? She'd only just welcomed me back. It was a big ask for anyone. She'd have to be superhuman to take my side, knowing the DNA results were about to corroborate Ali's rape claim. If I was struggling with the idea, how could I expect Marie to believe me when I tell her Ali had rifled through our waste? That she must have searched for a used condom and planted evidence inside her to frame me. That was the truth, but it sounded incredible. In the face of scientific proof, only a desperate, guilty man would make up such an implausible story, right?

Maybe I could go back to the police. Before the results came in, I could tell them how Ali had just tried to blackmail me into having a relationship with her and that she'd admitted to fabricating the evidence on which they were building their case. I could even show them her latest text messages. Before I even finished the thought, I knew it wouldn't work. The texts proved nothing. If Marie was likely to dismiss my crazy-sounding reasons why the DNA evidence shouldn't be trusted, what would Hudec and Epps think? It would be worse than pleading guilty.

There was still a way out, one that had crossed my mind more than once in recent weeks. If I ended it all now, at least it would spare Marie, Freya, and Mom the torment of a trial. They wouldn't have to live through months of anguish with the public spotlight on them. It would be over quickly, and they could move on with their lives. It would be cruel, but much less so than the humiliation of having to watch me being dragged through the court process, only to try and build a new life while I languished in prison. And what kind of life would I have whenever I was released? My marriage would be over, my family would despise me, and I'd be forever known as the local realtor who raped a young client. I might as well be dead.

It was the best solution for everyone. As I slipped my seatbelt on, a calmness came over me. I knew what had to be done. I started the engine and headed north, the opposite direction from Owen Bay.

Passing along the backroads through North Saanich, I thought about the first home Marie and I bought near here not long after we married. It was a 1950s-built doer-upper with a self-contained suite on the lower level, which we rented out. It was the only way we could make the monthly mortgage payments. Happy times made even more so when Freya came along. Our daughter had learned to ride a bike along these country lanes. Every year she loved it when we'd take her up Horth Hill to pick blackberries, usually eating more than we put in the containers.

West Saanich Road took me to the end of the peninsula. In front of me, rising majestically on the far side of the Satellite Channel, Mount Tuam reflected on the water, its huge brown scar from a forest fire years ago reminding me of a ski run without the snow. I headed east along Lands End Road. On my left, palatial homes, set back on their one-acre lots along the waterfront, hid behind expensive gates and manicured hedges. Marie and I had always dreamed of living in one those properties when we'd made it. Silly, really, what we sometimes think is important. I realized now the life before Ali descended on us was every bit as perfect and fulfilling as any man could wish for. Back then, I was already the wealthiest man in the world. I just didn't know it.

At the eastern end of Lands End Road, I turned left into the parking lot for the BC Ferries terminal, found a space, then walked to the ticket hall. The next ferry to Tsawwassen on the mainland was due to leave in fifteen minutes. I bought a ticket, walked on board, and found a quiet spot outside on the top deck. Marie, Freya, and I had often sat there on daytrips to Vancouver. I'd lost count of the times we'd spotted orcas and humpbacks from that raised vantage point.

The breeze coming from the southeast was chilly, but I didn't mind. I was hoping it would dissuade most people from sitting outside. When we hit open water, the fewer people around to witness me jumping over the railing the better. I knew just the spot. Once we cleared the smaller islands, there was a large stretch of deep water a few miles before we hit the mainland. When no one was looking, I planned on leaping into the sea. I'd never been a strong swimmer. If anyone did see me hit the water, by the time the ferry had turned around, I'd be long gone.

There was little more than an hour before we reached that point, long enough for me to compose an email to Marie and Freya, apologizing and begging for their forgiveness and under-standing. I would use the onboard Wi-Fi to send it at the last moment.

Ten minutes after we left Swartz Bay ferry terminal, my phone rang. I saw it was a call from Bekah. Part of me wanted to ignore it, but then I realized it would be the last time I would ever communicate with my sister, so I answered.

"Hi Beks," I said, trying hard to sound normal.

"You haven't called me today," she said. "You promised to call every afternoon, remember?"

"I'm sorry. I...I've been busy."

"Anyway, Mike and I have found a great new lawyer for you. Mike's spoken to him already to put him in the picture. He's expecting a call from you first thing in the morning. Got a pen?"

"Look, I'm not sure I need one now. There's been...things have...it's hard to explain, Beks. I just don't think I need one any longer. I'm sorry I didn't call to let you know. Please thank Mike for me."

"What? Of course, you need one. If it's the money, don't worry, Tom. We'll pay for it. I just want you to have the best chance of beating that bitch into submission."

I didn't know what to say. My sister had worked hard to find me another lawyer, and here I was throwing her kindness back in her face. "Okay. Can you email me his contact details?"

"Are you alright, Tom? You sound a bit weird."

"I'm fine."

"What's all that noise in the background? Sounds like you're in a wind tunnel or something."

"I can't talk now. Can I call you tomorrow?"

"Something's not right. Where are you? Don't tell me you're okay, because I know that's not true."

I couldn't say goodbye to my sister like this. It wasn't right. It wouldn't be fair to her. She deserved an explanation. I sighed. "The truth is, Beks, I don't think I need a lawyer, because she's already won."

"What's that supposed to mean? You're not the first man to be wrongly accused of rape. You'll feel a lot better once you've spoken to this new guy. You mustn't let it get you down. We'll get through this, I promise. Where are you, anyway?"

"On the ferry to Tsawwassen."

"You're heading this way? Why didn't you tell me?"

"I don't know."

"I don't care where you're going, but I want to see you before you head back. Okay?"

She didn't know it yet, but that call from my sister saved my life. Hearing her grounded tone and unconditional acceptance, shook some sense into me. "Beks, would you do me a favor?"

"Of course."

"I don't have my car. Would you be able to meet me off the ferry? I'll explain everything when I see you."

"I'll be there."

"I love you, Beks."

Bekah waved frantically the moment she saw me walking off the ferry. When we hugged, I didn't want to let her go.

"You look dreadful," she said, her hands still gripping my shoulders when she stepped back and examined me.

"I can't tell you how glad I am to see you," I said.

We climbed into her car. "What were you doing coming over as a foot passenger?" she asked, as she started the engine. "You always bring your car."

"It's a long story." I looked out of the side window and watched the vehicles streaming off the ferry.

While Bekah fought the rush-hour traffic heading around Vancouver, I did most of the talking. By the time we reached her home, I'd told her all about Templeton, our visit to Victoria police headquarters, and what Ali had done to frame me for rape. I held nothing back.

Bekah's response was one of controlled rage. I watched her reactions as she drove and listened, noticing her grip grow steadily tighter on the steering wheel. Every now and then, a muscle in her jaw twitched. "Unbelievable," she kept repeating. I suspect it was only for my sake she didn't lose it altogether. Neither did she push me to explain why I was on the ferry as a foot passenger at that time of the evening. Although she never said anything, I suspected she'd already worked out what I had planned to do had she not intervened. As I said, unconditional acceptance.

Nor did I sense any doubt from Bekah that I was telling the truth. Knowing that she truly believed me, despite the seemingly fantastical story about Ali searching through our garbage, gave me a great sense of comfort, hope even. If my sister had that much faith in me, then maybe Marie would, too.

Mike came out of their house and greeted us when we stepped out of the car.

"I'm sorry to intrude on you like this," I said, shaking his hand. I didn't know how much he knew, but he must have been curious as to why his wife had rushed over to Tsawwassen to pick up her brother without any notice.

"Hey, buddy," he said, "it's no trouble at all." He put his arm around my shoulders. "Come on in."

While Mike and Bekah made coffee in their kitchen, I went through to the lounge and telephoned Marie. She would be starting to worry by now. I hadn't called to say I'd be late, and I knew she'd be waiting to hear how things had gone at the police headquarters that morning. For now, I kept things to the bare minimum. I told her Bekah had called late in the day and that she and Mike had arranged for me to meet a new lawyer they'd found in Vancouver first thing in the morning, and that's why I'd traveled to the mainland at short notice. It was the truth, but not exactly everything. When she asked about Templeton, I promised to tell her about him when I got home. She didn't know it yet, but there was much more I needed to share with her.

The thought of telling Marie about Ali still filled me with dread.

Chapter 46

My morning meeting downtown with the Vancouver lawyer Bekah and Mike had found was brief and less than positive. Once I told him about the potentially incriminating DNA evidence the police were waiting for, his initial bullishness about my defense soon evaporated. While he didn't say as much, I knew he was struggling to believe me when I described how Ali had obtained my semen. By the time the meeting was over, he was already hinting a negotiated plea deal with the prosecutor would be the best outcome. That told me all I needed to know about my chances of beating the rape charge. I wasn't surprised. Even my sister looked deflated as we left the building.

Afterward, Bekah drove me to the terminal at Tsawwassen for my ferry back to the island. While she tried to put a brave face on things, I could tell she was finding it difficult to accept the advice we'd just heard. She kept saying, "Maybe we should find another lawyer." This time it was my turn to cheer her up. I told her I'd be okay, and we'd get through it somehow. But she looked anxious, no doubt fearful I might try something stupid when she wasn't around to stop me.

As we headed south from Vancouver, my mind turned to what I was going to say to Marie when I got home. It was bad enough I still had to tell her about the fabricated DNA evidence. And now I knew my legal position, I'd have to prepare her for my likely conviction and incarceration. Despite Bekah's continued faith in my innocence, I'd be lying if I said I was confident Marie would be as accepting.

A couple of minutes before we hit the ferry terminal, my phone rang.

"Mr. Harper?" the caller asked when I answered.

"That's me," I said. I didn't recognize the voice, but I could see it was a Victoria number.

"This is Detective Epps."

Despair wrapped itself around me. I closed my eyes. This was it; the storm was about to hit, only much quicker than I'd hoped.

Please, let me have time to speak to Marie.

"We'd like you to come in to see us today," Epps continued.

The DNA results had to be in. They were preparing to charge me. "I'm about to catch the ferry to the island. Does it have to be today?" I knew the answer before Epps said anything. All I needed were a few hours to sit down with Marie. I wanted her to hear it from me before we were all crushed by the legal process.

"When will you be back on the island?"

"I'll be on the one o'clock ferry, so just after two thirty."

"Let's say three thirty, here." Epps didn't make it sound like an invitation I could refuse.

"Okay. I'll be there."

Bekah looked at me when I finished the call. "Problem?" she asked as we pulled into the parking lot at the terminal.

"That was Victoria police. They want me to go in this after-noon."

Bekah's face looked pained. We both understood what this meant. "Do you want me to come with you?"

I reached across and squeezed her arm. "Thanks, but I think I have to deal with this one on my own. I'll call you as soon as I can to let you know how it goes. I promise."

We hugged each other, and I watched my sister get back into her car and start the engine. She managed a half-smile through tearful eyes as she drove away. I waited for her to disappear be-fore I turned and walked to the office to buy my ticket.

Chapter 47

Ali wore a smart business suit as she waited in the reception area at Victoria police headquarters.

"I'm sorry we kept you waiting," Detective Constable Epps said when she came to collect her.

Ali smiled. "That's okay, but I hope this won't take long. I have to get back to the office for a meeting this afternoon."

"Shouldn't take too much time."

Epps led the way to an interview room on the ground floor. Detective Sergeant Hudec was already seated at the table, slurping coffee out of a paper cup.

"Thanks for coming in again," he said, standing. He pointed Ali to a chair on the opposite side of the table. Epps joined her colleague on his side, so they were both facing their visitor.

"We wanted you to come in to clarify a few things in your statement before we move forward with Harper," Epps said. "Once again, I need to remind you that everything is being recorded."

"Sure," Ali said. "I understand. Happy to do all I can to help."

Hudec opened the file on the table in front of him and started reading from it. "In your statement, you said Harper caused the bruising around your neck. Can you remind me how that happened?"

Ali leaned forward, her forearms resting on the edge of the

table, hands knitted together. "It was right after he kicked in my door," she said. "I'd opened it to see who it was, and he burst in. I was thrown backward and the next thing I knew, he had a hand around my neck. I couldn't breathe, his grip was so tight."

Epps scribbled some notes on her pad.

"How did he go from holding you by the throat to getting the knife?" Hudec asked.

"I don't remember, exactly. I know he threw me onto the floor. I was gasping for breath, not really watching what he was doing. He must have got it from the kitchen while I was distracted. Anyway, the next thing I remember was him dragging me into the lounge and holding it in front of my face."

"Did he say anything?"

"He threw a whole load of insults at me. I'd rather not repeat what he said, if that's okay."

"Doesn't matter." Hudec turned over a couple of sheets of paper on his file. "We need some more details on how the sexual assault occurred."

Ali looked down at the table. "Is that really necessary?"

"I'm afraid it is."

Ali sighed. "He told me to undress."

"What were you wearing?"

"It was late. I was about to go to bed. I had my bathrobe on." Ali cradled her upper body with her arms, as if she was cold. "I kept asking him not to do this. He said he would slit my throat if I didn't do exactly as he wanted."

"Take your time."

"I remember he was smiling when I slipped the bathrobe off. He just stood there and looked at me for what seemed like forever. All the while, he had the knife in his hand. I kept begging him to stop."

"What happened next?" Hudec scanned the file as he spoke.

"Do I really have to go through this again?"

Hudec nodded. "The details matter. I'm sorry."

Ali looked away. "I was terrified. I thought he was going to kill me." She made a face as she recalled the memory.

"We can take a break whenever you want," Hudec said.

Ali closed her eyes. "He unzipped his pants. It was weird. He kept telling me how beautiful I am." She opened her eyes. "Then he…he made me take him in my mouth." She looked right at the officers. "I wanted to be sick."

"I know this is difficult," Hudec said. "What exactly happened next? Is that when he ejaculated?"

"No, not then." Ali looked away again. "He told me to turn over. He made me get on my hands and knees on the floor. That's when he…"

"You need to tell us, Ali. We need to get the facts exactly right."

"He pushed me face down into the floor and he…he entered me."

"And then he ejaculated?"

Ali's body shivered. "Yes. When he finished, I pleaded with him not to hurt me. I still didn't know if he was going to kill me."

"Did he say anything?"

"Not much. By then, I was so traumatized, everything was a blur. I do remember him warning me that if I told anyone, he'd come back to finish what he'd started."

"That's when he left?"

"Yes. And as he did, he threw the knife on the floor."

Epps stopped writing and rested her pen beside her pad. "I'm sorry to have to ask you this, Ali," she said. "It's important that we know. Were you sleeping with anyone at or around this time?"

"No. Why?"

"It's all to do with the DNA. We need to eliminate every possibility. So, you had no sexual partners at the time this took place?"

"No. None."

"Okay. Thanks." Epps glanced at her colleague.

Hudec turned the pages of his file. He stopped and read something before he spoke. "I have another sensitive question for you, I'm afraid."

"That's okay. I know you have a job to do."

Hudec stroked his chin. "Is there any reason you would make up what happened that night?"

Ali knitted her eyebrows. "Why would I lie about something like this? Do you think I want to be here? Going over it again makes me want to throw up."

Hudec pointed to his file. "It's just that we heard from someone else who says you've done this kind of thing before."

"What do you mean? Done what before?"

"Lied about being raped."

Ali shot backward in her chair. "That's not true."

"You sure about that?"

"Absolutely. I think I'd remember if something like that happened."

"So, you've never heard of a Professor Templeton?"

Red patches surfaced on Ali's neck. "He was my law professor at UBC."

Hudec ran his finger along the open page on his file. "He told us you accused him of raping you, but the whole thing was made up."

"I don't know what he told you, but he did assault me. I'm not lying about anything."

"So why was he never tried?"

"They dropped the case. He convinced one of his other students to cover for him. She said she was with him the night he attacked me. I don't know what he promised her in return, but she was the one who lied, not me." Ali kept shaking her head. "If I had made it all up, don't you think he would have wanted to see me convicted? I assume you asked him why that never happened."

"Sure, we did."

"And what did he say?"

Hudec didn't answer the question. He leaned back in his chair and stared at Ali.

"What could he say?" Ali continued. "He knew he'd bought an alibi. The arrogant pig couldn't wait to put it all behind him. That man almost ruined my life."

"I don't get it," Hudec said. "If he wanted to bury the whole thing, then why do you think he came in here with Harper to tell us all about you? That doesn't make sense. It's certainly not the action of a man with something to hide."

"Who knows? Maybe Harper put him up to it. You need to ask him."

"How would Harper know about the professor? There's no way he could have found him."

Ali shrugged. "It doesn't really matter. When the DNA results come back, we'll see who's lying and who's telling the truth."

Hudec turned over some more pages. "Actually, the report came in yesterday."

Ali's shoulders rose as she sat forward. "Good. Because DNA doesn't lie, right?"

"Not in my experience," Hudec said in a matter-of-fact tone. "Thing is, though, the report raises a few questions."

Creases formed across Ali's brow. "Like what?"

"Do you have any siblings? Brothers, sisters?"

"I know what siblings are. I have one brother. Why do you ask?"

"What's his name?"

"Simon, but what does he have to do with anything?"

"How old is he?"

Ali cocked her head. "Sixteen. He's sixteen."

Hudec glanced at Epps and then made eye contact with Ali. "Thing is, we'd like you to explain how your brother's DNA turned up on the rape kit sample you gave us."

The red blotches now enveloped the whole of Ali's neck. Her cheeks looked like they were on fire, and her left eyelid began to twitch. "I don't…that's…that's just not possible."

Epps stopped writing. "Ali Page," she said, "I am arresting you for…"

Chapter 48

The Pat Bay Highway from Swartz Bay to Victoria was quieter than usual, and I made it to the police headquarters fifteen minutes early. My stomach churned when I entered the building. From this moment on, my life wouldn't be my own. Once they'd charged me, every step from here would be dictated by others. The best I could hope for was not having to be holed up in prison while I waited for the trial. That morning, I'd forgotten to ask my new lawyer whether it was normal to be let out on bail when facing such serious charges. I guess I'd soon find out.

Epps came to collect me from reception. I had no idea how these things worked. Part of me expected her to slap cuffs on me right away. Instead, her face was a little kinder than the last two times I'd met her. I swear I caught a slight smile as she greeted me.

"Please come this way," she said, leading me down the same corridor as Templeton and I had used a couple of days earlier, when I'd been filled with confidence the professor's testimony was going to rescue me.

Detective Sergeant Hudec was already in the room when we arrived. He was wearing the same tie as before, but it was pulled loose. He looked like he'd had a hard day and was desperate for another of his coffees. On this occasion, he stood and shook my hand. That was a first, too. Maybe now they had what they wanted—all the evidence they needed to lock me away—the officers could afford to be less adversarial and a touch more

265

human. Whatever it was, given my vulnerable state of mind, I was grateful for their small gestures of civility.

"We've got the DNA results back from the lab," Hudec said, holding up in his hand a bunch of papers. "We wanted to go through them with you."

"Listen," I said, "can't we just cut right to it?" I couldn't see the point dragging this out. I didn't need to know the details. We all knew what was coming.

"Sure. The bottom line is the rape kit sample has come back with a match."

I waited for the bullet. There was no point me trying to explain what Ali had done to frame me. That morning, my lawyer had told me he would know when the right time was to use that information. For now, he'd advised me not to say anything until I'd been charged. It would only hurt my defense if I did.

"But not with you," Hudec continued. "We owe you an apology."

Was I hallucinating? Had Hudec just told me there was no match with me? I stared at both officers, not knowing what to say. Time seemed to stop while my brain caught up.

"So, who did you match it with?" I asked, unable to mask the shock in my voice.

"I'm afraid we can't share that with you."

My mind went into overdrive. Was this really happening? I knew Ali had been through our waste. Maybe she'd made that up to get under my skin. But Hudec just said the results showed a match. How could that be when no one else was there that night? Nothing made sense.

"So, what does this mean?" I asked.

Hudec played with the knot in his tie. "There was no rape."

"I kept trying to tell you—"

"Ms. Page made the whole thing up. We know that now. Once again, we're sorry. I hope you can understand we had to investigate."

Confused and exhausted, right then I didn't have the energy

to argue.

"Looks like she did the same to you as she did to Professor Templeton," Hudec continued. "We've already spoken to him. He's confirmed we can use his statement and that he'll do everything he can to assist in the case."

"What case?"

Hudec grinned at me. "This morning, Ms. Page was charged. Not only has she wasted our time, but she tried to fabricate evidence to wrongly convict you. Those are serious crimes."

"If convicted, she'll serve up to five years," Epps said. "Plus, she'll never be able to practise as a lawyer again. This is going to cost her dearly and rightly so. Women like her make it hard for genuine sexual assault victims to come forward, to say nothing of the harm she has done to you."

I can't tell you how good it felt to hear the officers' words. Finally, the truth was out and Ali was going to pay for what she'd done. If I'd had my way, she would never be allowed out of prison. No one should ever have to go through the torment Templeton and I had suffered.

"We hope we can count on your help?" Hudec asked. "Your testimony will be crucial."

"Try stopping me," I said. I began to absorb what this meant for me and my family. The horror of these past few months was finally over, and we were going to get our lives back. "Where is she now?"

"She's out on bail," Hudec said, "but don't worry, there's a court order preventing her coming anywhere near you or your family. If she breaks that, she'll be facing even more charges. It would be an immediate breach of her bail conditions. You won't see her again until the trial."

Standing on the steps outside the police building, I felt the warmth of the late afternoon sun on my skin. I raised my head toward the clear blue sky and closed my eyes. Relief mixed with elation.

Finally, it was over.

Chapter 49

Three days later, the *Times Colonist* ran another piece, only this time I wanted everyone to read it. The headline said it all: *Wrongly Accused*. And because Ali's initial appearance was in open court, the newspaper named her as the woman behind the false rape allegation. They even had a photo of her, dressed in a smart business suit. It looked like it had been taken from her firm's website.

Next day, the Vancouver papers picked it up, and it also made the local TV news. I never did find out for certain how the press managed to get hold of so many details, but the fact that their stories all mentioned Professor Templeton was a strong clue. I wouldn't be human if I didn't confess to feeling a large amount of schadenfreude, knowing Ali was now having to deal with the same public humiliation and contempt she had visited on me and the professor. If she hadn't been already, I guessed it would only be a matter of time before she was fired by her new employer.

My relationship with Marie grew stronger with each day. I lost count of the times she apologized for not standing by me when I'd needed her or asked for my forgiveness. I kept telling her there was nothing to forgive. Had I not had that stupid affair years earlier, she wouldn't have had any reason to doubt me in the first place. Ali was to blame; no one else.

Freya returned to school, much relieved to learn her friends had nothing negative to say about her father. She'd been fretting over that. It had been worrying me, too. Thankfully, it didn't take Freya and I long to rekindle our relationship. The only negative was that she stopped seeing Simon, and that upset her for quite a while. I'd been so distracted over the summer I hadn't appreciated how close they were. I tried to explain how it was natural for him to take his sister's side, but Freya didn't see it that way. The upside for us was that Marie and I had no reason to keep in contact with Ali's parents. It would have been awkward, to say the least, if Freya was still dating their son. In fact, we hadn't seen Bob or Sonya in weeks and we hoped that would continue, at least until the trial.

Soon after the story broke, I went to see Brenda and managed to persuade her to return to my firm. Actually, she didn't need much persuading. She said she'd been hoping to have her old job back ever since she'd read about Ali's arrest in the newspaper, but she'd been too embarrassed to ask me. I missed working with her. The place just wasn't the same without her, and there was no way I could cope on my own. New listing inquiries began to come through the door like never before. The people of Owen Bay were rallying around, showing their support, something I found deeply humbling.

I'd spent so long looking over my shoulder, worrying what Ali would do next and fearing for our safety, that it took a good month or so for me to adjust. It wasn't easy getting my life back into its old rhythm. Gradually, however, Ali dominated my thoughts a little less each day. The one thing I couldn't shake off was my reaction to the phone. Whenever it rang, or when a message pinged, I'd hold my breath until I looked at the screen and saw it wasn't her. That said, not once did she try to call or text me after she was charged. For a while, it was as if she had never existed.

Then, exactly nine weeks after my last meeting with Hudec and Epps, it happened.

Marie and I had gone to bed around eleven. We were asleep.

At first, I thought I was imagining it, like a bad dream. A searing, burning pain swathed my face as if suddenly my skin was on fire. I bolted upright, screaming. I couldn't see out of one eye and, through the blurred vision of the other, I caught the silhouette of someone next to my side of the bed.

The shape moved, and a split second later liquid splashed the top of my head, scorching my scalp before eating into my flesh.

Shrieking, I lunged at the intruder, grasping and feeling my way as I had virtually lost my sight. I missed and fell facedown on the carpet.

More fluid squirted onto my naked back. Within seconds I could feel layers of my skin peeling back, as if I was being skinned alive.

"Your daughter's next, Tom," the intruder said. The voice was calm and controlled, but there was no mistaking it as Ali's.

Panic replaced agony. *Freya.* My survival instinct kicked in, and I reached out for Ali's legs. I had to stop her while Freya was still unharmed. I wasn't going to allow this monster to touch our daughter even if I died in the process. What about Marie? Had she already been attacked while I was asleep?

"Marie," I shouted, both of my hands clutching what felt like Ali's lower leg. "Marie."

More liquid doused my lower back and ran between my buttocks. I was on fire again, but I didn't release my grip. I could smell my own skin burning. Later I discovered I'd been showered in sulphuric acid.

Consumed by the pain, I used what little strength I had left to haul Ali's leg toward me.

I felt her topple, head backward into the bedroom wall. Sensing where she was, I rammed my body in her direction, crushing her against the wall.

"Tom!" It was Marie's voice.

Thank God she's alive. "Run, Marie."

"She's got a knife."

At first, I thought it was a punch, but then I realized it had to be the hilt of a knife as it penetrated deep into my shoulder. When Ali withdrew the blade, waves of agony rippled through me. Still unable to see, I wrapped my hands around my head, preparing for the next strike.

"Get out of here, Marie," I shouted. "Get Freya and run." I used my weight to keep Ali pinned to the wall, bracing for the next stab.

Three blows of the knife came in quick succession, the first glancing off the back of one of my hands, the next two striking my collar bone with such ferocity I felt it break. I knew I was dying. I prayed I'd be able to hold Ali off long enough for Marie and Freya to escape. Nothing else mattered. I didn't care what happened to me. I remember the pure clarity of thought that came with acceptance of my imminent death. I understood what had to be done.

No longer concerned with the knife and where it would strike next, I took my hands away from my head and wrapped them around Ali's waist. I bear-hugged her spine and pinned her ribs up against the wall with the weight of my shoulder. She was going nowhere. Adrenaline coursed through my veins as I crushed her with every ounce of energy I could summon.

In those vital seconds, I lost count of the number of blows she inflicted on my back, but I felt no pain. Every fiber of my being was focused on saving my wife and daughter. They had to live. No way would this wild beast be allowed to get near them.

Then stillness.

A gunshot reverberated around the room. Ali's flailing had stopped. I felt her body go limp in my arms.

Another shot, which I later learned went through Ali's head, shattering her skull across the wall.

"Bitch!" Marie said. "Die you fucking bitch!"

Ali's lifeless body slumped to the floor when I released her.

A second later, I passed out.

* * *

271

There was my life before Ali Page, and there is my life now.

Five years have passed since that night when she broke into our home. Thankfully, Marie had started keeping my pistol in her bedside cabinet right after she threw me out of the house, fearing another visit from Mahoney or some other loser while I wasn't there. I dread to think what might have happened had Ali not been stopped by those bullets.

We'll never know what made her the person she was. Even after the hell she put us through, I still can't accept some people are born evil. Where's the hope in that?

Sadly, a year after the break-in, I had to close my real estate brokerage. The pain from the acid burns across sixty percent of my body meant working was impossible. My eyesight has almost gone, and I lost most of one lung through the stab wounds. Money is tight, but we get by. We still live in Owen Bay, but in a much smaller property. Material things never did matter that much to me. The important thing is that we feel rooted here. It's where our friends are. It's where our life is.

Freya is in her last year at UBC, studying law, of all things. Professor Templeton even teaches some of her classes. Funny how life works out. She wants to practise property law one day. I'm so proud of the young woman she has become.

As for Marie and me, our relationship has never been stronger. I owe her everything and, health permitting, I pray we get to spend many more years together. She is, and always has been, the love of my life.

ACKNOWLEDGMENTS

Thanks to Henry Heinicke for his invaluable help during my research.

MARTIN BODENHAM was born in the UK. He is the author of the crime novels *Crime and Justice*, *The Geneva Connection*, *Once a Killer*, and *Shakedown*.

After a thirty-year career in private equity and corporate finance, Martin moved to the west coast of Canada, where he writes full-time. He held corporate finance partner positions at both KPMG and Ernst & Young as well as senior roles at a number of private equity firms before founding his own private equity company in 2001. Much of the tension in his thrillers is based on the greed and fear he witnessed first-hand while working in international finance.

MartinBodenham.com

BOOKS

On the following pages are a few
more great titles from the
Down & Out Books publishing family.

For a complete list of books and to
sign up for our newsletter,
go to DownAndOutBooks.com.

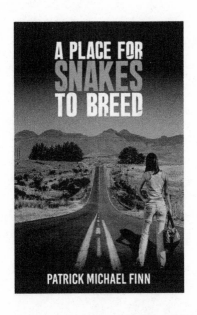

A Place for Snakes to Breed
Patrick Michael Finn

Down & Out Books
June 2021
978-1-64396-207-8

The desert spares no souls.

Set in the scorched and unforgiving deserts of the American Southwest, *A Place for Snakes to Breed* follows Weldon Holt's desperate search for his daughter Tammy, who is lost in the vicious landscape of interstate truck stop prostitution and its nightworlds "where the fruit of human trade is harvested by razor blades and cheap pistols."

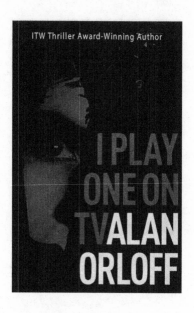

I Play One on TV
A YA Thriller
Alan Orloff

Down & Out Books
July 2021
978-1-64396-213-9

All's great for sixteen-year-old actor Dalton Black as he portrays a teen killer on a crime reenactment show—until he comes face-to-face with the real killer. But Homer Lee Varney isn't after revenge—he wants help, claiming he's been framed.

Will Dalton and his drama friends be able to catch the real killer? Or will they be his next victims?

Stay tuned to find out!

To Bring My Shadow
Matt Phillips

All Due Respect, an imprint of
Down & Out Books
July 2021
978-1-64396-222-1

A haunting, hardboiled tale that follows detective Frank "Slim Fat" Pinson and his partner as they try to unravel the vexing mystery surrounding a who-done-it drug murder in San Diego, *To Bring My Shadow* is the first detective novel from acclaimed pulp writer Matt Phillips.

Meet a fascinating detective of indefensible fault, immense morality, and incalculable demise.

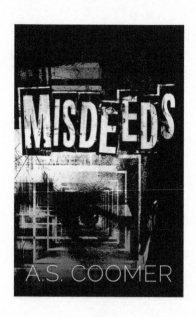

Misdeeds
A Criminal Collection of Crime Fiction
A.S. Coomer

Shotgun Honey, an imprint of
Down & Out Books
May 2021
978-1-64396-110-1

This is a book of *Misdeeds*. The stories between these covers will shock, appall, and enthrall.

There are killers in here. Thieves & vagabonds, needy sisters & disgruntled brothers, cops & kidnapers, not to mention a corruptor of children, all slide around the pages of *Misdeeds* like burning grease in an overheated pan.

These stories pop, sizzle, and burn. Consider yourself warned, fresh meat.

Made in the USA
Monee, IL
28 August 2021

76736148R00173